THE BRIDAL SWAP

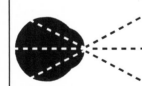

This Large Print Book carries the
Seal of Approval of N.A.V.H.

THE BRIDAL SWAP

KAREN KIRST

THORNDIKE PRESS
A part of Gale, Cengage Learning

GALE
CENGAGE Learning®

Detroit • New York • San Francisco • New Haven, Conn • Waterville, Maine • London

GALE
CENGAGE Learning®

Copyright © 2012 by Karen Vyskocil.
Smoky Mountain Matches Series.
Thorndike Press, a part of Gale, Cengage Learning.

Thorndike Press® Large Print Gentle Romance.
The text of this Large Print edition is unabridged.
Other aspects of the book may vary from the original edition.
Set in 16 pt. Plantin.

LIBRARY OF CONGRESS CATALOGING-IN-PUBLICATION DATA

Kirst, Karen.
  The bridal swap / by Karen Kirst. — Large print ed.
    p. cm. — (Smoky Mountain matches series) (Thorndike
  Press large print gentle romance)
  ISBN-13: 978-1-4104-5047-0 (hardcover)
  ISBN-10: 1-4104-5047-3 (hardcover)
  1. Long-distance relationships—Tennessee—Fiction. 2. Sisters—Fiction.
  3. Large type books. I. Title.
  PS3611.I76B75 2012
  813'.6—dc23   2012017033

Published in 2012 by arrangement with Harlequin Books S.A.

Printed in the United States of America
1 2 3 4 5 6 7 16 15 14 13 12

I have swept away your offenses like a
cloud, your sins like the morning mist.
Return to me, for I have redeemed you.

— *Isaiah 44:22*

For Jacob.

Your dad and I are so proud of
the thoughtful, caring young man
you've become.

Just remember to keep God
first in your life.
I love you!

CHAPTER ONE

Gatlinburg, Tennessee
September 1880

Josh O'Malley's life was about to change. Standing on the boardwalk in front of Clawson's Mercantile, a bouquet of wildflowers in his hand, he watched intently as the carriage rolled to a stop. The team of midnight-black horses snuffed and tossed their heads, their massive chests quivering with exertion. The driver, dripping sweat and wearing an inch-thick coating of dust, remained seated while a second, well-dressed man climbed down with haste and swept open the door as if royalty waited inside.

Time stood still. The sounds of the town — snatches of conversations, the bell above the mercantile's entrance, wagons lumbering past — all faded as he waited for a glimpse of his fiancée, Francesca Morgan. Six long months had passed since he'd last seen her.

Anticipation swelled within him like the Little Pigeon River after a heavy downpour. His fingers tightened on the stems. Would she like it here? Not for the first time, doubts flickered in his mind. How would this oil heiress from New York City adjust to his small town, tucked deep in the Smoky Mountains?

He shoved such thoughts aside. Together they would deal with any hurdles.

Then she was there, in the doorway, placing her gloved hand in the man's and floating down the steps in a cloud of seafoam green. All he could see was the top of her fancy hat. This was the first day of their lives together.

"Hello, Francesca."

Her head whipped up, and he found himself staring into a stranger's face.

"Pardon me, Miss." Josh retreated a step. He glanced around her to find the carriage interior empty. Confused, he looked at her once more. "Excuse me, I was under the impression this was the Morgan carriage."

The young lady's eyes flared wide as if she recognized him. But that was impossible.

With a slight incline of her head, she dismissed the man at her side. "Thank you, Mr. Crandall." Her eyes held a mix of compassion and apprehension.

"Mr. Joshua O'Malley?"

His gut clenched. She couldn't know his name unless . . . "Yes, that's me."

"My name is Katerina Morgan. I'm Francesca's younger sister."

Sister? Surely not. This lady and his fiancée looked nothing alike.

Francesca was tall, lithe and graceful, her peaches-and-cream complexion the perfect foil for her corn-silk hair and baby-blue eyes. The young lady standing before him was altogether different. Petite and fine-boned, yet in possession of captivating curves, the top of her head barely grazed his chin.

Katerina was a delicate lady . . . like a doll come to life. Her face was a perfect oval, with rounded cheekbones and dainty chin. Her almond-shaped eyes shone the same hue as her pale green dress, and her pouty, pink lips could've been sculpted by an artist. Her hair was the color of decadent chocolate and arranged in elaborate twists and curls.

"Where is Francesca? Has something happened?"

"Please — is there somewhere we can speak in private?"

Curious townsfolk had stopped to watch

11

their exchange. Gatlinburg was a small town, and most knew his fiancée was arriving today.

"Over here."

They would be out of sight behind the mercantile. Taking gentle hold of her arm, he helped her across the grass and caught a whiff of her perfume, a subtle scent with notes of citrus. Like her elegant outfit, it was most likely the latest fashion from Paris. And worth more money than he'd see in a lifetime.

"What lush beauty." Her steps faltered. "Why, I doubt I've ever seen its equal. You are fortunate, Mr. O'Malley, to wake up to this day after day."

He followed her uplifted gaze to the rounded mountain peaks on all sides, the clear blue sky a perfect backdrop against the autumn foliage visible even at the higher elevations. He understood her reaction. Most newcomers agreed this part of East Tennessee was a tiny slice of paradise.

"I can't imagine living anywhere else," he murmured.

The hushed hum of rushing water met his ears as they neared the bank's edge. Releasing her arm, he warned, "Mind your step. There's a steep drop-off." About ten feet below, the water's surface reflected the trees' changing colors — dusky green with patches of red and orange.

"It's lovely," she breathed.

Enough small talk. "Why isn't Francesca here?" *Instead of you?*

She faced him, shoulders squared and hands clasped at her slim waist. "I'm afraid I have unsettling news." She paused, clearly uneasy. "Francesca has married another man."

Married? "That's impossible." Josh struggled to make sense of her words. "She promised to marry me." The date was set. Saturday next, they were to stand before Pastor Monroe and exchange vows. Friends and family had already been invited.

Her lips compressed in lines of regret. "I am truly sorry."

"I don't understand."

What about all those letters? Had she only pretended to be excited about starting a new life with him?

"Who is he?" he ground out.

"Someone she knew before she met you," she said gently. "They had a falling-out a few days before she left for her visit with the Meades."

He'd met the lovely heiress at the Meades' home in Sevierville, had gone to deliver a pair of rocking chairs and nearly run her

13

over in the doorway of the grand mansion. Nothing in her behavior had hinted of another attachment. Surely he would've seen the signs!

"I realize this is difficult news —"

"How long ago did she go back to him?" he demanded. "And why did she send you to do her dirty work?"

She blanched. "They were married two weeks ago. And she did not send me. Despite my insistence that you should be told in person, she refused to come."

Whirling away from her, Josh battled conflicting emotions. Anger. Outrage. Disbelief. If the marriage had taken place two weeks ago, then they'd reconciled some time before.

He'd been duped.

His head pounding by this time, he strode to the edge of the embankment and hurled the bouquet, the kaleidoscope of colors cascading to the water's surface and swirling downstream. He needed to be alone, needed to think through this upheaval in his plans.

"I appreciate your coming here, Miss Morgan. Now I must go." He gave her a half bow. "Good day."

Kate's gaze lingered on the tender petals

being crushed by the current before skittering to his retreating back. Collecting her skirts, she hurried after him. "Mr. O'Malley?"

When he stopped and glanced back, the tortured look in his eyes nearly took her breath away. "Yes?"

Kate stared at the man Francesca was to have married, unable to utter a word.

She'd looked at his picture when no one else was around, memorizing each feature. Intelligent brows, patrician nose, square jaw. His was a photogenic face.

On paper, he was merely a handsome stranger. The flesh-and-bone man was another matter entirely. In a word, he was intoxicating.

His dusky-gray, pin-striped suit, with its simple lines and understated elegance, molded to his broad shoulders and lean torso. His tan skin glowed with health and vibrancy, and his honey-brown hair was short, the ends bleached blond by the sun.

The neatly trimmed mustache and goatee covering his chin were new. Not usually taken by facial hair, Kate found his fascinating. He looked . . . mysterious. A bit untamed.

"Did you need something?" he prompted.

He dwarfed her by at least a foot. That

wasn't unusual. Most men did. "Can you direct me to Charlotte Matthews's house?"

A muscle in his jaw jumped. "You know Mrs. Matthews and her son?"

"She was my governess for many years. I haven't met Tyler, but she mentions him quite often in her letters."

"I see." His eyes were an intriguing color, the shimmering, metallic blue of a blue morpho butterfly's wings, pale around the pupil with a deeper ring of blue around the edges. So beautiful it made her wish for color photographs.

"Their farm is a mile or so outside of town. What time is your driver planning to leave?"

"As soon as I get settled at Charlotte's."

"You're staying here tonight?"

"Actually, I'm planning to be here for at least a month, perhaps longer."

His brows slashed down. "That long? May I ask why?"

"I'm here to take photographs of the mountains. I'm considering publishing a book about this area."

"A book," he repeated, clearly displeased. "You're a photographer?"

Was he one of those men who disapproved of female professionals? "I am."

His brilliant blue gaze assessed her. No

16

doubt he was comparing her to her sister. She inwardly winced. She'd learned long ago that she didn't measure up, would forever be in Fran's shadow.

Men adored Fran. Women wanted to *be* her. Even their parents favored her — their mother especially.

Patrick and Georgia Morgan had wanted only one child. Francesca — the epitome of grace and loveliness — fulfilled their every dream of what a proper daughter should be. So when dark-haired, demanding Katerina arrived unexpectedly, Georgia had been less than thrilled.

A lengthy bout of colic made matters worse. For months, Georgia refused to visit the nursery, leaving Kate in the care of nannies. Perhaps that rough beginning had cast a pall over their relationship. Whatever the case, the distance between them seemed to grow wider with time.

Kate had given up trying to earn her mother's love.

"If you'd rather not help me," she said after a lengthy silence, "I'm sure I can find someone else."

He blew out a breath. "It's too far to walk. Mind if we take your rig?"

"Not at all." They fell into step, as he

matched his stride to hers. "I appreciate this."

He merely nodded, his mouth set in grim lines. Once he'd given directions to her driver and tethered his horse to the rear of the carriage, he settled his tall frame in the seat across from her. Holding his hat in his hands, he took in the sumptuous mahogany fabric that covered every square inch of the carriage interior. What was he thinking?

His letters, which Fran had read aloud in the drawing room during afternoon tea, had been filled with descriptions of his family's home and the town of Gatlinburg. Fran had laughed, calling him provincial. Kate disagreed. Josh's letters had revealed a charming, thoughtful man who dearly loved his family and hometown.

Glancing out the window, she caught sight of Clawson's Mercantile, the post office and a quaint white church framed by the mountains.

"Everything looks just as I'd imagined it," she said without thinking. "Your description of Main Street makes me feel as though I've been here before."

His voice dripped icicles. "You read my letters?"

"I . . . We . . ." she sputtered. "Well, y-yes. Fran read them aloud." Mortified at her slip, Kate pretended an exaggerated interest in the tips of her tan leather ankle boots.

"Those were my private thoughts, intended for no one but Francesca."

Silence settled heavy and oppressive between them.

"I am truly sorry," she murmured. "I've hurt you —"

"No. Your sister did that all on her own." He turned his head to glare out the window. "It's becoming quite clear she did not hold me in the same regard as I did her."

What could she say? That Fran was interested only in social standing and wealth? Why she'd ever accepted Josh O'Malley's proposal was beyond Kate. Perhaps to make Percy jealous, so he'd come crawling back to her? If that was the case, the ploy had worked.

The man across from her looked lost. Adrift in a vast ocean with no rescue in sight. Fran had done this to him, but Kate had delivered the news. Did he despise her for listening to his letters? Did he consider her the enemy — guilty by association?

The carriage soon slowed and turned onto a rutted lane. The vegetation was thick on either side, and tree branches scraped along the sides of their rig, slapping against the half-open glass. Pine needles littered the

19

bench seats and carpeted floor. Mr. Crandall, her fastidious footman, would be none too pleased.

Anticipation curled through her at the prospect of seeing her former governess again. For a time, kindhearted Charlotte Matthews had been the one bright spot in her otherwise lonely existence. They'd reconnected through correspondence, and the older lady had made it plain that Kate was welcome to visit anytime.

They rolled to a stop before a squat, haphazard dwelling nearly engulfed with ivy. Only the window and the door had not succumbed to the ivy's onslaught. She frowned. Would there be room for her here?

The door swung open, and Mr. Crandall stood ready to assist her. Joshua O'Malley descended the steps after her, his expression an inscrutable mask.

Hands clasped at her waist, she turned to thank him, but he was already headed for his horse. It appeared he'd had all of her company he could stand. With a mental shrug, she approached the cabin and knocked twice.

A chair scraped against the floor and the vibrations of heavy footsteps could be felt on the porch. That didn't sound like a lady. Instead, a disheveled, dark-haired man about her age appeared in the doorway. "What do ya want?"

"Hello, I'm looking for Charlotte Matthews —"

She wasn't prepared for the hand that shot out and gripped her wrist in a painful hold. The stranger yanked her forward, and her free hand flew up to stop her fall, only to encounter an unyielding wall of muscle. Gasping in fright, she stared into his shocked brown eyes.

"Lily?" he ground out.

"N-no, it's Kate."

He tugged her against his long length. "I can't believe you've come back to me." His stale breath, reeking of whiskey and tobacco, washed over her.

She recoiled. "You're mistaken! I don't know you."

His dark brows lowered, and anger flashed in his eyes. "Don't play me for a fool, Lily."

His fingers dug into her flesh, and she flinched. "Please," she whimpered, "let me go."

Somewhere behind her, she heard the click of a gun hammer. "I'd advise you to get your hands off the lady."

She couldn't see Mr. O'Malley, but his voice rang with deadly promise.

Uncertainty flickered in the glazed eyes.

21

"My wife is my business."

"The booze has scrambled your senses, Matthews." He came closer. "Kate Morgan just arrived today. Look at her fancy clothes. She's from New York City. A Yankee."

This man was Tyler Matthews? Charlotte's son was a dangerous drunk?

"I don't understand." His grip loosened, but he didn't release her. His bloodshot gaze roamed her features. "You aren't Lily?"

Her mouth suddenly dry, she croaked out a response. "No."

His hands dropped abruptly to his sides. Immediately, Mr. O'Malley took her elbow and eased her to his side so as not to draw the other man's attention. Her knees felt like gelatin. Unsteady, she held on to his arm as if it were a lifeline.

He appeared calm, but Kate sensed the tension humming through his body. His jaw was set in rigid lines. "Why don't you go back inside and sleep it off?"

Head bent, Matthews rubbed the back of his neck. "I, uh, haven't been sleepin' too good lately."

"Then maybe you should lay off the drink."

Mr. O'Malley obviously knew this man and his history. What had happened to his

22

wife? And why had he mistaken Kate for her?

"Yeah." Turning, he went inside without another word.

Her rescuer angled his face down toward hers. "Are you all right?"

His low, easy drawl flowed over her like decadent, sugary caramel.

Kate gulped. She avoided all sweets, in particular caramel. One taste was never enough.

Suddenly conscious of her viselike grip on his arm, she let go and took a quick step back.

"I'm fine," she said, tugging her snug-fitting jacket down. Her arms smarted from where Matthews had held her prisoner, but she wouldn't mention that to him. "Thank you for intervening."

Mr. Crandall rushed forward. "I second that sentiment, Mr. O'Malley. Are you quite certain you're unharmed, Miss Morgan?"

"Yes."

The brim of his black hat shading his eyes, Mr. O'Malley slid his weapon back in its holster and nodded to the carriage. "Let's go before he has a change of heart."

"Go where?" It suddenly dawned on Kate that she had no place to stay.

"My house."

CHAPTER TWO

This was not the day he'd had planned.

He should've been acquainting his intended with her new home. Instead, he was saddled with her sister. Troubled and pale after her ordeal, Kate stared out the carriage window, seemingly a million miles away.

"Where do you suppose Charlotte is?" Her gaze settled on him, seeking answers.

He hitched a shoulder. "I don't know."

"I thought everyone knew everyone else's business in small towns."

"That's true to a point. However, I personally don't keep track of everyone's comings and goings." He shifted on the swaying seat. When a worried crease appeared between her brows, he added, "We'll ask my mother. She's friendly with Mrs. Matthews, so there's a good chance she'll have an idea where she's gone, if anywhere. For all we know, she could've been visiting a friend or picking up necessities."

Her expression brightened, then dimmed an instant later. "Even if she is nearby, I can't possibly stay there. Not with her son." The fingers plucking at the lace edging her sleeves stilled. "Where is Lily Matthews?"

"Dead."

Her lips parted. "I don't understand. Then why —"

"You resemble her." He shoved a hand through his hair. "Matthews used to be a productive member of this town, but he hasn't been the same since the accident." He'd heard of the man's tendency to drink, but he hadn't realized the severity of the problem. If he had, he wouldn't have taken Kate out there.

"Does Gatlinburg have a hotel? Or a boardinghouse?"

"No hotel. No boardinghouse. The Copelands occasionally have rooms to let, but their son and his family are visiting from out of town."

Again, she got that worried look.

"My parents may know of somewhere you can stay," he tacked on. "Or you could go back to New York."

She stiffened. "That's not an option."

"Why not?"

"I came here to do a job." At his puzzled

25

expression, she sighed. "The book, remember?"

"Ah, yes. I remember. You're a photographer." While he had no issue with working women, he couldn't picture this elegant, delicate young lady as anything other than a privileged socialite. "Your coming here proved to be very convenient for Francesca, didn't it? Why not let you deal with the unnecessary groom?"

"Mr. O'Malley, I'm sorry —"

He held up a staying hand as the driver halted the team outside of the livery. "It's not your place to apologize. Forget I said anything."

Kate didn't speak as they exited the carriage. Replacing his hat on his head, he gave instructions to the driver and footman.

"We'll leave your trunks here until we figure out where you'll be staying."

She glanced up and down the busy street. "I thought we were going to your house."

"We are. It's not far. I thought you might like to stretch your legs after being cooped up much of the day."

Surprised that he cared one whit for her comfort, she fell into step beside him.

Passing the last business on the right, Leighton Barbershop, he led her across a quaint, wooden bridge overlooking the river.

The shaded lane enveloped them in a vibrant cocoon, leaves hanging mere inches from their heads. To the right and left stood an endless parade of stately trees reaching for the Heavens, the thick, dark trunks anchored in a sea of gold created by the shorter tulip trees' golden leaves.

What beauty! *How many are your works, O Lord! In wisdom You made them all; the earth is full of Your creatures.*

She wished suddenly for a cushioned chair, a steaming cup of Earl Grey and a copy of *Scientific American.* She'd stay here in this lane for hours if he'd allow it.

Around the bend, the trees opened up to an expansive clearing, the green grass a lush carpet leading to a two-story cabin with a long, narrow front porch and beyond, a weathered barn and several outbuildings. It was just as he'd described, but of course the reality far surpassed her imaginings.

Pigs squealed in the distance. The sizable garden was bursting with jewel-toned vegetables — plump orange pumpkins, glossy eggplant, striped squash of different sizes and shapes, and green peppers.

Temporarily forgetting her dilemma, Kate grinned, ecstatic to see a real farm up close for the first time.

Pointing to impressive rows of trees, she

asked, "Are those apple trees?"

He nodded. "McIntosh apples. They'll be ripe in about a week."

"That's a lot of apples."

"We won't eat them all fresh. They'll be used to make cider, vinegar, applesauce and apple butter, not to mention pies and other desserts."

"You have a beautiful home," she breathed, a note of wistfulness in her voice.

He glanced over at her. "The good Lord has blessed us."

As they drew nearer to the house, Kate's nerves assailed her. How would his parents react to her presence once they learned her awful news? Mouth dry and palms damp inside her buff-colored lace gloves, she slowed her steps.

The front door opened. A man and woman emerged, their faces alight with anticipation. "It's about time, Joshua!" the woman exclaimed. "We were beginning to think something had happened." Advancing down the steps, she crossed to meet them, her husband not far behind.

"Sorry to worry you, Ma," Josh said. "This is —"

"Francesca!" To Kate's surprise, Mrs. O'Malley clasped her hands in hers. "I'm so pleased to meet you!"

Oh, no. This was not good.

"I —"

"This isn't Francesca." Josh ran a finger beneath his shirt collar as if to loosen it. "May I present Kate Morgan? My ex-fiancée's little sister."

"Ex-fiancée?" his mother repeated, brow wrinkling in disbelief. "What's happened, Joshua? Isn't Francesca coming?"

More than once during her long journey to Tennessee, she'd faced Josh in her imagination. Rehearsing what she'd say. Envisioning what he might say. She hadn't considered his family's reaction. Standing here with Mr. and Mrs. O'Malley regarding her as if she were a creature from another planet, she regretted the omission. Not a word came to mind.

Josh's level gaze was on her as he spoke. "Francesca changed her mind about the marriage. Kate thought it best to bring the news in person."

"I'm sorry, son," said Mr. O'Malley, as he placed a comforting hand on Josh's shoulder.

His mother approached, questions lingering in her eyes. Her tremulous smile lessened Kate's apprehension a notch. "Kate, I'm Mary. And that's my Samuel. It's a brave thing you did, coming here in your sister's place. Thank you."

Kate released the breath she'd been holding. She wasn't going to be berated, after all. "I regret to have to deliver such dreadful news."

Unlike Georgia Morgan's cool, aloof beauty, Mary O'Malley's appearance was one of sweet femininity, her wavy brown hair styled in a casual upsweep and a simple gold chain with a cross to complement her blue calico dress. And tall, lean Samuel O'Malley, with brown hair much like Josh's, had a pleasant face.

"We appreciate your consideration of Josh's feelings," Samuel added.

The tips of Josh's ears reddened. "I'm sure Kate would appreciate something to drink after her long trip."

"Where are my manners?" Mary gasped. "Come on in! I've a fresh batch of crybabies already cooling on the table."

Crybabies? What on earth?

Josh's parents went inside first, and he gestured for her to go ahead of him. She felt the weight of his gaze on her back as they passed through the doorway.

Her first impression of the O'Malley home was that it could've fit inside the dining hall of her parents' estate. Instead of silk damask wall panels, these walls were bare wooden planks. There were no ornate candelabras or wall sconces, only kerosene lamps placed in key areas about the room. Compared to her estate's marble hallways, plush Oriental rugs and the finest furnishings money can buy, this home was indeed humble.

However, there was no denying it was an inviting space, cozy and cheerful and decorated with care. Blue-and-white gingham curtains hung at every window, and landscape scenes of mountains and meadows hung on the walls. A serpentine sofa with blue brocade cushions and walnut trim, along with two matching chairs, were situated around a charming stone fireplace.

"Not exactly what you're used to, is it?" Josh stopped at her side.

"It's lovely."

He studied her, weighing her words and expression as if trying to gauge her sincerity.

"Please, make yourself comfortable." Mary gestured to the sofa. "I'll get the refreshments. Samuel, can you give me a hand?"

The couple passed through the dining area and rounded the corner into what she assumed was the kitchen. She couldn't make out the words of their quiet conversation, but no doubt they were discussing her sister's cowardice and lack of decency.

"Would you like to have a seat?"

Kate swallowed hard. Josh's steady assessment set her nerves on edge.

"Yes, thank you."

Moving to the nearest wingback chair, she sank gracefully onto the cushion and arranged her skirts with care. He didn't join her. Instead he began to pace the length of the couch, hands in his pockets. Every now and then a muscle in his cheek twitched.

She could just imagine his thoughts. Wringing Fran's neck, perhaps?

His parents returned at last with a tray of glasses filled with ginger water and a plate piled high with cookies, which they placed on the low coffee table in front of her. The sweet aroma of molasses teased her nose. Were these the crybabies, perhaps?

Mary handed her a glass. "Here you are."

"Thank you." The tart liquid washed the dust from her throat.

When they were settled in the sofa across from her, Mary said, "You've traveled a great distance, haven't you, Kate? What are your plans now that you're here?"

"I'm actually here to take photographs. And to visit my former governess, Charlotte Matthews." Her gaze shot to Josh, who was still pacing. "Everything was arranged and she knew to expect me. She wasn't at home, however."

Absently, she rubbed the tender spot on her wrist where Tyler had held her.

"We thought you might know her whereabouts." Josh had stopped pacing. Resting his weight against the sofa, his hands gripped the wooden trim. His gaze caught her movement and narrowed. Kate covered the spot with her hand.

"You know Charlotte? She's a dear lady." Mary frowned. "She's been facing some hard times lately. Tyler isn't coping well with the death of his wife. And now his sister, Carrie, is expecting and has been terribly ill. Charlotte left last week to be with her until the baby comes. I'm afraid she won't be back for quite some time."

Kate lowered her gaze to her lap. This wasn't welcome news. Charlotte must've been too preoccupied to send her a letter explaining the situation.

"Miss Morgan needs a place to stay," Josh spoke into the silence. "Do you know of anywhere?"

"You can stay here, of course." Mary beamed. "With four males stomping around this house, I get lonesome for female company."

"Mary, I'm not sure . . ." Samuel shot a meaningful glance at Josh.

Her smile faltered. "Oh, yes, I didn't think —"

"She can sleep in my cabin," Josh announced bitterly. "I won't be needing it after all."

"Are you sure?" Mary peered up at him, her eyes full of concern.

"Positive. It won't take all that long to move my things back into my old bedroom."

"Wait." Kate hastily replaced her drink and came around the sofa to face him. "The last thing I want to do is push you out of your home."

"A home I built for my future wife." The pain of betrayal flashed hot in his eyes. "But she's not here, is she?" Turning his back, he strode for the door. "You're welcome to it."

His boot had connected with the bottom step when he heard the door open and close and Kate call his name. What now? Couldn't she see he wasn't in the mood for company?

With great reluctance he pivoted back, squinting in the afternoon sunshine. She edged forward, her face shadowed by the hat's brim. Loosening the ribbons of her reticule, she withdrew a long parchment envelope and held it out to him.

"I have a letter for you. From Francesca."

He stared at the letter, not sure he wanted to read it. "What does it say?"

Her lips parted, and dark lashes swept down to hide her eyes. Pink washed her cheeks. "I don't know. She didn't share the contents with me and, to be honest, I'm glad she didn't."

Tucking the letter in the inside pocket of his suit jacket, Josh nodded in silent farewell and left her standing on the porch. If he didn't get alone soon, he was going to come undone. What he wanted to do was hunt down the man who'd stolen his future and plant a facer on him. Then he'd confront Francesca and force her to confess her perfidy to his face.

But that wasn't an option. Not today, anyway.

With effort, he ruthlessly tamped down the emotions clawing at his insides.

Ignoring the letter burning the lining of his suit, he gathered his clothes and books from his home, not stopping to linger and mourn his loss. To his relief, his mom was showing Kate the kitchen when he went inside the main house, so he was able to put his things away, change clothes and duck back outside without being seen.

During the entire trip to town and back

to retrieve her luggage, the letter and what it might say dominated his thoughts. Why hadn't Francesca had the decency to face him herself? Why put it off on her little sister?

Finally, when the wondering became too great, he pulled the envelope from his pocket and sank onto the top step of his porch.

Heart thumping against his rib cage so hard it hurt, he unfolded the paper and, holding it to his nose, inhaled her flowery scent. He felt achy all over.

Dearest Josh,
I am not sure what to write, for I know nothing I say will change your low opinion of me. Katerina was adamant that I give you some explanation, and I admit she was right. You must know that I care for you, but you and I together for a lifetime never would have worked. Percy can provide the type of life I need to be happy.

Sincerely,
Francesca Morgan

Stunned, Josh flipped the paper over and found the other side blank.

There was no apology. She'd basically

admitted to wedding this man for material gain.

Francesca's nonchalant attitude, her utter lack of remorse, stung. Anger boiled up once again, threatening to overwhelm him.

Once again, he was facing a lonely future.

In the shade of the back porch, Kate leaned against the wooden railing and stared out at the idyllic scene. Gently rolling fields of green, knee-high stalks waving in the breeze, gave way to rounded mountain peaks rising in all directions in a patchwork display of burnished reds, golds and greens. God's magnificent handiwork for all to see and savor.

She was eager to explore, to seek out potential images for her book.

But first she had to find Josh, as Mary requested. Supper awaited.

Above the lowing of cattle, she heard the insistent pounding of an ax.

Following the sound, she strolled across the yard toward the barn, casting a glance inside the shady interior as she passed by the open doors. Dust motes hung suspended in the dim light, the smell of hay and animals reminding her of the stables back home.

Rounding the corner, she came to an

abrupt stop.

A flash of sunlight on glistening skin, sculpted muscles straining, stretching, Josh handled the ax with ease, slicing through the wood like butter. He'd exchanged his neat suit for a pair of dark denim trousers and sturdy brown work boots. His sleeveless undershirt gave her a clear view of molded shoulders, thick biceps and corded forearms.

She gulped. Oh, dear.

Glancing away, she saw the high stacks of kindling by the barn wall. Surely they didn't need more. Then it struck her. He wasn't doing this out of necessity. He was venting.

Compassion for his plight brought moisture to her eyes. She blinked hard. She couldn't let him see her tears. He'd assume she was feeling pity for him, and she had a feeling he wouldn't like that.

When she moved into his line of vision, he wedged the ax into the stump, turned his back and, retrieving his white shirt, shrugged into it. Still working the buttons, he faced her, brows raised in question.

"Sorry to interrupt," she ventured. "Your mother sent me to tell you the meal is ready."

"Just a minute."

She stood by quietly, fingers toying with

the lace peeking out of her sleeves as he quickly stacked the wood before joining her. He was a rumpled mess, his short hair mussed and shirt untucked, the sweat-dampened material sticking to his frame. It only added to his appeal.

"Have my parents kept you entertained this afternoon?"

"Your parents have been welcoming and friendly."

Strangers who were more attentive than her own parents.

Walking beside him, she sensed the coiled tension in him. Had he read the letter? She wondered what it had said, feared Fran's words had inflicted further pain. Her sister wasn't known for her tact.

He stopped at the pump to clean his hands and douse his face. When he'd wiped off the excess moisture and tucked the cloth into his back pocket, he startled her by taking hold of her hand.

"What are you —"

Carefully, he slid her sleeve back, revealing the purple marks marring her pale skin. His eyes darkened. "Matthews did this?"

The scent of pine clung to him. Kate couldn't think with him standing so near, his strong, warm hands cradling hers with such tenderness. Back home in Francesca's room, gazing at his portrait and committing his face to memory, she couldn't have guessed the impact of his physical presence.

She dragged in a breath. "I'm fine, really."

"Steer clear of him, Kate. He's unpredictable."

It was his first use of her name. She had to admit it sounded good on his lips.

"Kate?" he prompted impatiently.

"You don't have to worry. I won't go near the man."

"Hey, Josh!"

Two men were headed in their direction. Josh's brothers?

Releasing her, he crossed his arms and waited. Their attention didn't waver from her as they approached. Feeling like a specimen underneath a microscope, she fought the urge to squirm.

"Kate Morgan, these are my brothers, Nathan and Caleb."

Nathan shot a startled glance at Josh, but he quickly masked his confusion. His eyes were kind as he welcomed her. "It's nice to meet you." Two years younger than Josh, he was twenty-two.

Twenty-year-old Caleb scowled and said nothing. Josh had mentioned in his letters that his youngest brother didn't like to be around people, something to do with a scar he'd gotten from a recent accident. She didn't see evidence of one, but she noticed he kept his face turned to one side.

"Where's Francesca?" Nathan asked.

Josh stiffened, his voice flat. "She isn't coming, after all."

"Did something happen?" Nathan asked quietly.

"Yes." Josh's voice held an edge. "She decided to marry someone else." At Caleb's intake of breath, Josh held up a staying hand. "Kate is her sister. She's staying with us for the time being."

He didn't seem pleased with the turn of events. And why should he be? Her sister should've been standing here meeting his family, not her.

Mary pushed open the door. "Supper's ready."

She didn't miss the flash of relief on Josh's face. No doubt he was growing weary of explaining her presence to everyone.

Sitting at the far end of the table, Josh listened to the ebb and flow of conversation without contributing to it. This was the last place he wanted to be, surrounded by people pretending nothing was wrong. Pretending he hadn't just been cast off.

Suppertime in the O'Malley household

was typically loud and lively, and tonight was no exception. His father and brothers made sure of that. One glance at Kate Morgan's mystified expression suggested family dinners at the Morgan estate were a much more sedate affair.

Her regal bearing and expensive clothing set her apart from everyone else at the table. She'd removed her hat, gloves and jacket. Beneath her brocade vest of matching material, she wore a filmy cream-colored blouse with lace at her neck. The color of her eyes matched the peridot earrings dangling from her ears, the vivid green gems flashing with every turn of her head.

Watching her, Josh realized he'd been a fool to think Francesca could ever be satisfied with his way of life. The Morgans lived a life of luxury. Nothing was out of their reach.

He lived simply. He worked hard to carve out a life for himself, yet he had no complaints. He loved these mountains, this land. And he wanted someone to share his life with.

God, I don't understand Your ways. Nothing is turning out the way I thought, and it's hard. So hard.

"Time for dessert." His mother placed a warm pecan pie in the middle of the table.

Standing, Josh brought his empty plate to the counter. "I'll pass tonight."

"But it's your favorite," Mary protested, carrying dishes into the kitchen.

He squeezed her shoulder. "Save me a piece for tomorrow?"

Kate approached, her plate still half full. "You are a marvelous cook, Mary. However, I'm afraid I couldn't finish it all." She smothered a yawn.

"Oh, my. You've had a long day, haven't you, dear?" Mary said. "Joshua, will you walk Kate out to the cabin?"

His and Kate's gazes clashed. Then her lashes swept downward, her expression neutral.

What could he say? *No, I don't want to spend even a second alone with her? This woman reminds me of Francesca's treachery and my glaring failure.*

He swept out his arm. "After you."

CHAPTER THREE

With her hat in one hand and her skirts in the other, Kate swept past him onto the narrow porch, her shoulder brushing against his chest and a stray chocolate curl caressing her cheek. The creamy skin of her nape glowed alabaster in the moonlight. Her fresh, citrusy scent, carried on the gentle breeze, filled his nostrils and stirred his blood.

Closing the door behind him, Josh inhaled the cool, pine-scented air in an effort to displace her scent. Kate was a lovely woman, and he was a man craving comfort. Disgusted with himself for even noticing, he gave her a wide berth and started across the lawn.

"Mr. O'Malley?"

She hadn't moved an inch. From the soft golden glow spilling through the windows, he saw her hesitation and retraced his steps.

"It's Josh. What's wrong? Did you forget

something inside?"

"No. I, um — It's pitch-black out there." Her voice faltered. "Back home, gas street-lamps line the streets and give off quite a bit of light."

He held the kerosene lamp aloft. "This will light our way."

An owl hooted. Kate's gaze darted to the dense woods. "What about wild beasts? I've read a few books about this area. There were accounts of black bears attacking people."

He suppressed a smile. "While it's true there are bears in these parts, they normally stay in higher elevations. Bear attacks are rare and most likely the result of someone coming too close to a momma bear and her cubs."

He approached and held out his arm, but she didn't immediately take it.

"So you've never seen a bear anywhere near here?"

"I didn't say that. But mostly they keep to themselves."

Her slender hand curled around his biceps, the warmth of her light touch seeping through his shirt. "I'm safe out here then?"

He guided her across the yard. "I can pretty much guarantee a bear isn't going to break into the cabin while you sleep. You should watch out for snakes, though, especially rattlers and copperheads."

Her nails dug into his skin. "Snakes?"

"And spiders," he added, disregarding the twinge of his conscience. He was only telling her the truth. "Black widows and brown recluses are the ones to watch out for. Nasty bites. You could lose a limb."

"Oh, dear." She shuddered. "My books didn't mention any of that."

"Just be careful around tall grass. And don't reach into dark corners and crevices where crawling insects like to hide." He pulled away from her. "Here we are."

Opening the door for her, his gaze fell on the burst of color in the corner of the room. More wildflowers. He'd borrowed his mother's only crystal vase and placed the arrangement on the dining table as a small token for his wife-to-be.

He frowned. This night was supposed to have played out much differently. He'd imagined Francesca's reaction to the home he'd built for her, had hoped she'd be pleased.

Instead, a stranger stood beside him.

Moving forward, her skirts whispering in the silence, Kate's gaze assessed the airy, open space that made up the seating area and kitchen.

"You built this yourself?"

He nodded. "With help from my father and brothers."

"You did a great job." The admiration shining in her eyes was a soothing balm to his battered soul.

"Thanks."

In the kitchen, she trailed her fingers along the gleaming walnut tabletop. Her gaze shot to his, a small wrinkle between her brows.

"This is similar to the one at your parents', only smaller."

It was one of his most recent pieces, carved with his own hands. For some reason he couldn't identify, he was reluctant to tell her about his furniture business. Not even Francesca knew.

Slipping his hands into his pockets, he asked casually, "Do you like it?"

She stepped back to study it. "It's sturdy, solid. Simple lines. But here —" she traced a fingertip along the carved edge "— this is truly magnificent. The detail of the leaves and flowers is amazing. Was it done by a local craftsman?"

He hesitated. "Yes."

"Does he live nearby?"

Closer than you think. "Yes. Very near."

"You should tell him his furniture would sell extremely well back East." Her praise brought a rush of pleasure, especially con-

47

sidering her family's estate was most likely furnished with the finest money could buy.

"I'll do that."

She smothered another yawn. Time to go. He wasn't sure why he'd lingered anyway.

"Good night, Kate." He paused. "Lock the door. You'll feel safer."

Kate stared at the closed door a full minute before crossing the room to slide the wooden bar in place. His woodsy scent lingered in the silent room. He'd been stiff, watchful, his blue eyes revealing his misery. *Oh, Fran. How could you?*

Her heart ached for the pain he was enduring.

Turning, she relaxed against the rough wood and stared at the home intended for her sister. Prestige and money were everything to Fran. If she were here, she would scorn this rough-hewn dwelling, no larger than her private bathroom. She would not appreciate its charm, the love and care poured into it. Everywhere she looked, Kate saw little touches meant to cheer.

The bouquet on the table. The floral-print high-backed chair beneath the curtained window. A rainbow-striped rug in front of the stone fireplace. A painting of a waterfall on the wall behind the sofa.

Josh obviously loved her sister. What would it feel like, she wondered, to be loved like that? Sadness pressed in on her. She couldn't recall hearing the words *I love you* a single time.

Her parents weren't given to displays of affection. That was for the lower classes, her mother had said when Kate questioned her.

She recalled walking through the park with her nanny, envious of the children holding hands with their mothers, the little boys balanced on their father's shoulders looking happy as could be. The longing for love and affection had only grown with time.

God loves you, a small, still voice told Kate. Her eyes smarted with unshed tears. *Help me remember, Father, that You love me even when I'm unlovable.*

The stillness reminded her that she was alone. For the first time in her life, there were no ladies' maids waiting behind the scenes to help her undress or fetch her a soothing cup of tea. The realization was both heady and daunting. What would it be like to be an independent woman?

Exhausted from days of travel, not to mention emotionally drained, Kate decided to deal with unpacking later. Instead, she began the tedious process of undressing. First the skirt, then the underskirt. Bustle.

Corset cover. Petticoat.

The ivory satin corset presented a problem. Without assistance, it was next to impossible to undo the tight stays. Huffing and grunting, arms twisting every which way, she was at last able to free herself from the rigid contraption. She resisted the unladylike urge to toss it across the room.

Tucking the despised article beneath her arm, she went to investigate the bedroom. Covering the wide bed was a handmade quilt similar to the one on the sofa, this one in pale blues and pinks done in the pattern of interlocking rings. She thought of the thick, luxurious silk coverlet on her own bed. Beautiful, yes, and expensive, but not unique. Before she left, she would ask Mary if she'd be willing to sell her one of hers.

Locating her satchel, she changed into her night rail. Next to the bed was a waist-high table where the oil lamp stood. Extinguishing the flame, the room was plunged into inky darkness.

Kate froze. The blackness closed in on her. Images from her childhood flashed through her mind. Her nanny's contorted, angry face. The dark closet. Musty-smelling coats, piles of boxes and broken, discarded toys distorted by the shadows. Her lungs struggled to draw in air.

How she hated the dark!

This room was small, the ceiling low. And there were no windows to open, as in her spacious, airy bedroom at the estate. No gentle light from the row of streetlamps to ease her fear, or the occasional sound of horses clomping down the lane to comfort her.

No. I mustn't give in to the memories.

But they came anyway . . . of another time, another place. The wine cellar. A man she'd adored. The extinguished candle. Her panic. His calm reassurances and mesmerizing touch. She'd felt so loved . . .

No! Reining in her thoughts before the shame consumed her, she scrambled beneath the covers and tugged them up to her chin.

Father God, I need You. I don't want to remember.

He will keep him in perfect peace, whose mind is stayed on Thee. She repeated the verse until her muscles relaxed and she drifted off to sleep.

Dressed to go visiting Saturday morning, Mary placed fresh-baked loaves of sourdough bread into the basket on the counter. "How are you holding up? I know it must be difficult having Kate around. I could ask

Betty if she'd mind her staying over there."

Leaning back in his chair, Josh toyed with the handle of his coffee mug. A dear friend of his mother's, Betty Stanley would welcome Kate into her home. He didn't doubt she'd treat her with kindness. On the downside, she had five sons. All single. And a touch wild. Sending a delicate beauty like Kate over there would be like throwing a rabbit to a pack of hungry wolves. He couldn't do it.

Besides, he wasn't sure he wanted to sleep out in the cabin. All alone. With nothing but his thoughts to keep him company.

"No. I'm fine, Ma." At the questioning arch of her brow, he added, "Honest."

"If you change your mind, let me know. I'm sure Kate would understand."

"I'll do that."

"What are your plans for the day?"

"I'm working on Mr. Wilcox's dining table. He's anxious to have it before his in-laws arrive next weekend."

She paused in her preparations. "Could you put it off for a couple of hours? I need someone to keep Kate company while I deliver this." When he opened his mouth to speak, she tacked on, "I wouldn't ask, except Nathan has been up all night with Bess. I took his breakfast out to the barn about an hour ago, and the calf still hasn't made an appearance. And your father and Caleb are milking the cows."

He didn't want to play babysitter for Francesca's little sister, but what choice did he have? His mother went out of her way to make life comfortable for him and his brothers, so whenever she asked a favor, he did his best to comply.

"Fine. I'll do it."

"You're a sweetheart, you know that?"

"Don't tell anybody."

Amid her soft laughter, there came a light knock on the front door.

"That's probably her. Do you mind, dear?"

Swallowing a sigh, he went to greet their guest. At the sight of her, the greeting on his lips fell flat. Her clothing, fancier even than the previous day's, was utterly out of place here.

Her silk brocade ensemble put him in mind of the eggplant growing in his ma's garden — deep, luxurious purple. The slim jacket had sleeves that bloomed out at the shoulders and tightened at the elbow on down to the wrists. A beribboned V emphasized her trim waist, erupting into a six-inch ruffle. The straight skirt below had slits revealing pleated skirts underneath. Corded rosettes adorned both the jacket and skirt, and frothy white fringe peeked out of the wrists.

Her elegant look was spoiled by the mass of chocolate waves tumbling past her shoulders. My goodness, she looked all of sixteen with her hair down. Young and vulnerable. Sweet.

Nope. He took a step back. *He refused to be drawn in by her beauty.* If anything, Francesca had taught him outward beauty, no matter how innocent-looking, didn't guarantee a beautiful heart.

"Good morning, Josh." Her cheeks were a becoming pink. "Might I speak with your mother, please?"

"She's in the kitchen."

With a stately nod, she walked past him. He remained where he was, unable to pull his gaze from her retreating form. She moved with grace and poise, head high and spine straight as an arrow, like a queen before her royal subjects.

Frowning, he shook his head. How many hours of practice had it taken to perfect such posture? Time better suited to more productive pursuits.

Bits and pieces of their conversation drifted out to the living room.

He heard the self-deprecating humor in

Kate's voice as she asked for help with her hair. "It appears I'm helpless without my staff."

"Don't worry, dear. Let's go up to my room and see what we can do."

"Since I'll be on my own for a while, maybe you can give me some pointers."

Josh stuffed his hands in his pockets, finding it odd that a young lady would need help fixing her hair.

As the pair ascended the stairs, he wondered how Francesca would've coped without servants to do her bidding. He hadn't given it a thought before this moment, all the changes he'd expected her to make. Instead of being waited on hand and foot, she would've had to do everything herself. While he'd been blinded by love, she'd obviously been thinking of more practical things.

In less than ten minutes, Kate and his mother were making their way back downstairs. His mother reached the bottom steps first. "Will you make Kate a cup of hot tea? Her breakfast is on the stove."

To Kate, she said, "I'm sorry to run off, but Laney Hedrick has been ill. The ladies in our sewing circle are taking turns delivering meals, and today happens to be mine. Would you mind spending the morning with Joshua? He's agreed to show you around."

Pausing on the last step, Kate's fingers tightened on the banister. Her gaze shot to his face, then away.

"I'd like that."

His gaze narrowed. Kate Morgan's perfect manners couldn't conceal her wariness. Was it him? Did he make her uncomfortable? Did she think he'd lash out in anger at her because of what Francesca had done? Or was she simply a timid young lady?

Their temporary guest was a stranger to him. Francesca had spoken at length of her parents but when it came to her sister, she'd been strangely reticent. He wondered why that was. Was theirs a strained relationship?

"I'll be back in time to fix supper, I hope. If not, there's smoked ham and bread for sandwiches."

"Don't rush, Ma. We'll rustle up something if you're late."

The back door clicked shut. Silence hung thick in the air. Kate avoided his gaze, staring with great interest at the white pine floorboards.

Clearing his throat, he headed for the kitchen. "I'll get your breakfast."

While he set the water to boiling and retrieved a teacup and saucer from the cabinet, she stood gazing out the windows overlooking the front yard. He wondered what she was thinking. Why the forlorn expression? Did she miss the big city already?

At the sight of the heaping portion of eggs, bacon and biscuits, her eyes widened and she pressed a hand against her midsection. "I can't possibly eat all that."

Swallowing his irritation, he gripped the top rung of the chair in front of him. "You want me to make something else?" *Your Royal Highness?*

She looked doubtful. "I normally have a bowl of oatmeal or a slice of toast with marmalade."

He thought back to the few weeks in March he'd spent with Francesca. "Your sister has quite the appetite."

Hurt flashed across her face, which she quickly masked. "My sister can eat anything she likes and it doesn't affect her figure."

Josh stood mute. What had he said to cause her pain? His heart beat out a warning. He'd known Kate Morgan less than twenty-four hours, and already she was getting under his skin.

"Well, you certainly don't look as if you need to worry about that," he said brusquely. "I'll check if we have oatmeal."

Her eyes flared with surprise. "Wait. Please don't go to the trouble." Lowering herself into the chair, she indicated the plate. "This smells delicious."

At least she wasn't sulking. Francesca would have.

He retrieved her tea from the kitchen and set it on the table, along with a crock of honey, then sank into the chair across the table. He watched her eat, thinking he'd never seen such refined manners. She ate carefully, her jaw barely moving as she chewed, dabbing her mouth with her crisp napkin.

"What would you like to do today?"

"I'd like to scout out some possible sites for photographs. Can you suggest any particularly interesting spots?"

"First I need to know what you're interested in photographing. What kind of book is this going to be?"

"A sort of travel guide. I'd like pictures of the mountains, of course." Her eyes sparkled as she warmed to her topic. "Churches make interesting photos. Barns. Wagons. Everyday scenes of life on a farm. Would you show me your farm?"

"Sure."

"I also like to take portraits of people. I noticed the one of your family on the fireplace mantel. Perhaps I can take another one and give your mother a print."

"She'd like that, I'm sure. That was taken many years ago." He sipped the stout, black brew. "As to possible sites, I'll have to give it some thought."

"Thank you."

"How long will it take you to gather all the photographs you need?" *In other words, how long before you leave?*

"I'm not certain. But I'm not in any hurry to go back. My parents are touring Europe for the next two months. Francesca is on her honeymoon —" She broke off, her gaze shooting to his. Flustered, she rushed ahead. "Anyway, I didn't like the idea of rattling around the estate with only staff for company."

"I'm curious why you didn't go with your parents. Surely Europe is a more interesting subject than our mountains."

"Simple. They didn't ask. My parents prefer to take their vacations alone."

"I see." Taken aback by her candid response, he said, "Well, I imagine you'll soon be bored here."

"If that happens, then I will know it's time to go home."

"Don't you have fancy parties to attend? Shopping to do? I'm sure you noticed our one and only general store."

Her eyes dulled. "If my presence here is

inconvenient, I will leave immediately."

Now he felt like a heel. He'd been insensitive. "Forgive me. I didn't mean to make you feel unwelcome."

Lashes lowered, she sipped her tea. Her fingers were elegant, nails trim and shiny, skin like satin. One gold filigree ring adorned the fourth finger of her right hand. They were the hands of a privileged lady, unblemished by hard work.

How would he handle the strain of seeing Francesca's sister every day? Reminding him of all he'd lost. And the gossip her presence would stir up . . .

Undoubtedly, he was going to be the subject of a lot of talk. That's simply the way things worked in small towns. Wasn't every day a man's fiancée up and married someone else.

"Are you ready for that tour?" He pushed back his chair.

She hesitated. "If you have something you'd rather do, I can entertain myself. I brought quite a collection of books with me, as well as my harp. I'll be fine on my own."

"You brought your harp?" Who traveled with musical instruments? He'd never understand the whims of the wealthy.

"It's a Celtic harp, small enough to hold on my lap. I've played for many years. The music soothes me."

"I know what you mean," he said, surprised they had something in common. "About the soothing part. I play the fiddle."

"Oh?" Interest stirred in her expression. "I would like to hear you play sometime. Fran didn't mention that you played an instrument."

"That's because I didn't tell her."

One pitfall of relationships conducted at a distance was that important details were often overlooked or left out entirely. In Francesca's case, details like another suitor. Thoughts of her with another man churned up unpleasant emotions. The betrayal affected him deeply. If and when he ever decided to court another lady, he'd be certain to keep things simple.

And the lady sitting across from him was anything but.

CHAPTER FOUR

Strolling about the O'Malley farm, Kate's gaze was drawn repeatedly to her handsome guide. Sunlight filtered through the leaves overhead, showering patches of light on the navy cotton shirt stretched taut across his back and shoulders. Josh's rich drawl made each word sound like a caress. Listening to him explain the names and uses of each structure lulled her into a state of contentment.

He'd spoken hesitantly at first, his expression guarded, as if he expected her to be bored. Her many questions had brought about a change in his tone and manner, however. He was clearly proud of his family's farm. And from what she'd seen, he had reason to be.

She surveyed her surroundings with a practiced eye. People back home would enjoy seeing these rural images. The wealthy would use them as a guide to plan sojourns to the mountains. Those who couldn't afford to visit would at least be able to glimpse the beauty of East Tennessee. She could hardly wait to get started!

Kate found the workings of a farm fascinating. Here people had to be self-sufficient, working with the land and its offerings to provide for their needs.

She would never tell him Francesca would've been less than thrilled with her new home. No doubt, she would've taken one look and hightailed it back to the city.

Pushing away from the corn crib, he jerked a thumb over his shoulder. "All that's left to show you is the apple house."

"Apple house?" Five rows deep, the orchard fanned out in both directions behind him. There wasn't a building in sight.

"It's where we store the apples we don't immediately use." He extended his arm. "The ground is uneven in places. I wouldn't want you to stumble and fall."

She slipped her hand into the crook of his arm, his muscled forearm bunching beneath her fingers. They strolled at an even pace to the orchard. A gentle breeze stirred the trees, carrying with it the fragrant, tangy scent of the fruit hanging from the branches.

"I don't see a house."

He pointed to the steep hillside beyond

the trees. "Look there. See the door?"

Squinting, she could just make out a low roofline and a child-size door. "It looks like a child's playhouse."

He laughed. "Come, I'll show you."

As they drew closer, she saw that it had been built into the hillside and only the front facade of stone and timber was visible. When she questioned him, he said it was to maintain the temperature inside at an even level and thus keep the apples from spoiling. Again, she was impressed by the family's ingenuity.

Using his shoulder, he edged open the door. With a flourish of his hand, he said, "Ladies first."

She bit her lip. From where she was standing, the interior looked awfully dark and cavelike. But he was waiting patiently, assessing her with those intense blue eyes.

She didn't have to stay inside, she reasoned. What could a quick peek hurt?

Drawing a deep breath, Kate stepped through the doorway, bowing her head to avoid the low crossbeam. Cool, musky air filled her nostrils. Stacks of empty baskets filled the long, narrow space.

It wasn't so bad.

Then Josh came in behind her, his body blocking out the light.

Her heart tripped inside her chest. Nausea threatened, and she felt strangely light-headed.

Memories from the past swept over her, and spinning on her heel, she collided with his solid chest. "Please, I need to get out."

His hands came up to steady her. "What's wrong?"

Without answering, she ducked beneath his arm and shot out the door. Once again in the open field, she sucked in a lungful of air. *Please don't pass out.* Pressing a palm against her clammy forehead, she willed herself to remain calm.

"Hey." He came abreast of her, his hand cupping her upper arm. "You're as white as a sheet. Let's go over here and sit for a spell."

Kate leaned on his strength as he guided her to a fallen log beneath a nearby apple tree. He helped her settle, then sat close beside her. She couldn't dwell on his near-ness, only her acute embarrassment.

What must he think of her?

"I — I'm all right now."

"What happened back there?" he prompted, his voice thick with concern. "Did I do something to make you uneasy?"

"No, it wasn't you." Eyes downcast, she plucked at the ruffles on her sleeve. "I don't like small, confined spaces. I tend to panic, as you've just witnessed." Her heart rate was slowing to normal, the nausea fading.

"I wouldn't have insisted on your going inside had I known. I'm sorry."

She shifted her gaze to his hands, resting on his knees. Tanned and smooth, they were strong, capable hands.

"It wasn't your fault. I knew better."

"Have you always felt this way?"

No, not always. "For a long time, yes." *Please just leave it at that.*

He was quiet. Then, reaching up to the limb suspended above their heads, he plucked two apples and offered her one. "Feel like eating something? The natural sugar might put some color back into your cheeks."

She met his assessing gaze and got lost in the blue depths. The quirk of his lips in a friendly smile broke the spell.

Accepting the fruit, she balanced it in the palms of her hands, wondering how she'd be able to eat it without making a mess of herself and her outfit. Come to think of it, she hadn't eaten an uncut apple since she was a little girl. It was one of those simple acts classified as unladylike. A young lady of her social standing should never appear less than picture-perfect.

Beside her, Josh was already enjoying his.

A tiny seed of rebellion sprouted in her mind. She wasn't in New York. This wasn't the estate. She was on a farm in the Tennessee mountains. Surely the rules of what her mother considered proper conduct could be bent a little.

Sinking her teeth into the firm flesh, Kate relished the sweet-tart explosion on her tongue. Maybe it was the combination of warm sunshine and fresh air or Josh's presence beside her, but she was certain this was the most delicious apple she'd ever tasted.

When the core was all that was left, she glanced over to find him grinning at her.

"What?"

"You, ah, have juice dribbling down your chin."

"I do?"

He caught her wrist. "Wait. Use my handkerchief."

Pulling a clean white square of cloth from his pants pocket, he reached over and wiped her chin. His other hand still held her wrist, the pads of his fingers pressed against her skin so that surely he could detect the spike in her pulse.

He lowered his hand. "There," he murmured with a distracted air, "good as new."

"Thanks," she managed in a weak voice.

Then, as if just noticing he still held her, he dropped her wrist like a hot coal.

Surging to his feet, he put distance between them, stroking his goatee in a nervous gesture. "Well, that's all there is to show you. Tour's over." He jerked a thumb over his shoulder. "Guess we should head back to the house so that I can warm up the soup Ma made for lunch."

What had just happened? Whatever it was, he'd been affected the same way she had. And he didn't seem at all pleased.

What was he thinking? Allowing himself to be affected by Kate Morgan. Of all the foolish, irresponsible . . . Hadn't he learned a thing from his tangle with one spoiled heiress?

Annoyed, he was quiet on the walk back and throughout the meal. Kate, perhaps sensing his mood, was quiet as well, seemingly content to listen to his father, brothers and himself discuss farm business.

With the afternoon stretching before them, he'd decided to show her around town. Strolling beside her, he glanced at her profile.

She was soaking in their surroundings as if imprinting the scene upon her memory.

Was this city girl a nature lover or was this intense observation a result of her profession?

Her expression brightened. "Look!"

He followed her gaze to a hollowed-out tree trunk where a momma raccoon and four kits lay curled up in their nest, a tangle of gray-and-white fur.

"What an adorable sight!" she whispered, her smile full of girlish excitement. "How old do you think they are?"

"I'd say four or five months." He matched his voice to hers so as not to disturb the sleeping family.

"To see them in real life is such a treat!"

"What? You don't have raccoons in the big city?"

She appeared thoughtful. "Perhaps in Central Park. The deer are plentiful there, I'm told, as are foxes."

The largest city he'd visited was Knoxville. Amid the noise, crowded streets and hectic pace, he'd quickly discovered he preferred country life.

"You've never been there?" he asked, wondering for the first time what she did to pass the time.

"A handful of times. I wasn't fortunate enough to see any wildlife."

"Well, there's plenty of it here."

Her gaze was drawn once again to the sleeping raccoons. "I'm continually struck by God's handiwork. His imagination and creativity. Nature reflects His majesty, wouldn't you agree?"

Josh was surprised to hear her speak about God. He'd tried on several occasions to engage Francesca in a conversation about faith, but she'd skirted the issue, saying only that she was a frequent church attendee. Was this another area of difference between the sisters?

"I agree wholeheartedly."

Something in his voice must've snagged her attention, for she turned and thoughtfully regarded him. They shared smiles of understanding, an acknowledgment that on this important subject they were in agreement.

Then, before he could get too accustomed to her heart-melting smiles, he resumed walking. She fell into step beside him.

Crossing the bridge into town, the first business they passed was his friend Tom's barbershop. Since it was midafternoon, the shop was empty of customers. Tom stood in back, polishing his tools.

Glancing out the window, he spotted Josh and waved, his brows hiking up when his gaze lit on Kate. He flashed Josh a wolfish grin and a thumbs-up. He must not have heard of Francesca's defection.

The tips of his ears burning, Josh slid his gaze to Kate, who appeared unaware of the exchange. Her stiff black bonnet shielded the sides of her face, so it was unlikely she'd seen anything.

Great. Everyone was going to assume she was his bride-to-be. He'd forever be explaining himself. It'd be easier to call a town meeting and set the record straight once and for all.

They walked in the direction of the mercantile. Out of habit, his gaze homed in on the empty store for sale across the street, the one he'd been saving up to buy. When he saw the owner, Chadwick Fulton, ducking inside, he stopped abruptly.

"I see someone I need to talk to. Would you mind if I met you at the mercantile in about fifteen or twenty minutes?"

"No, not at all." Curiosity marked her expression.

He hesitated, suddenly remembering his and Francesca's outings in Sevierville and her insistence that he stay by her side. "Are you sure? I wouldn't want you to feel ill at ease, you being new in town. I can put it off until another time."

"Don't worry," she surveyed the single

road of businesses and smiled, dimples flashing. "I'm fairly certain I won't get lost."

Pleased by her response, Josh smiled back. Apparently, Kate Morgan could take care of herself. "Clawson's is the last business on this side of the street. You can't miss it. I'll catch up with you."

He waited until she'd gone inside to cross the street and study the storefront. He imagined the words *J. D. O'Malley Furniture Company* scrolled in large letters across the plate-glass windows. His dream of opening his own furniture store was so close to reality.

"Good morning, Mr. Fulton," he greeted as he entered, closing the door behind him.

Seated behind the only piece of furniture left behind, a scuffed hunk of wood masquerading as a desk, the old man looked up and grunted. "O'Malley."

"How are you today?"

"What do ya want?"

Fulton's grumpy response wasn't unusual. He was an unhappy, crotchety old man.

"Sir, I came by to let you know that I've almost got the money to buy this place. I'll be paying you a visit as soon as I finish a few more orders."

"The sooner I sell it, the better," he groused, then shook a gnarled finger at Josh.

72

"Remember, I ain't holdin' this place for you. Cash talks, and so far you ain't shown me any."

Josh understood it was the way of business, but he didn't have to like it. Mr. Fulton wouldn't agree to accept a deposit. "Yes, sir. I understand." He tugged on the brim of his hat. "Good day."

"Yeah, yeah." He waved him out. "G'day."

After taking one last look around the space and mentally calculating how many pieces he'd need to fill it, he left. He eyed the mercantile across the street, deciding he had time to stop by the post office and see if he had any letters from his cousin Juliana. He wasn't consistent in his replies, but so far she'd overlooked that fact and kept the letters coming. They never failed to lift his spirits.

She'd only been gone a month, but it felt like a lifetime. He took comfort in the fact that her new husband was making her happy.

Inside the post office, he was surprised to see a line of people. He had time, though. Kate didn't seem to be the type to fuss if a man was a few minutes late.

Kate strolled along the boardwalk carrying the small brown sack of hairpins and hand mirror she'd just purchased. Though not a large store, she'd been pleasantly surprised by the variety and quality of goods. The proprietor and his wife had been friendly and helpful without being overbearing. And customers greeted her with either a nod or a smile.

The overall atmosphere of the town was one of easy-going charm. People back home seemed to be more formal, keeping to themselves as they went about their business.

Glancing up and down the street, she searched for Josh. She wondered what could be keeping him. He'd certainly been intent on some task. Perhaps it had taken longer than expected.

She decided to head in the direction of the shop he'd disappeared into. Waiting for a wagon to pass, she lifted her skirts off the dusty ground and hurried to the other side. She didn't notice the two men standing outside the post office until she was almost upon them.

The shorter of the two elbowed his companion in the ribs and muttered words too low for her to hear. That man, whose face had been obscured by his hat's wide brim, lifted his head and stared hard at her. She recognized him at once. Tyler Matthews.

Her feet slowed as his hungry gaze devoured her, looking her up and down as if she were a slice of pie to be savored. Feeling violated, she stopped, unwilling to go any nearer. When he advanced a step toward her, Kate whirled and walked as quickly as she could in the opposite direction while trying not to attract attention.

Glancing back to see if he still followed her, she collided with a muscled chest and her sack slipped out of her hands. It hit the weathered boards with a thunk. Hands came up to steady her.

"Kate?"

Josh. "I'm sorry," she panted, "I didn't see you."

"What has you upset?" Holding her steady with a gentle grip, he gazed down at her with concern.

"I saw Tyler. He started to follow me."

Lips compressing in irritation, he scanned the boardwalk behind her. "I don't see him. He must've ducked in between the buildings. Where did you first spot him?"

"Outside the post office."

Slowly she became aware of his thumb lazily stroking her arm, an unconscious gesture meant to soothe.

His brows came together. "You okay?"

"Yes, just a bit unnerved. This is something I've never experienced before, having someone fixated on me." She shuddered. His fingers flexed in response.

Josh was near enough for her to feel his body heat, to see the leap of his pulse in the hollow of his neck. The dark shirt complemented his tanned skin and brilliant eyes. Her gaze fell to his mouth, noting that his lips looked warm and generous. What would it be like to be kissed by Josh? she wondered suddenly.

Had he ever kissed Fran? Her sister had been surprisingly coy on the subject, never hinting either way. Jealousy gripped Kate's heart, startling her. She had no business entertaining such thoughts!

Tearing her gaze up to his, she sucked in a breath at the confused interest in his eyes. With an almost imperceptible shake of his head, as if to clear his thoughts, he swallowed hard.

"I want you to be careful." He bent and picked up her sack. "Stay alert to your surroundings, especially when you're alone."

"Of course, I —"

"Josh!" a female voice trilled. "Aren't you gonna introduce us to your fiancée?"

CHAPTER FIVE

Two young ladies stood watching them, eyes wide with curiosity.

Kate flushed with embarrassment. No doubt they were drawing their own conclusions to what appeared to be an intimate moment. What would they think when they realized she wasn't Francesca?

"Girls, I'd like you to meet Miss Kate Morgan." Josh put distance between them. "Kate, these are my cousins. Megan and Nicole O'Malley."

Like Kate and Francesca, the O'Malley sisters did not resemble each other in the slightest. With her dusky-blond curls and angelic countenance, Megan radiated a sweetness not present in Nicole, who was a striking beauty with raven hair and china-blue eyes.

Megan's friendly smile put Kate instantly at ease. Nicole stared at her with undisguised awe, her gaze taking in every inch of

Kate's attire. Compared to their comparatively simple dresses, she supposed her ensemble was a bit much.

"It's a pleasure to meet you."

"Welcome to Gatlinburg, Kate," Megan said.

"Kate? But I thought —" Nicole began, only to stop when Megan nudged her shoulder. "Uh, it's nice to meet you."

Hating that Josh had been put in the position yet again of having to explain this horrible situation, she saved him the trouble. "My sister, Francesca, isn't coming, I'm afraid."

"We'll discuss it later," he said firmly, searching the street for onlookers.

That was one advantage of living in a large city, she thought — a person could blend in with the crowd. No one knew your business, and no one cared.

It was obvious the girls respected Josh, for they dropped the subject like a hot potato.

"We were on our way to Plum's for tea. Would you like to join us?" Megan asked, her eyes hopeful.

"It's our town's very first café," Nicole gushed. "Mrs. Greene, the proprietress, says one day soon we'll have loads of people coming through here looking at our mountains and that they'll all need a place to eat.

Ma thinks she's lost her mind —"

"Nicole, please." Megan shot her an exasperated glance.

She waited for Josh to reply, who deferred to Kate. "It's up to you."

After the near run-in with Tyler and her disturbing awareness of Josh, a cup of hot tea might help her to relax. "That sounds like a splendid idea."

"Wonderful." Megan beamed her pleasure.

Kate hadn't always been the best judge of character, but she got the feeling Megan O'Malley would make a good friend. And she didn't have many of those. Most of the young socialites of her acquaintance were like Fran, interested only in the latest fashions, the finest parties and, most importantly, finding a rich, suitable husband.

While she liked nice clothes, she would much rather take photographs than spend hours poring through *Harper's Bazaar* or standing for fittings. Parties among her set were overrated. Same food, same music, same people. Different setting.

As for a husband, she did want one of those. Longed, actually, for someone to love who loved her heart, mind and soul. But after what had happened with Wesley, well, she worried no man would want her — a used woman.

He certainly hadn't wanted her. Once had been enough for him.

While she'd been sure he would show up the next day with a ring and a proposal, he'd boarded a ship for England instead.

Shoving the remembered pain and humiliation aside, she crossed the dusty street with Josh, the sisters walking ahead of them. They were chattering and laughing, seeming as close as sisters could be, and Kate experienced a familiar twinge of regret. She and Fran had never shared such a close bond, not even as children. Now that her sister had a new husband and a home of her own, Kate doubted they ever would.

Plum Café was an unexpectedly charming establishment. Mauve tablecloths covered the round tables, and matching curtains edged with gold ribbon adorned the windows overlooking the street, softening the harsh glare of sunlight.

An assortment of tantalizing aromas hung in the air. Voices and the clatter of dishes could be heard coming from the kitchen in back. Only one of the tables was occupied — an elderly couple who smiled and nodded but otherwise minded their own business.

Josh pulled a chair out for each of them

80

and once they were seated, lowered his tall form into the one beside her. He took off his hat and hooked it on the back of his chair, then ran a hand through his hair. It was impossible to judge his mood by his closed expression. Was he thinking of his canceled wedding?

The proprietress, a meticulously dressed, middle-age lady, appeared and took their orders.

Nicole leaned eagerly forward. "Kate, you must tell us about New York. Have you been to Macy's? What's it like?"

Kate smiled. "Macy's has the most amazing window displays. The staff is attentive and knowledgeable. There is so much to see, you could spend days browsing the aisles."

"Is there a library in the city?" Megan looked hopeful.

"There are two — the Astor Library, used primarily for research, and the Lenox Library, which has mainly rare, religious books. I don't visit either one, since our estate houses a grand library with both classics and recent works."

"What a treat to have all those books at your disposal. Why, I doubt I'd get much else done if I lived there!"

"What type of books do you like to read?" Kate asked. "I brought a crate full with me.

You're welcome to borrow as many as you'd like."

"Honest?" Megan seemed pleased with the offer.

"All she reads are love stories." Nicole rolled her eyes. "Nothing else."

"That's not true," the other girl protested. "I like adventure stories, too."

"If I have to hear about Mr. Darcy and Miss Bennet one more time," she exclaimed, "I think I'll be sick."

"Nicole!"

Kate dipped her head to hide a smile. Their drinks arrived then, along with a plate of gooey, pecan-sprinkled cinnamon rolls.

Josh held up a hand. "We didn't order these, Mrs. Greene."

"Consider it an engagement gift." The lady's smile encompassed Kate and Josh. "Congratulations."

Before they could correct her, she disappeared into the kitchen.

"Oh, dear." Cheeks burning, Kate lowered her gaze to her lap.

When she felt his touch on her shoulder, she looked up and got lost in his impossibly blue eyes. "Forget about it," he said quietly. "It'd be a shame to let these go to waste. I'll clear things up with Mrs. Greene later."

"Here you are." Megan set a roll in front

of her. "That woman is an amazing cook. You have to try one."

Nicole was already biting into the pastry, an expression of rapture on her youthful face. "Mmm."

She supposed she could set aside her self-imposed aversion to sugar-laden treats just this once. "Fine. But just so you know, I don't normally do this."

All eyes were on her as she lifted the first bite into her mouth. The rich, cinnamon pastry melted on her tongue. She stifled a moan of appreciation.

She attempted a stern expression. "Now I'm in trouble. I will have to make a point of avoiding the Plum Café from now on and maybe even this entire side of the street."

The sisters chuckled. Even Josh managed a smile.

"Want to know what I think?" He set down his coffee mug. The teasing light in his eyes was unexpected, stealing her breath. "Now that you've tasted them, you won't be able to resist."

"I disagree," she challenged with a lift of her chin. "When it comes to sweets, I happen to have unwavering willpower."

His gaze dropped to her mouth. His eyes darkened, all emotion hidden. "You, um, have a spot of cinnamon." He indicated the corner of her lips.

Self-conscious, Kate used her napkin. "Better?"

"Yes." Shifting in the chair, he addressed Megan. "I was at the post office just now and picked up a letter from Juliana."

"Oh?" She exchanged a pointed glance with Nicole. "What did she say?"

Nicole giggled.

"I haven't read it." He stared hard at them. "What's up?"

"Juliana's expecting!" Nicole blurted.

"You weren't supposed to tell," Megan admonished in a hushed whisper.

Beside her, Josh went very still. "Why keep it a secret?"

Eyes averted, Nicole toyed with her teacup. Megan met his gaze head-on.

"It's not a secret, of course. It's just that, well, Juliana wanted to tell you herself. No doubt it's in your letter." To Kate, she explained, "Juliana is our eldest sister. She was married last month and now lives with her husband, Evan Harrison, in Cades Cove. She and Josh were best friends."

Gulping the last of his coffee, Josh set the cup down with a thud. "Are you two going straight home after this?"

"Yes."

"Would you mind walking Kate home?"

"Not at all."

Grabbing his hat, he looked at her. "Is that okay with you?"

"Certainly."

Standing, he slipped Megan a banknote. "This will take care of the bill and tip."

"Josh —"

He silenced his cousin with a look.

The three sat without speaking as they watched him leave. As her seat was facing the window, she could see him striding purposefully down the street. He was obviously distraught by this sudden news. Her heart went out to him.

"Kate, did your sister call off the wedding?" Megan's troubled countenance revealed how deeply she cared about her cousin.

"Yes. In fact, she has already married someone else."

Kate cringed at Nicole's shocked gasp. Megan's eyes glistened with unshed tears.

"He must be heartbroken," she whispered. "He was already sad about Juliana's leaving."

"She and Josh were practically joined at the hip."

"He lost his best friend," Megan confirmed. "And now his bride . . ."

Lounging on a sun-warmed rock, Josh stared unseeing at the water coursing past. The fish weren't biting today.

He'd been in his workshop since leaving the café, working most of the day to finish Mr. Wilcox's dining table. His hands ached from the amount of sanding and polishing he'd done, but it was a small inconvenience. The table was finished. The money he'd get from it would bring him one step closer to his dream.

If someone else didn't beat him to the punch, that is.

A twig snapped. Josh whipped around, his hand going to the pistol in his holster. Spying Kate, he relaxed.

She'd abandoned her stiff jacket and wore only a long-sleeved, ruffled black blouse with her deep purple skirts. Slung over her shoulder were an odd-shaped bag and a leather strap attached to a square box. With the other hand, she carried a tripod stand.

Her porcelain skin was flushed pink. Chocolate curls had escaped confinement to brush against her cheeks. It was obvious she hadn't seen him. Her gaze scanned the woods, occasionally dropping to the ground as she maneuvered fallen logs and uneven terrain.

"Kate."

Her hand went to her throat. "You startled me!"

"Sorry." Standing, he removed his hat. "Do you need help?"

"I can manage." Changing direction, she headed his way.

He met her halfway and took the tripod.

With careful movements, she set the box and bag on the leaf-strewn ground.

She held out her hands for the tripod.

"I'm sorry about earlier," he said. "I shouldn't have left."

"I survived," she huffed. "Although you could've warned me about Nicole's propensity to talk endlessly of fashion." If it weren't for the teasing light dancing in her eyes, he would've thought she was serious.

Again, her reaction was unexpected. Francesca would've pouted over such carelessness on his part, no matter that he was upset, trying to absorb one change after another.

"It's a topic of great interest to her, I'm afraid." He sighed, a hint of answering humor in his voice. "She drove you to distraction, I take it?"

"Not at all! I like Megan and Nicole very

much. They are nicely mannered young ladies."

"Glad to hear it. I'm rather fond of them myself."

"The sisters you never had?"

"Living next door to each other, we were practically raised as one big family. They do like to accuse me of assuming the role of protective older brother."

"You were upset earlier. Is everything okay with the one who moved away?"

"Juliana's fine." He slipped his hands into his pockets. "Better than fine, actually. Ecstatic. I'm thrilled for her. It's just that so much has changed the past few weeks."

Her expression turned pensive. "Yes, I can imagine it's a lot to take in."

Certain she was thinking of his canceled wedding and not at all interested in going down that path, he resumed his post and picked up his rod.

Indicating his empty pail, he said, "I was hoping to have trout for supper, but so far the fish aren't obliging."

A ghost of a smile gracing her mouth, she surveyed the pebble-strewn stream and dense forest spreading out around them. It was quiet here. Restful. Nothing but the trickle of water and the rustle of leaves overhead.

"There's something magical about this place," she said, her voice hushed. "It's so beautiful it almost defies description."

With the onset of fall, the leaves were already beginning to thin out. "You should see it in spring and summer. The greenery is so thick you feel like you're the only creature for miles around, save the birds and squirrels."

Her gaze settled on his. "I'd like that."

He hadn't meant it as an invitation. It wasn't that he didn't like her. Kate seemed nice enough. But she didn't fit in here. And although the physical similarity wasn't there, in his mind he'd never be able to separate her from Francesca and her heartless betrayal.

He pointed to the box. "What do you have there?"

"My camera."

Crouching down, she flipped open the lid and lifted it out. Made of polished cherrywood with brass fittings, black accordion-like material in between the two ends, it appeared to be an expensive piece of equipment. "Would you mind if I took a photograph of you?"

"What? Now?" He wasn't primped and primed for a portrait. Far from it.

"Yes, now." She stood. "Not every photo

has to be staged in a studio."

"But I'm not dressed —"

"You look fine." Her gaze flicked over his shirt and trousers. "Natural. I wouldn't expect you to be fishing in a three-piece suit, and neither would anyone else." She paused in sliding a piece of square coated glass into the camera. "If you'd rather not, I understand. I don't want to make you uneasy."

"No, it's fine."

"Great." Her wide smile elicited one of his own. "I'm going across."

There was a natural bridge to the other side, a mound of earth and rocks she crossed without incident. When she was directly across from him, he said, "I thought photographers had to travel with portable darkrooms." The stream wasn't all that wide, so he didn't have to raise his voice.

"Not with the invention of the dry plate." She steadied the stand before placing the camera on top. "The image is fixed and doesn't have to be processed right away."

"I haven't heard anything about it."

"That's because they've only recently been manufactured for widespread sale. Okay, look directly at me. And sit as still as possible." Peering into the camera, she removed the cover and waited for a full minute before replacing it. Straightening, she seemed pleased. "That's going to be a good one, I think."

Crossing back over, she was replacing the camera in its box when he spoke.

"Tell me about Francesca's husband."

Her hands stilled. She looked uncertain.

"I don't even know her married name," he persisted.

"His name is Percy Johnson."

"Francesca Johnson. I think Francesca O'Malley has a nicer ring to it, but that's just my opinion."

Her mouth flattened. "I'm sorry."

"I know he's not a common laborer, like me. What does he do? Or rather, what does his family do? He probably hasn't worked a day in his life." He couldn't disguise the bitterness in his voice.

I'm sorry, God. I can't help envying the guy. He got the girl, and I'm left here to pick up the pieces.

Indignation flashed in her eyes. "There's nothing common about you. My sister chose flash and glamour over depth and substance. She made a foolish decision."

Her words sparked an odd pang in his chest. He couldn't figure out why she was defending him. She didn't know him. Not really. Except, she *had* listened to his letters and glimpsed into his soul without his consent.

"Don't get me wrong," she hastened to add, "I love my sister. It's just that we each have our own opinions of what's important in life."

He found that difficult to believe. They might disagree on specifics, but their outlook couldn't be all that different. They shared the same upbringing, the same advantages.

Proposing marriage to a woman so far above his station had been a colossal mistake. He should've realized from the beginning that their worlds were too far apart.

"I just don't get it," he wondered aloud. "Why not break off the engagement the moment she decided to patch things up with him?"

She edged closer to the water, stepping on a smooth, slanted rock scattered with orange leaves. "I wish I had an answer for you. Her behavior is as much a mystery to me as it is to you."

"The two of you aren't close?"

She frowned. "No."

He wanted to question her further, to ask why her parents hadn't invited her to join them in Europe, but it was none of his business. Soon she'd be gone and he wouldn't have to spare another thought on the Morgan family.

She pointed to a rounded shell bobbing above the surface. "Do you know what kind of turtle that is?"

"Can't rightly say, but there are a number of painted box turtles hereabouts."

"A pity it moves too quickly for my camera."

His eyes on the turtle, he hadn't noticed her getting closer to the rock's edge.

"Be careful," he warned, holding out a hand. "Those rocks can be slippery —"

"All I want is a closer look."

One moment she was standing, bent at the hip with hands braced against her knees. An instant later, she was facedown in the stream.

Dropping his pole, Josh strode through the thigh-deep water. Wrapping his arm around her, his hand curled around her waist, he helped her stand. "Are you hurt?"

A bubble of laughter escaped as she wiped the moisture from her eyes. Her mouth a breath away from his ear, the soft, husky sound shot liquid fire through his veins.

"I'm fine." Taking stock of her sodden clothing, she grimaced. "My pride is a bit bruised, however. You did warn me, didn't you?"

Josh couldn't stop his smile. "Did you get that closer look you wanted?"

"No. I guess he didn't want to stick around for all the excitement."

A shiver coursed through her body. Though it was a warm September day, the water was cool. And she was wet from head to toe, the layers of clothing clinging to her petite yet womanly frame. Water dripped from her hair onto his shirt.

His gaze dropped to her mouth. What would it feel like —

Stiffening, he dropped his arm and stepped back, the water swirling around his legs.

Have you lost your mind? This is Francesca's sister, remember?

"Let's get you back to the cabin," he muttered, avoiding her curious gaze.

Once he'd helped her to the bank, he was careful to keep his distance the entire walk home. Nor did he attempt conversation. If Kate wondered about his mood, she didn't comment.

Leaning the tripod stand against the porch railing, he directed his gaze to the blue mountain ridges framed by the sky. Anything to keep from looking at her. "I'll ask Ma to bring you a cup of tea."

"That's not necessary," she countered in a

subdued voice. "I'm certain she has more important things to do than wait on me."

He clenched his fists. Of course she would be gracious. He couldn't imagine that ever coming out of his ex's mouth. From what he'd seen, Francesca had relished being waited on.

Again, his mind discharged a warning signal. This woman was dangerous.

"You're our guest. She wants you to be comfortable here."

"Yet I don't make you comfortable, do I?"

He did look at her then. Even with her wet hair plastered to her face and head and her clothes disheveled, she was beautiful. The vulnerability he sensed in her touched a chord deep inside.

Setting his jaw, he hardened his heart. "You don't affect me at all, Miss Morgan. Evenin'." He tugged on his hat's brim and, pivoting on his heel, left her staring after him.

Chapter Six

Stung by his cool dismissal, Kate watched him stride away. He held himself stiffly erect, his broad shoulders taut with tension. Well, he'd certainly told her, hadn't he? She'd been forward and assuming. What did she expect?

Josh was merely tolerating her presence. She was an interloper, a painful reminder of loss and betrayal.

She didn't fit in at home, and she certainly didn't fit here.

Shivering in the late-afternoon sunlight, she went inside to change. The quiet that greeted her inside the quaint space compounded her loneliness. At the estate, she was never completely alone. Butlers, footmen, housekeepers, ladies' maids and manservants moved discreetly about, attending to their business, seeing to the day-to-day running of the expansive mansion and tending to the needs of its occupants.

Though New York was her home, she wasn't happy there. And while she gained immense satisfaction from her photography work and her gardening, she lived with the knowledge that her presence wasn't wanted or needed by anyone. She didn't brighten anyone's day or bring a smile to a loved one's face. No one was eager to share secrets with her or give her a hug.

From the time she was a little girl, she'd known something was wrong with her. Her mother had never looked at her with pride and pleasure, as she had Francesca. Instead, whenever her gaze lit on Kate, her mouth would tighten and a wrinkle would form between her brows, as if puzzling out an impossible riddle.

The nightmare with Nanny Marie underscored her feelings of inadequacy.

By the time Wesley Farrington IV entered her life when she was seventeen, she'd been desperate to forge a connection with someone, anyone.

Seated on the edge of the bed combing out the tangles in her hair, her eyes drifted shut as she recalled their first meeting. Her parents were hosting an elaborate party, and everyone who was anyone in New York society had made an appearance. The ballroom glittered and sparkled like the contents of a jewelry box with its crystal and gold chandeliers, gilt-edged mirrors and jewel-toned carpets. The air was sweet with the fragrance of fresh flowers spilling from vases placed about the room, the sets of French doors thrown open to the balmy night.

While Kate had watched from the sidelines as gaily dressed couples swirled and dipped across the marble floors, Francesca had been surrounded by a bevy of admirers.

She'd noticed Wesley the instant he entered the room. Darkly handsome, with a smile that hinted of secrets and promises, the Oxford graduate had captured the attention of nearly every female under the age of sixty. Kate watched him charm each one, in turn, never dreaming he'd spare a word for her.

So when he'd appeared at her side not an hour later and requested a dance, she'd gaped at him. He laughed and repeated the request. They danced the next two dances, then escaped outside to stroll through the gardens. By the end of the night, she was certain she was in love.

Over the course of two months, he took her on carriage rides in Central Park and showered her with trinkets and roses and boxes of chocolates from Paris.

Kate had never been happier. Wesley

treated her as if she were the most special girl in the world. He loved her. He hadn't voiced the words, but she could see it in his eyes.

It was that assumption that had ultimately led her to make the worst decision of her life. One night of pleasure had cost her not only her virtue, but a future with him.

Wesley never explained why he left. For months afterward, she'd waited impatiently for correspondence from him. Surely he would apologize for leaving so abruptly, reveal his reasons for abandoning her. She waited in vain.

She concluded that she must've done something wrong. Or disappointed him somehow.

When her mother questioned her, Kate made the mistake of confiding in her.

Georgia had railed at her. She had risked the family's reputation and ruined forever her chances of marrying a decent man. She was damaged goods.

A sharp rap on the door startled her, and the brush slipped out of her hand and clattered to the floor.

Her stomach flip-flopped. Was it him? Had he come back to apologize?

"J-just a minute," she called, her fingers going to her neck to make sure the buttons of her china-red housecoat were buttoned. She wasn't dressed to receive visitors, but this wasn't the estate. There was no one else to open the door.

Pulling it open, she found Nathan standing on the other side with a tray in his hands.

"Hi. Josh told me about your dunking." His smile was gentle. "He fixed a pot of tea and asked me to deliver it."

With a grateful smile, she gave him room to enter. Josh had ignored her refusal and sent the tea anyway.

Nathan set the tray on the table, and the tangy scent of ginger filled the cabin. There was a rose-emblazoned teapot, a matching cup and saucer, honey and a dessert plate bearing four pillowlike cookies. Her mouth watered. What was he doing, sending her sweets?

"Is there anything else you need?"

"No." Kate rested her hands on the top of the chair. "Thanks for bringing this over. Would you like to join me?"

"I wish I could, but I gotta check on the new calf."

She lifted the dessert plate. "Take at least one of these with you."

Grinning, he held up his hands. "There's a dozen or more of those in the kitchen.

I've already had my fair share." He started for the door. "See you at supper."

When he'd gone, she stared at the table, her gaze caught by the lone cup and saucer. Tears sprang up. It seemed she was destined to always be alone.

Seated at the end of the pew with Mary on her left, Kate admired the church's stained-glass windows and ornately carved wooden podium. It was not a large building, by any means, but it was well-maintained and the pews gleamed in the muted, rainbow-colored light.

"What a lovely church," Kate murmured.

Mary sat with her gloved hands folded primly in her lap. "Do you attend services back home?"

"Yes." Kate pictured the grand, overstated auditorium and the fashionably dressed men and women who attended the services. The preacher there was nice enough, though she often left feeling dissatisfied. "I'm eager to hear Reverend Monroe."

"He's a good speaker." She nodded. "I like his practical style. He's humorous, too."

"It was good of him and his wife to take in my driver and Mr. Crandall the other night. I'll have to personally thank them."

"I'll introduce you after the service."

"Thank you."

Mary leaned close, her voice hushed. "You didn't happen to see Joshua this morning, did you? He's never late."

"No, I didn't."

He wasn't at supper last night. When no one remarked at his absence, she'd assumed he'd informed them of his whereabouts. When he hadn't shown up for breakfast, Kate got the sinking feeling he was avoiding her. Why his behavior should bother her she hadn't a clue. So what if Josh O'Malley didn't like her? She wouldn't be here forever.

Glancing over her shoulder, she became aware of several people watching her with interest. Pretending not to notice, she stared straight ahead once more. Of course, the townsfolk would wonder about her. By now everyone must know she was not Josh's fiancée. She didn't like being the center of attention, however.

Maybe that's why Josh hadn't come. How difficult it would be for him to face these people — his friends and acquaintances — and admit he'd been cast off! *Father, please comfort him. Ease his hurt and disappointment.*

At last, the service began. With Mrs. Monroe at the piano, the reverend led the congregation in two familiar hymns. Its beauty was in its simplicity. Her spirit soared at the sound of the pure worship, voices lifted in praise to God.

When everyone was seated and the reverend opened his Bible, Kate sat unmoving, absorbing his every word.

Sitting in the very last row, two steps from the door, Josh couldn't tear his gaze from Kate. He studied the sweet curve of her cheek, the pink tip of her ear, the slender slope of her neck.

He should be listening to the sermon, he knew, but her rapt expression — the vulnerability and wonder he saw there — captivated him. She'd indicated faith in God, so why did she look as if this was the very first time she'd heard God's Word preached?

He tried to turn his attention to the reverend and failed. His conscience troubled him. He'd been callous and rude, and he was never rude. He prided himself on being a gentleman, yet look at how he'd treated Kate from the very moment he set eyes on her.

The fact was she scared the daylights out of him. Here he was supposed to be nursing a broken heart and instead he found himself intrigued by his former fiancée's little sister.

His instinct told him to steer clear of her. But he didn't want to hurt her. And avoiding her would not go unnoticed, not by her and certainly not by his family.

Remember, she won't be here forever.

Fall was a busy season on the farm, anyway. Hog killings, apple peelings, corn shuckings. When he wasn't helping his father and brothers, he'd be in his workshop, making furniture. The time would pass quickly.

Before he knew it, everyone was standing for the closing prayer. He'd missed the entire message because his mind had been filled with thoughts of her. Not good.

Wanting to skip the inevitable questions and looks of pity from the congregation, Josh ducked out the door and headed home ahead of his family. He waited for Kate in the shade of her front porch.

She hesitated when she saw him. What was she thinking?

"Hi." He stayed where he was, waiting for her to come to him. His parents and brothers waved but continued toward the house.

"Hello."

Kate appeared every inch the sophisticated heiress.

She was meticulously dressed, as usual, in a light brown linen suit with cutouts and dark cocoa piping on the sleeves. Her gloves and bonnet were also dark brown. With the help of his mother, she'd styled her hair differently today — the top half caught up in ribbons while the mass of dark waves tumbled about her shoulders. Sunlight glinted in the strands with each movement of her head.

"What did you think of the service?" Arms folded, he leaned back against the railing.

She climbed the three steps and stopped, her hands folded primly at her waist. "I've never heard anything like it."

That surprised him. "Francesca said your family attends church every Sunday."

"That's true. Our pastor's sermons are mostly about helping the less fortunate. Not once have I left there feeling as I do now, convicted yet encouraged."

Interesting. "Your sister didn't care to discuss her faith. I realize it's a private topic for some people, but now I'm wondering if she didn't have a foundation to draw from."

"A couple of years ago, a friend of mine walked me through the Scriptures, showing me how to become a follower of Jesus Christ. I shared this with both my parents and Francesca." She bowed her head, her fingers now clamped tight. "They weren't interested."

A slow hiss escaped his lips. "I'm sorry."

And he was. Sorry for them, because they were missing out on a precious relationship with the God of the universe. Sorry for Kate. He, too, had loved ones who didn't know Christ and didn't care to know Him. It was tough. And he was sorry for himself. In his longing for a family of his own, he'd neglected to discover the important things about his future bride. As hurtful as it was, he was beginning to think Francesca had done him a favor.

"Me, too. I hold on to hope, however, that one day they will change their minds."

"I'll pray for that."

"Thanks, Josh. That means a lot."

In her eyes he saw sadness and something more, an emotion he himself struggled with. Loneliness. But how could *she* be lonely?

Kate was the member of a prominent, influential New York City family. Certainly she mingled with other socialites her age. Francesca had written in detail about the grand gatherings they attended each week.

Another thought struck him with the full force of a sledgehammer. Not only was Kate lovely and sweeter than pecan pie, she was the eligible daughter of oil magnate Patrick Morgan. Single men must be lining up to court her. The image soured his stomach.

He hadn't asked if she had a steady beau, and he didn't plan to. He was *not* interested in Kate's love life.

Pushing away from the railing, he moved toward her. "Are you joining us for lunch?"

His mother and aunt had planned a picnic.

"Yes, I'm just going inside to choose a couple of books for Megan."

When he drew near, she stepped aside to let him pass. He didn't. He inhaled her citrusy scent. "Romance is her favorite."

Her long lashes swept down to hide her eyes. "I remember."

"And what is yours?"

"I prefer science and nature books."

"You surprise me, Kate."

"Why?" Her gaze shot to his. "Because socialites as a rule must only be interested in the latest fashions? Learning cross-stitch and backgammon?"

"Exactly," he drawled. "For if you women exercise your vast intelligence, you'll soon realize you have no need for men."

Kate burst out laughing. The musical sound warmed him straight through to his soul.

"You have a nice laugh," he said softly.

She blushed and looked away. He could've kicked himself. Why had he said that out loud?

"Well, I'd better change and get the wagon ready."

He did move on then, before he said something else best left unsaid.

It was a perfect afternoon for a picnic, a flawless autumn day with startling blue skies and sunshine that soothed the soul. Perched on the patterned quilt spread out across the grass, Kate was content to listen to the conversation flowing around her.

Megan and Nicole sat on her left and directly across were Nathan and Josh. While she and the girls sat primly with their skirts arranged just so, the men had removed their boots and stretched out their large frames so that they were half sitting, half lying on the quilt. Josh was nearest to her, his pant-clad leg an inch or so from her taupe linen skirt.

Kate felt the weight of his every glance as if it were a physical touch.

His classical features put her in mind of the marble statues in the estate gardens — Roman soldiers of noble beauty and strength. His skin wouldn't be cold to the touch, of course, but certainly as smooth. His trim mustache and goatee gave him a dangerous air, and it wasn't difficult to picture him as a fierce warrior, a leader among men.

The sunlight made the tips of his hair shine liquid gold. No doubt its texture was that of the finest silk . . . *Enough.* Like every other upstanding, morally upright man, he was out of reach. Him especially. To daydream about her sister's former fiancé was utterly unacceptable.

Wrenching her gaze away, she scanned the lush, green fields sloping gently to the stream and the trees along the bank. On distant hills stood row upon row of corn. Black shapes were some farmer's cattle grazing. The landscape's verdant beauty imprinted itself on her mind and settled deep in her soul. Never before had she been so affected by her surroundings.

As Josh had said, this place really was a slice of paradise.

Kate turned her head at the sound of Mary's laughter. She and Sam, along with Alice, Sam's late brother's wife, occupied a second quilt closer to the water. Mary had introduced Kate to the girls' mother that morning at church, and she had seemed sincere in her welcome. In fact, everyone who'd gathered around at the completion of the services had been kind, expressing their delight at meeting her. It had been as pleasant as it had been unsettling. Their lack of formality had been wholly unexpected. She couldn't picture the affluent people of her church acting in such a manner.

Megan and Nicole's younger sisters, fifteen-year-old twins Jessica and Jane, strolled arm in arm along the bank. Caleb wasn't here. He'd escaped immediately after breakfast. Kate wondered where he spent all his time.

"Kate, tell us more about New York."

Nicole's eyes sparkled with curiosity. Of all the O'Malley sisters, the seventeen-year-old wore the finest dresses, and her glossy black mane was at all times meticulously styled, not a hair out of place.

"What would you like to know?"

"How far do you live from the dress shops?"

"There are a number near our home, but oftentimes the designers come to us with new arrivals from London and Paris. If my mother, sister or I need an outfit for a special occasion, they bring sketches and materials to choose from."

Josh scowled in disapproval. She hoped he didn't assume those things were important to her.

"Can you believe that, Megan?" Nicole nudged her sister, her eyes like saucers. "I am so envious!"

Kate lifted a shoulder. "It's convenient. I'm not an avid follower of fashion, like my mother and sister. There are certain colors and fabrics I prefer, of course, but my interests lie elsewhere."

Megan looked up from the book in her lap, a volume of poetry Kate had lent her, blond curls tumbling across her forehead. "How did you come to be interested in photography?"

"My father has friends in that field — both amateurs and professionals. Whenever he visited their studios, he didn't mind my tagging along if I promised not to disturb anything. The cameras fascinated me — the different sizes and wood grains and gadgetry."

"When did you decide to try it for yourself?" Josh shifted, and his knee brushed hers.

The casual contact jolted her. Swallowing hard, she struggled to keep her voice steady. "I wanted my own camera for a long time, but my father made me wait until I was fifteen. Up until the last year or so, the process of taking a photograph and exposing the image was a daunting one. Chemicals were — and still are — involved, although now with the dry plates it isn't rushed." She addressed Megan. "I could take photographs of you and your sisters if you'd like."

"That would be wonderful! Thank you."

Nicole appeared thoughtful. "What should I wear?"

Nathan chuckled. "Clothes."

She stuck her tongue out. "Hilarious, Nathan."

"You've looked fetching in every outfit I've seen you wear," Kate assured her. "Anything you choose will do splendidly."

She blushed prettily. "That's nice of you to say."

Kate caught Josh's appreciative smile, his eyes communicating his approval. It was obvious he cared deeply for his family. Unlike the ambitious, shallow men of her acquaintance, Josh stood for honor and compassion. He was the kind of man who put the needs of others before his own and would sacrifice everything for those he loved.

"What did Kate bring for you to read, Megan?" he asked, his gaze never wavering from Kate's face. Like a moth to a flame, she was drawn to him. She couldn't look away.

"*The Count of Monte Cristo, Great Expectations* and *Mansfield Park*."

"That should keep you occupied for two

or three days." He winked at Kate.

"Maybe one day Megan and I can come and visit you in New York," Nicole said wistfully.

Kate did break eye contact then. "I'd like that," she said, meaning it.

"Honestly?"

"Yes." She laughed. "You're welcome anytime."

"Josh said Francesca is the same age as our eldest sister, Juliana. Twenty-one. How old are you?"

"Nicole." Josh's voice deepened in warning.

"Nineteen."

"The same age as Megan," she gushed. "Do you have a steady beau?"

"You shouldn't ask such things, Nicki," Nathan admonished with a nudge of his foot.

She whipped her head around. "Don't call me that!"

Kate sensed rather than saw Josh's sharpened gaze. "You don't have to answer."

"I don't mind." Nicole hadn't meant to be intrusive. She was young and in awe of Kate's life in the big city. "I don't have anyone special in my life."

"All three of my cousins are single, you know. Well, I suppose Josh isn't ready to court anyone just yet after what your sister did to him. And Caleb —" she scrunched up her nose "— is not what I'd call a catch. A bigger grump I've never met! That leaves Nathan. He's real nice most of the time."

Nathan had tugged on his boots and was hauling Nicole to her feet before anyone could utter a word. He led her, sputtering her displeasure, toward the water. The three of them sat there in heavy silence for what seemed like an eternity. Finally, Megan cleared her throat.

"I think I'll join Jessica and Jane."

Face averted, her gaze on the distant trees, Kate wished she could disappear. Her cheeks burned with humiliation.

"Kate."

"Hmm?"

"Will you look at me?"

His eyes seemed to see straight into her soul, exposing her secrets. "I'm sorry about that. My cousin rarely thinks before she speaks. I'm sure she didn't set out to embarrass you."

"Poor Nathan." She dredged up something resembling a smile. "He won't be able to look me in the eye."

"Nathan may seem shy and unassuming, but he can be tough when the need arises."

She glanced to where Nathan was walking

with Nicole beside the water, his arm around her shoulders. She was a spirited girl. For any man to calm her would take a strong will and finesse.

Kate moved to rise. "Now is probably a good time to speak with your parents about arranging for another place to stay. It slipped my mind yesterday."

A tiny gasp escaped her lips when Josh took abrupt hold of her hand. She'd forgone gloves for this outing, and the sensation of his rougher skin against hers shot fiery tingles up and down her arm. His grip was both gentle and firm, anchoring her to the spot.

"There's no need to go anywhere else. Unless you want to, that is."

She bit her lip. "I do enjoy being around your family. They've been extremely kind to me."

His expression remained neutral. "Then it's settled. You're staying."

CHAPTER SEVEN

East Tennessee was weaving its way into Kate's heart.

The more she explored, the more enthralled she became. At Mary's urging, Kate had set out after lunch Monday with her camera and supplies. She'd returned to their picnic spot and spent the better part of two hours setting up the equipment and taking various shots. Though hot from working in many layers of clothing, she was satisfied with her efforts. She couldn't wait to develop the prints!

Walking back to Sam and Mary's, she soaked in her surroundings. Sunlight streamed through the trees overhead, dappling the firm, brown earth. The forest was both mysterious and peaceful and, above all, breathtaking in its beauty. A testament to God's limitless imagination.

The prospect of leaving and returning to city life saddened her.

Spotting the stream she'd tumbled into the other day, Kate decided to stop and rest. Her equipment was heavy, the tripod awkward to carry. Her neck was damp with moisture, her hair heavy and straining against the pins.

Setting everything at the base of a sugar maple, she lowered herself onto the same rock Josh had occupied. The sparkling water meandered past. Wouldn't it feel wonderful to dip her sore feet in?

The woods stood silent and empty. No one was around to see her unladylike behavior. And her mother's voice seemed further away today.

Unlacing her boots, she tugged them off and removed her stockings, wriggling her stiff toes. Pulling her skirts up to her knees, she plunged her feet in the water. The bracing cold stole her breath at first, but she quickly adjusted to the temperature.

Leaning back, supporting her weight with her hands braced against the rock, she lifted her face to the sun. *Thank You, Father, for the gift of Your creation.*

She wondered where Josh had disappeared to after lunch. Since establishing that she would remain in his cabin for the duration of her visit, his manner had been polite yet reserved, his expression carefully neutral.

"Lily."

Startled out of her reverie, Kate bolted upright. When her gaze connected with that of Tyler Matthews standing on the opposite bank, her stomach lurched. Apprehension shot through her limbs. Her ears buzzed. What did he want with her?

Her precarious position wasn't lost on her. She was well and truly alone — far enough away from the cabins that no one would hear her if she screamed.

"Don't be afraid." He held his hand out. "I would never hurt you. You know that, don't you?"

Tyler's dark eyes pleaded with her. Judging by the expression of profound sorrow on his face, he must've loved Lily very much. A tiny part of her felt sorry for him. Still, he must be drunk to mistake her for his dead wife. And that meant he was unpredictable.

"I — I'm not Lily, remember? My name is Kate. Kate Morgan."

Expression hardening, his large hands curled into fists. "My eyes work jus' fine, Lily Matthews." He slurred his words. "I'm weary of living without you. So you can either —" Closing his eyes tight, he pinched the bridge of his nose between his thumb and forefinger. "You can —"

Her movements slow and calculated, Kate eased her feet from the water and stood up.

Opening his eyes, he stumbled forward. "Come back home of your own free will or I'll take you by force."

"I'm not going anywhere with you!"

Adrenaline pulsing through her system, she bolted. The sticks and rocks scraping her bare feet hardly registered.

"Lily!" he gasped.

She heard a splash. He was following her!

"You can't run forever!" His breathless voice was a mix of anger and desperation.

Kate's confining skirts tangled around her legs. Terror turning her blood to sludge, she yanked them up and ran faster. Her lungs burned. Her side ached under her ribs.

Where was he? She couldn't hear him behind her. Still, she expected to feel his beefy hands on her any second. Suddenly his yell rent the air and she stumbled, glancing over her shoulder in time to see him crash to the ground, his feet twisted in a thatch of overgrown ivy. Gasping, she pushed herself to the edge of her limits. She didn't see Josh until she was almost upon him.

"Kate?"

"Josh!" she gasped.

Seeing her distress, he ran to intercept her.

Shaking now, she fell against him. His strong arms closed around her, sheltering her. She was safe. *Thank You, God.*

"Is it Matthews?"

Her cheek pressed against the hard wall of his chest, she fought to catch her breath. "He appeared out of nowhere."

He eased back to peer into her face. "Are you all right?"

At her nod, he pulled his troubled gaze away to scan the forest behind her. "He's gone now, but don't worry. I'm going to have a talk with him. This has to stop." He curled his arm around her shoulders. "Let's get you back to the cabin."

She took a step and swift pain radiated across the soles of her feet. She sucked in a harsh breath.

Josh stopped. "What is it?"

She didn't want to admit to being barefoot. "Nothing. I'm okay."

His eyes narrowed. "What hurts, Kate?"

"I left my boots back at the stream. My feet are just a little scraped up."

"You ran all this way barefoot?" he demanded. Without warning, he scooped her up and strode in the direction of the cabin.

"What do you think you're doing?"

"Put your arms around my neck."

Hesitantly, she complied. Pressed against

him as she was, it was impossible not to notice the strength of his chest and muscular arms. He didn't seem bothered at all by her weight, supporting her with ease as his long strides ate up the distance.

The honey-brown hair at his nape tickled her fingers, tempting her to explore the soft strands. Her gaze traveled along his temple and the sun-bronzed skin cloaking his cheekbones down to the mustache and goatee framing his firm mouth.

Josh O'Malley was the epitome of strength, confidence and masculine beauty.

And he was her sister's ex-fiancé. She had to remember that.

Thankfully no one was out and about when they arrived, and Josh headed straight for her cabin. Kicking the door closed with his foot, he deposited her gently on the sofa.

"Don't move."

He rifled through the cupboards and shelves in the kitchen and disappeared into the bedroom, returning with a bowl and a pitcher of water, and a towel draped over his wrist. When he knelt at the far end of the sofa and reached to brush aside her skirts, Kate panicked. Her mother's cold recriminations marched through her mind. This was not proper in the least!

"What are you doing?" she exclaimed.

His expression was calm and controlled. "Your feet need attention." His voice deepened. "I promise to be gentle."

"I can do it myself then."

Crossing his arms, he dared her with a look. "I'd like to see you try."

Kate knew with her restrictive clothing, especially the tight corset she'd barely managed to fasten that morning, it would be difficult to bend and doctor her feet. Josh knew it, too. He was too much of a gentleman to voice that fact out loud, however.

When she broke eye contact, he pressed her shoulders back against the cushions. "Close your eyes and relax. Think of something pleasant. It'll be over before you know it."

Mortified, certain her face would burst into flames, Kate squeezed her eyes tight and clenched her hands. Her body tensed at the first brush of his fingertips on her tender skin. Gradually though, she relaxed. True to his word, his touch was gentle and efficient as he cleaned off the dirt and applied a medicinal cream to the scrapes and scratches.

"All done."

Kate opened her eyes. Face averted, he smoothed her skirts back down and stood to clear the coffee table. She eased her feet to the rug and sat up, watching as he washed his hands and folded the towel into a neat square. Bright red stained the back of his neck, indicating that he wasn't as unaffected as he pretended.

"Tell me about Tyler," she said, partly to ease the sudden tension in the room and partly to satisfy her curiosity.

Leaning a hip against the cabinet, he leveled an inscrutable look at her. "What do you want to know?"

"You said he hasn't always been the town drunk. What was he like before his wife died?"

His lips turned down. "A good man. He and I grew up together, though he was two years behind me in school." Stroking his goatee, he appeared lost in thought. "Tyler was never happier than the day he wed Lily. He was crazy about that girl."

Kate didn't hold out much hope that a man would ever love her like that.

"Do I resemble her that much?"

His gaze shot to her face. "You share similar features and hair, although she was taller and her eyes spaced farther apart. You could certainly pass for sisters."

Kate digested that information. She looked remarkably like Tyler's dead wife. The one he'd loved and tragically lost. How could she ever convince him she wasn't Lily? When would his obsession with her end?

"What do you think he wants with me?" her voice wobbled.

Josh crossed the room and lowered his large frame to the cushions. Sliding one arm behind her along the sofa's edge, he leaned in close and cupped her cheek. "I won't let him hurt you, Kate. I'll protect you."

Kate's expressive eyes revealed her innocent trust in his ability to uphold that promise. He meant it. He would do everything in his power to keep her safe.

Silence thick with expectation hung between them. Josh stroked her silken skin with his thumb. His gaze dropped to her parted lips, and he could no more deny his wish to kiss her than stop breathing.

He lowered his mouth, brushing her lips with the slightest pressure. His heart lurched and took off like a runaway wagon. *Easy. Don't rush it.*

Sliding his hand beneath her thick tresses to curl around her nape, Josh settled his mouth on hers, testing and tasting her sweet offering. Her hand came between them to press against his chest, directly over his heart, not pushing him away yet not allow-

124

ing him any closer. The heat of her fingers seeped through the cotton fabric of his shirt, branding him.

Josh inhaled deeply her subtle, pleasing scent. She clung to him with timid devotion, and his heart swelled with a fierce protectiveness. Never before had he experienced such a sure, swift thrust of emotion. Not even Francesca had made him feel this way.

Francesca! He broke off contact and, ignoring her whimper of protest, set her away from him. Surging to his feet, he began to pace, thrusting his hands through his hair. What had he done?

He was recently jilted, a man on the rebound. Kissing Kate was the last thing he should be doing!

"Josh?"

"I shouldn't have done that. I don't know what I was thinking." He continued pacing. "I apologize."

"Right," she said on a shaky breath, "I'm not Fran."

He jerked to a stop and shot her a dubious look. "You think I don't know that?"

"Hard to ignore the differences between us." Hurt bloomed in her eyes. "You regret kissing me because you love her."

"I don't —"

There was a knock at the door. Talk about bad timing. With a long look at Kate, he went to open it. Nathan stood on the other side, her belongings in his hands.

"My camera!"

Moving toward the dining table, Nathan's gaze darted between Kate and Josh. "I was out walking and spotted your things. Is everything all right?"

He set her boots on the floor and placed her equipment on the tabletop.

"Did you see Matthews out there?" Josh said.

"No. Why?"

"He was on our property. And he frightened Kate."

"Are you okay?" Nathan's face clouded as he assessed her.

"Fine. Thanks for bringing my things." Her gaze connected with Josh's. "I'd forgotten."

Because they'd been too wrapped up in each other and that kiss. *A kiss he wouldn't be repeating.*

"What are you planning to do?"

"It's time I paid Matthews a visit."

"I'm coming with you," Nathan said.

"Fine." Josh paused in the doorway and turned to Kate. "Take it easy. Try to stay off your feet."

Eyes troubled, she nodded. "Be careful."

Pulling the door shut behind him, he followed Nathan down the steps. "You're prepared, right?"

He touched a hand to the gun in his holster. "Yep."

Josh hoped there wouldn't be trouble, but a man had to be ready just in case. Entering the barn, they saddled and mounted their horses. The first half of the ride was made in silence. Josh's thoughts weren't on the coming confrontation, however. They were centered on Kate.

He growled low in frustration. He'd hurt her feelings. The apology had made things worse.

Nathan edged his mount closer. "You gonna tell me what's going on between you two?"

No use denying it. Try as he might, he'd never been able to hide anything from Nathan.

He shifted in the saddle. "If I knew, I'd tell you."

"She feel the same way about you?" Humor laced his words.

Josh whipped his gaze to Nathan's face. "I was engaged to her sister up until a few days ago."

"I'm aware of that," he drawled.

"I have no business thinking about any woman," he stated with force, as much for his own benefit as for his brother's. "I should be heartbroken."

"And the fact that you're not bothers you."

"This attraction to Kate doesn't make sense."

"Matters of the heart rarely do."

Josh fell silent, forcing his attention to the task at hand. They were nearing Matthews's spread. Emerging from the trees, he noticed details he missed that first trip out here. Then he'd been too distracted to notice the overgrown yard, the sagging barn doors, the chickens roaming free. Apparently Matthews had more important things to do than tend his property.

"Do you think he's home?" Nathan came to stand beside him.

"Hard to tell." His narrowed gaze scanned their surroundings. The place appeared to be deserted. "Keep your wits about you."

Adrenaline surged through him. "Matthews! It's Josh O'Malley." He pounded on the door, one hand resting on his weapon. "Open up!"

Standing at the base of the steps, Nathan continued to eye the outbuildings.

Josh waited another minute before trying

again. When no response came, he moved to peer through the single window. It was coated with grime to the point of being opaque. He could only make out bulky shapes. Moving back to the door, he tested the latch. Unlocked.

"Josh." Nathan's voice held a note of warning.

"I'm just gonna see if he's in there. Knowing him, he's probably passed out on the bed."

He pushed the door open and the stench of old grease and stale food filled his nostrils.

Quickly he took stock of the interior. Matthews was nowhere to be seen. If Charlotte were to see how her son had let this place go, she'd be fighting mad.

"He's not here. Go on home. I'm gonna wait for him."

"You said yourself he's dangerous. Why don't we come back tonight after supper?"

He had work to do, but this was important. Matthews was threatening Kate, and it had to stop.

"I'm staying. And I need you to go check on Kate for me."

Frowning, Nathan turned and mounted. "If you're not back by eight o'clock, I'm coming to check on you."

■ ■ ■ ■

Kate pushed the food around her plate in hopes that no one would notice her lack of appetite. Sam and Mary were doing most of the talking. Caleb was his usual reserved self, and Nathan hadn't uttered a single word. His uneasiness only added to her disquiet.

Josh's empty chair mocked her. Had he confronted Tyler and met with trouble? What if he was hurt? The prospect of him lying injured somewhere, helpless and bleeding, set Kate's nerves on edge.

His kiss haunted her. He'd been both gentle and possessive, a curious combination that had simultaneously comforted and thrilled her. For a brief moment, she'd allowed herself to pretend she deserved a man like Josh.

That she wasn't a woman who'd been used, found wanting and cast aside.

And then reality had reasserted itself. He'd pulled away because *she* wasn't the one he wanted. She wasn't Fran.

What had he been about to say just when Nathan arrived? "I don't." "I don't" what? Regret kissing Kate? Or still love Fran?

But of course Josh loved Fran, Kate

chided herself. Everyone loved Fran. And he'd been all set to marry her, hadn't he?

The clock on the sideboard chimed, startling her. Eight o'clock. On the other side of the window stood impenetrable darkness — the one thing about the mountains she didn't like. She hadn't imagined she'd miss the sometimes annoying sounds of the city as it settled into evening and the streetlamps warding off shadows.

Across the table, Nathan stood so abruptly his chair nearly toppled over. Conversation ceased as all eyes turned to him.

"Excuse me," he said over his shoulder before depositing his dishes in the basin that served as a sink. "Ma, thanks for the meal. Sorry to rush off, but I've got things to take care of."

Grabbing his jacket off the hook near the back door, he tugged on his hat and slipped out into the night. The door clicked softly behind him.

He was no doubt going to Tyler's homestead to check on Josh. Clenching her hands beneath the table, it took every ounce of self-control not to rush outside and demand that he take her along.

Mary slid a plate with a fat slice of chocolate cake her way. "Dessert, Kate?"

He was fast losing patience. Not only did the rundown cabin reek, but the rapidly cooling wind gusting outside whistled through the missing chink in the walls, making him regret not grabbing his jacket. So far Matthews was a no-show.

Rising from the lone chair in the room, he resumed his pacing. If Matthews didn't return within the next half hour, Josh would have to try again tomorrow. Nathan was probably already on his way.

His gaze settled once again on the amber-hued bottles scattered across the table, and he grabbed the oil lamp he'd lit earlier to get a better look. At first glance, they appeared to be empty bottles of alcohol, but the labels said otherwise. Dr. J. Collis Browne's Chlorodyne claimed to heal asthma, bronchitis and catarrh. Hostetter's Celebrated Stomach Bitters warded off rheumatism.

In the wagon accident that had claimed Lily's life a year earlier, Matthews had suffered severe injuries. He'd spent a month at the home of Dr. Owens, teetering between life and death. The townsfolk had called it a miracle when he'd finally pulled through.

Somehow Josh had the feeling the man didn't share their sentiments.

He sniffed one of the bottles and reared his head back. Disgusting. Setting it down, he wondered why Tyler would need medicine after all this time.

A muffled sound outside drew his attention. Muscles tensing, he snuffed out the lamp, crept to the window and, rubbing a spot clean with the threadbare curtain, peered out at the front yard. In the shadows stood a horse, its owner sliding to the ground and stumbling toward the cabin. Matthews.

One hand on his holster, Josh walked out of the cabin. "Had a bit too much to drink tonight?"

"What?" He brought his head up fast, squinting in the darkness. Then he moaned, his hands gripping the sides of his head. "What'd ya want, O'Malley?"

"What I want is for you to stay off my property. Leave Kate Morgan alone."

His hands dropped to his sides. "Kate," he mumbled, staring down at the dirt. "I dunno any Kate. Do I?" He started for the stairs. "Need sleep."

Watchful, Josh stood motionless. When Matthews's foot caught on the bottom step and he went sprawling, Josh rushed forward to haul him upright. And when the man didn't struggle, he decided it wouldn't do a bit of good warning him off Kate. At least not tonight. He was just about passed out.

Resigned, Josh helped him inside and guided him toward the bed in the corner. He landed facedown and was snoring before his head hit the pillow.

He shook his head. What a wasted life.

"Josh?"

Nathan. He strode for the doorway and jerked his thumb over his shoulder. "He's out for the night."

"Let me guess," he said from the saddle, he thumbed his hat up. "You didn't get to have that discussion, did you?"

"Nope. Sure didn't." Josh rounded the cabin to where he'd left Chestnut. Nathan's horse, Chance, followed. "But he hasn't seen the last of me."

They rode at a brisk pace through the darkness, Josh eager to get inside and get warm. As soon as they reached the yard, he looked toward Kate's cabin. Light in the window told him she was still up, and for a moment he thought about going to her.

Nope. Too risky.

That kiss was still fresh in his mind. He'd be a fool to go anywhere near her.

CHAPTER EIGHT

Kate couldn't breathe. Darkness pressed in on her. Panic rose up to claw at her throat. She must not scream, must not make the tiniest noise. Nanny said so. Else something much worse would happen to her.

The musty odor merged with the acrid tang of mothballs, burning her nostrils. She hated it in here! But there was no one to rescue her.

Father and Mother were at the seashore and wouldn't be back for another month. Fran was with her tutor in the opposite wing of the estate. And the other employees were scattered throughout, tending their chores.

Nanny Marie had sole charge of her. She would decide when Kate could come out, when her punishment was over. Not that she knew exactly what she'd done to anger Nanny. Kate tried to be on her best behavior, but she ran afoul of her nanny nearly every day.

Suddenly, she wasn't in the closet anymore. The darkness remained, but now the walls were lined with wine bottles. It was the estate's wine cellar. A pleasant, earthy smell hung in the still air. Wesley's handsome, shadowed face appeared, his eyes gleaming and his voice coaxing.

No! This was all wrong. And yet . . . he was so confident and reassuring. Everything would be fine. He wanted to show her what love was really like.

She didn't have to drink a drop of wine to be intoxicated. His touch drove all reason from her mind. With every fiber of her being, she yearned to be loved.

Wesley? The shadows morphed and he was gone. Shame stained her heart. What had she done? Tears spilled down her cheeks.

Gradually, Kate woke to wetness on her pillow. It took a minute for her mind to grasp her surroundings. She wasn't in New York, but in Tennessee. Josh's cabin. His bedroom.

The horrible reality of the dream lingered, and she couldn't help but think of that night with Wesley. No matter how much she wanted to despise him, she couldn't, for the burden of guilt didn't rest entirely on him.

Kate could've stopped him at any moment. She hadn't. His words, like blessed rain, had fallen on the parched soil of her soul. She hadn't been able to resist.

Fumbling in the dark, she crossed to the window and pushed the curtains aside. The moonlight, though weak, enabled her to see enough to light the lamp's wick. The golden flare soothed her somewhat.

She'd gone to bed troubled. Worried about Josh and Nathan, she'd stared at the low ceiling — unable to sleep until she heard the sound of horses entering the lane. Careful to conceal herself, she'd watched from the edge of the glass the brothers riding tall in their saddles, relief filling her at the sight of them safe and sound.

Tonight's emotional upheaval had stirred up disturbing memories of the past, hence the dreams.

Cold through to her soul, Kate rubbed her arms, hugging herself against the whirlpool of gloom and shadows tugging her down. Her gaze fell on her Bible on the bedside stand.

Remember the truth, Christ forgives us because of His faithfulness and goodness. We don't have to do anything to deserve it — nor can we. He chose to love each and every one of us, despite our failures.

Her old friend Danielle's voice echoed in

her head. A young ladies' maid working at the estate at the time of Wesley's betrayal, Danielle had seen Kate's misery and, flouting protocol, befriended her. Told her about God's love. Talked to her about the Scriptures. It was because of Danielle that Kate had turned to God.

God knew her inside and out — her fears and dreams, strengths and faults — and loved her anyway.

That truth had the power to drive out her uncertainties and worry.

Sliding the Bible into her lap, she turned to the book of Psalms and began to read.

Hard at work in his shop the following night, Josh was still kicking himself. Kissing Kate, allowing himself to feel things for her, was reckless. Against his will, she affected him. Not only had she captured his thoughts, she'd enslaved his senses, sharpening his awareness of her every move. He felt her every sigh like a soft caress. Her tender smiles weakened his resolve.

Hers was the face he saw in his dreams. Not Francesca's. And that bothered him. Was he really that shallow? Or worse, had he mistaken admiration and affection for love? The romance with Francesca had happened so fast — that initial meeting at the

Meades' and then picnics beside the river, strolls through the park, shopping excursions. Three whirlwind weeks of shucking his work in order to spend time with her.

He'd been in awe of her classic beauty, her coy playfulness and breezy confidence. Francesca was fun. That last night before she left for New York, he'd blurted out a proposal. She'd laughed outright. Then, realizing he was serious, she'd smiled in that carefree way of hers and said sure, she'd be happy to.

His heart ached from the loss of her. Or was it the loss of his dream?

Unsettled, he concentrated on measuring out the chair legs for the walnut dining set he was making for Mr. and Mrs. Calhoun. After that he had a pie safe to build for their daughter, who was getting married next month and setting up her own house. He had six more pieces on order. It was enough work to keep him busy from dawn until dusk. And he had furniture yet to build to showcase in his shop once he bought it.

Bent over his worktable, he'd barely acknowledged the quiet knock before the door scraped open and in stepped the object of his turmoil. Kate. The smell of fried chicken reached him before she did.

Laying aside the cloth tape measure, Josh

grabbed a towel and wiped the sawdust from his hands.

As she approached, her wide-eyed gaze surveyed the workshop with interest. She stopped a footstep away, the plate of food held out as an offering. Her eyes brimming with questions connected with his. Her finely etched brows arched up.

"I take it you're the local craftsman?"

Feeling exposed, he jerked his head. "Did Ma send you out here?" Careful to avoid touching her, he accepted the plate and utensils. "She knows I'll eat when I have time."

He ground his teeth in irritation. This wasn't the first time he'd skipped supper. His family understood his heavy workload and knew he'd be in to eat as soon as he could. So he was suspicious now. Was his ma trying to push them together?

He hoped not. He was still wrestling with Francesca's decision. And he was smart enough to know not to fall for her little sister.

"Why didn't you tell me?" She folded her hands at her waist and waited for his explanation.

Focusing on the meal, he tried not to notice how beautiful she looked in the yellow light of the oil lamps. She was dressed casually in a filmy green blouse that matched her eyes and a simple, unembellished black skirt. Her brown hair, caught up in a French twist, gleamed like the rich walnut wood he often worked with.

Swallowing, he said offhandedly, "I didn't see the need. You're a visitor here, Kate. You'll take your photographs and go back to New York. What does it matter what I do?"

Out of the corner of his eye, he saw her stiffen. "You're right, of course. You don't owe me any explanations."

Josh winced at the hurt in her voice.

"I'm sorry I bothered you," she exhaled. "Good night."

Her whole body rigid, she swept toward the door. He willed himself to be silent. Only when it closed behind her did he let out a ragged breath.

His appetite gone, he pushed the plate aside and went back to measuring. Only, he couldn't concentrate. He kept picturing the wounded look about her eyes. He'd hurt her feelings, and that made him feel like an insensitive boor.

Kate didn't deserve his harsh attitude. She couldn't know that whenever she was near, a warning hammered in his skull. If he wasn't careful, she would be his undoing.

One agonizing hour later, he gave up. It was no use. No matter what the reasons, he couldn't excuse his churlish behavior.

Tossing aside the tape, he untied his apron and hung it on the nail. He washed his hands in the basin and extinguished all the lamps but one, which he carried with him out into the night.

Time to apologize.

There was a nip in the night air, and clouds like stretched cotton obscured the stars. Angry, deep-throated yowls echoed off the barn walls, and he could make out two shapes tussling in the grass. Cats fighting over territory. Or a female.

He rapped on the cabin door and waited, not sure exactly what he planned to say. He heard the scrape of a chair, then her faint footsteps on the planks.

"Who is it?"

Not expecting her to speak through the closed door, he hesitated. "It's me. Can we talk?"

Quiet. "I'm tired, Josh. Can it wait until morning?"

Even though her voice was muffled, he could make out the defeated undertones punctuating her words. Laying his palm flat against the wood, he resisted the urge to bang his head in frustration. Fool. In protecting himself, he'd hurt her.

"What I have to say won't take long."

"I — I'm not dressed to receive you."

Sighing, Josh pushed away from the door and stuffed his hands into his pockets. "Good night, then. Rest well, Kate."

"Good night."

Discouraged, he stopped in the shop to get the forgotten plate of food. Back inside the house, he placed the leftovers in the icebox for tomorrow and walked into the living room. His father, relaxed in his chair, looked up from the Bible in his lap.

"Late night again, son?" Sam pushed his spectacles farther up the bridge of his nose.

"Yes." Josh moved to stand near the hearth, where his father had built the first fire since early spring. The heat seeped through his pants legs to warm his skin. The thought struck him that Kate needed a fire.

He turned to go. "I'll be back. I forgot to start a fire in Kate's fireplace."

"Already done." His father's voice halted his progress. "I showed her how to let it die down before she retires for the night."

Darn, he'd hoped for a solid excuse to see her. "Thanks, Pa."

His mother sat on the far end of the sofa piecing quilt squares. "What did she think of your workshop?"

"She didn't say." Not that he'd given her a chance to say much of anything.

Pulling a cushioned stool nearer to the fire, he sank down and rested his hands on his knees. Exhaustion overwhelmed him. He resisted, pushing aside the need for sleep for a little while longer.

While he loved his work and the hours passed quickly, the heavy workload took its toll on him physically. And he missed his family's lively conversations around the supper table. If the shop proved successful, he'd be forced to hire help. A good problem to have, he supposed.

"What's bothering you?" his father regarded him thoughtfully. "Is it too difficult? Having her here?"

"No, it's fine."

"She seems like such a sweet girl." Ma peered at him.

"She is."

Kind and generous, she didn't use her status and wealth as an excuse to act superior. A forgotten moment from his time in Sevierville slid unbidden through his mind.

He and Francesca had been dining in a finer dining establishment than he could reasonably afford, and the young waitress, nervous and unsure, had accidentally tipped a glass of water over into his lap. Much of it missed him, wetting only a small part of his pants, but Francesca was livid. She'd been ready to demand that the "unskilled peasant," as she'd called her, be relieved of her job. It had taken some fast talking, but he'd managed to calm her.

He couldn't fathom Kate ever acting that way. She'd shown nothing but kind regard for everyone she'd come in contact with. The way she'd taken to his cousins pleased him. Anyone who could meet Nicole's sassy, and, at times impertinent remarks with patience and even understanding was a rare person in his book.

"Do we have any more pie left over from supper, Mary? Maybe Josh would like a slice."

Setting the fabric aside, Ma rose. "Would you like one, too, dear?"

"Yes. Thank you, dearest wife."

"You're welcome, sweet husband."

He winked at her, and she blushed. All those years together and his parents loved each other more than on the day they married. It was the kind of love he craved for himself.

At twenty-four years old, he was ready to settle down and start a family. Maybe that's why Francesca's decision to marry another man chafed so. She'd cheated him out of his dream.

When Ma had left the room, his father closed his Bible and folded his hands on top. His wise gaze settled on Josh's. "What's on your mind, son?"

"I want what you and Ma have. Now that the wedding has been called off, it's not likely to happen anytime soon. Francesca is with another man and Kate . . ." He stroked his goatee, unable to voice his concerns. His forbidden, mixed-up feelings for her.

"Choosing a bride is one of the most important decisions a man will ever make. Did you consult God about your decision?"

Wincing, he shook his head. "Everything happened so fast. She was leaving, moments away from boarding the train, and I panicked at the thought of never seeing her again. I wanted her connected to me somehow, so when she went back to her glittering world she wouldn't forget me."

He'd made a mistake. Should've prayed about the matter first. God, in His ultimate wisdom, would've led him to the right choice.

Of course, his father didn't condemn him, only nodded in understanding. "I realize it's difficult for you to accept her decision, but maybe it was God's way of saving you from a regrettable marriage."

Was it difficult? He'd thought so at first. His pride had certainly taken a beating. Now, he realized the harder part was sorting through his unforeseen reaction to Kate.

Restless, he stood. Laying one arm across the mantel, he leaned against it, staring into the popping, hissing flames. If he didn't get this attraction sorted out, it could very easily burn out of control and he'd wind up making another rash mistake.

Kate was off-limits. An heiress to a vast fortune. Soon she would return home and, in time, marry a man possessed of a vast fortune. Together they would live a life of untold luxury.

"Something else besides the canceled wedding is bothering you."

He passed a tired hand over his face. "It's Kate. I can't think straight whenever she's near. She's very different than her sister, you know."

"Funny. Your mother had the same effect on me."

He straightened and met his father's level gaze. "I'm confused, that's all. I'll get it sorted out."

"With God's help, right?"

"You can count on it." Sometimes, instead of taking his problems to God right away, he tried to figure things out on his own. Not a wise course of action. "I'm going up to bed. Will you explain to Ma about the pie?"

"Sure." He chuckled. "I'll eat yours, too, if I have to."

"Thanks."

"I'm proud of you, son."

Josh dipped his head, grateful beyond words for the wonderful man who was his father. "Thanks, Pa. Good night."

He may as well have been invisible for all the attention she was paying him.

Seated across the breakfast table from Kate, Josh had yet to catch her gaze. Having overslept, he'd come downstairs last. She hadn't looked up at his family's chorus of greetings, nor had she acknowledged his presence once he sat down.

He didn't blame her. After his cold rebuke last night, he deserved the cool reception.

He hoped she'd go along with his idea to make it up to her. First, he had to get her attention. Shifting his boot beneath the table, he nudged the toe of her shoe.

Her green eyes shot to his over the rim of her teacup. Lowering it to the saucer with a clink, she gazed at him with uncertainty. Now what? He really didn't want to have this conversation in front of his family, did he?

In lieu of words, he smiled at her. She didn't reciprocate. Instead, she shifted her gaze to her plate, brow furrowed.

Thwarted but not defeated, he shoveled in the last of his breakfast and drained his coffee mug. He took his dishes into the kitchen and, placing everything on the counter, went out to the front porch to wait.

He didn't have to wait long. She emerged ten minutes later. When she didn't immediately notice him, he called out to her.

Kate's footsteps faltered at the sound of Josh's low drawl from the far end of the porch. Framed by the multihued forest behind him, arms crossed and one hip propped against the railing, he watched her with an expression akin to regret.

She hadn't wanted to face him today. It had been difficult, that meal, with him sitting so close and her trying to pretend his presence didn't affect her. She'd failed miserably.

Somehow this man had become important to her, and that gave him the power to hurt her.

Straightening, he slowly approached her spot near the steps, his boots scuffing the planks. His woodsy scent clung to his clothes. "I'm sorry about last night." In a familiar stance, he slipped his hands into the pockets of his brown trousers. "I know I haven't been the best host. With everything that's happened, I —" he hitched a shoulder "— I've been out of sorts lately. That's not an excuse to take it out on you, though. Forgive me?"

"There's nothing to forgive. You were right. I'm just passing through."

You're a visitor here, Kate. What does it matter what I do?

She'd been unable to push his words from her mind. His flippant remark had cut deep, flaying open her innermost fears. Not belonging. No one to love. No one to love her.

Even if she did fall in love, what man would want her?

"That doesn't mean we can't be friends. Right?"

"Friends?" She was fairly certain friends didn't kiss each other. But that wouldn't happen again. Friends is all they could ever be. "I'd like that."

"Well, then, friend, what've you got planned for the rest of the day?"

"Nothing. Why?"

"There's a place I'd like to show you, but it's a little ways from here. We'd have to take the horses. Do you ride?"

"Yes. Sidesaddle."

"I happen to have one of those in my barn." He grinned.

"Oh?"

"You'll need your camera."

Curious, she cocked her head to one side. "Where is this place?"

"Uh-uh. You have to come with me if you wanna find out."

CHAPTER NINE

Her horse followed close behind Josh's through the brightly hued forest, which to Kate seemed like a golden sanctuary. The moist, still air, scented with moss and decaying leaves, filled her lungs. It was not unpleasant. Merely different.

They didn't speak. The only sounds stirring the silence were the plodding of the horses' hooves on the soft ground and the snap of branches that their hulking bodies brushed aside. When she wasn't studying their surroundings, she was admiring the ripple of muscle evident beneath Josh's brushed cotton shirt. His was controlled strength, ready to be unleashed at a moment's notice.

She felt utterly safe with him. Physically, at least. Her emotions were another matter.

They'd been riding about an hour and a half, the terrain growing ever steeper. She was glad for the frequent rides back home, else she might've had trouble maintaining her seat. It must be nearing noon. She couldn't see the sun for the treetops, but the hollow feeling in her stomach was a good clue.

When the sound of water reached her ears, Josh slowed Chestnut to a stop. "We'll dismount here."

Tugging gently on the reins of her mare, Kate waited for him to come and assist her. Striding toward her, his eyes sparkled with anticipation beneath the brim of his brown hat. He'd lost the brooding expression, and in its place was one of contentment. Seeing him this way pleased her. Was it possible he was slowly coming to terms with Fran's decision?

Reaching up, he spanned her waist and lifted her down with ease. He grabbed her hand to lead her in the direction of the water. "Wait! What about my camera?"

"I'll come back for it."

Hearing the eagerness in his voice, she hurried to keep up with him. She was out of breath by the time they reached the clearing. Fifty feet above their heads, water rushed over the side of the mountain to cascade in a brilliant white stream to the dusky green pool below. Framed by sleek, slate-gray boulders and thick green overgrowth, it was a glorious waterfall.

Still holding her hand, Josh assessed her reaction. "Well?"

"It's amazing," she breathed, her gaze on the massive, moss-covered tree trunks lying sideways across the mouth of the fall. "Does it have a name?"

"Hidden Oak Falls." He gave her hand a tug. "Come, there's more."

His pace more sedate this time, they circled around the pool, stepping carefully over sharp-edged rocks. From this angle, Kate could see a rock overhang and a dark, open space behind the falls. And Josh was headed straight for it.

Delighted, she grinned with pleasure. What a discovery!

He paused at the opening. A knee-high log blocked the entrance. "I'll go over first, okay?" His long legs made it easy for him. Turning back, he held on to her hand. "Just step up on it, and I'll help you down."

Glancing down at her outfit, a petal-pink shirtwaist and brown-and-pink paisley skirt, Kate regretted her choice. While her wardrobe may be fitting for city life, it was highly unsuitable for the great outdoors.

"Don't look," she warned, knowing her pantaloons would show.

"I wouldn't think of it," he shot back with

a grin, then dipped his head so that she was staring at his hat's brim.

Scooping up the voluminous material with one hand, she tightened her grip on his with the other and levered herself up. Immediately he curled his free hand around her waist and swung her to the ground. The sound of thundering water masked all other sounds, and water droplets splashed against the hem of her skirts. The air was much cooler here. Goose bumps raced across her skin.

When he started to lead her farther into the dark space, Kate resisted. It wasn't enclosed like a closet, but the rock ceiling hung low and light didn't reach very far into the opening. The last thing she wanted was to become distraught in front of him again.

"What's wrong?"

"I don't like the dark, remember?" she said lightly.

"All right. We can stand right here and still have a spectacular view."

Releasing her hand, he tugged off his hat and set it on the log. He thrust his fingers through his hair, giving him that mussed look Kate found irresistible. With effort, she focused on the scene before her.

She'd forgotten her hat at the cabin, a fact her mother would lament if she knew. *Ladies must always present themselves with poise and decorum,* Georgia's voice paraded through her head. *Stand up straight, Katerina. Look at how your sister comports herself, tall and graceful like a ballerina.*

"You can walk behind the waterfall and come out on the other side." Josh moved in close in order to be heard above the noise. "There's a trail leading south."

"How did you find this place?"

"As kids, my brothers and I spent much of our free time exploring these mountains. We just happened upon it one day."

"What was it like? Growing up here?"

Leaning back against the gnarled rock, he folded his arms. "These mountains are all I've ever known. Growing up, we were expected to work hard and pitch in where help was needed. When the work was finished, though, we were free to explore. Hunt. Fish. Torment our cousins." He flashed a roguish grin.

"You didn't."

"I most certainly did." Still grinning, he shook his head. "Juliana didn't take it lying down, either. She fought back."

"What about Megan and Nicole?"

He rolled his eyes. "They went home crying to momma. Most of the time, Aunt Alice and my parents let us sort things out among ourselves. They were harmless pranks."

Josh was such a gentleman Kate had a hard time imagining him as a young, infuriating prankster. "I can't see it."

"Oh, ask Megan. She'll tell you enough stories to make you question your friendship with me." He paused. "What about you? What was it like growing up in the big city?"

Kate sorted through the memories. "I remember wishing for brothers and more sisters. Our cousins lived far away, and their visits were limited to two weeks during the summer and one at Christmas. I played with the staff's children until the year I turned ten. That's when my mother decided it was not in my best interest to fraternize with the hired help." Tucking a stray curl behind her ear, she avoided his gaze. "But I was fortunate in that there were many diversions at the estate. I split my time between the library, the gardens and the stables."

"Did you go to school?"

"We had private tutors."

"Sounds lonely."

"It was." She squared her shoulders. "But I had a roof over my head, clothes to wear and plenty of food to eat. And many luxuries not available to most people."

"Tell me, what's a typical day for an heiress?"

"Easy. Lie in bed until noon, spend much of the day ordering the servants about, fritter away money on useless frippery and consort with other heiresses who have equally meaningless lives."

His laughter echoed off the rough surfaces. "Let me rephrase that. What's a typical day for Kate Morgan?"

"If the weather's nice, I have breakfast on the terrace overlooking the gardens. Then I go in search of my mother to see if she has anything in particular for me to do that day. If not, I sometimes assist our head gardener, Mr. Latham, in the planning and upkeep of the gardens and solarium. I prefer to be outside, my hands in the soil." Her gaze followed the fairy flight of a yellow butterfly above the water. "We have many fountains and koi ponds, but they can't compare to this."

"When you're not helping Mr. Latham, you're . . ."

"Taking photographs. Or in my darkroom developing prints."

"What do you do with them all?"

"Frame some of them. Lucky for me, we have ample wall space." She smiled. "I have special albums for the rest."

"I'd like to see a sample of your work sometime."

"I didn't bring the chemicals or equipment with me to develop the prints. I decided to wait until I'd settled in to have everything shipped out here." She watched a pair of cardinals swirl and sashay through the air, a streak of red in the azure sky, their song swallowed up by the waterfall. "I've been considering opening my own studio."

His brows lifted. "Oh? That's interesting. Would you do mainly portraits, then?"

Pleased he hadn't outright condemned her idea, she answered, "I would split my time between the studio and the field. Clients wouldn't have to always come in for sittings. I could go to them. Some prefer the formal atmosphere of the studio, while others prefer a more natural setting. And I'd still do landscapes and perhaps have some of the finer images for sale."

Relaxed against the rock, Josh drank in the beauty of her complexion, the bloom in her cheeks and the sparkle in her jeweled eyes. Pink suited her. She'd gone hatless, and her dark tresses had been caught in a neat twist.

Because of his own love of woodworking, he was able to appreciate her passion for photography, even though he knew nothing about it. And he admired that she had set a goal for herself. Being an heiress, she didn't have to work. He somehow doubted that Francesca would put effort into anything worthwhile.

"You've obviously given this a lot of thought. What do your parents think about your plans?"

She broke eye contact. "I haven't told them."

That was odd. Again he sensed that something was off in that relationship. He opened his mouth to question her, but she headed him off.

"I'm getting chilled," she said, rubbing her arms. "Would you mind if I set up my camera now?"

"Of course." He pushed away from the wall and, grabbing his hat, took hold of her arm. "The sunshine should warm you right up."

He helped her back over the log, and they returned to where the horses stood grazing. Gathering their supplies, they selected a spot near the waterfall in full view of the sun. Kate set about readying her equipment while Josh spread a blanket on the grass and unpacked their lunch. His ma had included thick slices of ham on sourdough bread, a jar of sweet pickles, coleslaw, baked beans, lemonade and, for dessert, peach turnovers.

Hungry now, his mouth watered at the enticing smells assaulting his nose. "Would you like to go ahead and eat now or take photos first?" He waved away a pesky fly.

She looked up from attaching her camera to its stand. "Let's eat first. Once I get started with the photos, I sometimes get carried away. I wouldn't want to keep a hungry man waiting." Her mouth kicked up in a playful grin.

Her skirts sweeping the green grass, she approached and lowered herself onto the blanket with graceful ease.

"Does it take long?"

She paused in the arranging of the billowing material about her person to give him a quizzical look. "Does it take long for what?"

Sitting cross-legged, he gestured to her skirts. "To learn to maneuver in those fancy getups."

"Every young lady is given instructions in deportment and manners. Besides, I've dressed like this since I was a little girl, so I'm accustomed to it."

"Don't get me wrong — your clothes are beautiful. I mean, you look beautiful in everything you wear."

He clamped his lips together. He shouldn't be saying this. And yet, it was true.

"Thank you." A blush tinting her cheeks, she lowered her gaze to her lap.

Unlike Francesca, who'd preened whenever he'd complimented her, Kate was modest and shy in the face of praise.

There was so much about her that he found appealing. Her beauty wasn't only skin-deep. She had a beautiful soul, as well.

She'd make some lucky man a fine wife one day. If circumstances were different — *if* she wasn't his former fiancée's little sister and a wealthy, privileged city girl — then just maybe he'd let himself feel something for her. But they weren't. And he wasn't about to make the same mistake twice.

When he did decide to seek out a wife, he'd choose a young lady with an upbringing similar to his. Someone who loved the Lord and who strived to live each day with honesty and integrity. Never again would he allow himself to be involved with a woman who harbored secrets. Secrets destroyed people. Relationships suffered.

If Francesca had been honest with him, he'd have avoided much grief and embarrassment.

Placing bread and ham on a plate, he handed it to Kate, along with utensils. Aware of her small appetite, he allowed her to serve herself from the other containers.

As suspected, she took only minimal amounts and didn't touch the turnovers. But she ate everything on her plate, and her smile was one of satisfaction.

"I like picnics. There's something refreshing about eating outdoors, especially with a view like this."

Taking a swig of his lemonade, he nodded. "I agree."

Soon she rose and went to her camera. Feeling lazy from the heat, his stomach full, he was content to recline on the blanket and watch her work. In between shots, she told him about the recent advancements in photography. She was well-informed on the topic, and her enthusiasm was evident.

Not only was Kate a joy to watch, she was easy to be with. He wouldn't mind spending the entire day out here. But projects awaited him back in his workshop. And after an hour, she was ready to pack up and go home, so they did.

After tending to the horses in the barn, he walked with her to the cabin, somehow reluctant for the outing to end.

"I had a wonderful time today." She smiled over at him. "Thank you."

"You're welcome. I enjoyed it, as well."

"Will you work in your shop now?"

He nodded. Wanting to tell her more, he

said, "You know, I have plans to expand my furniture business."

Her face lit up. "Josh, that's wonderful! I have no doubt you'll be successful. Perhaps you can give me some pointers."

Her enthusiasm warmed his insides. "Well, I'm not quite there yet. But close. It's something I've wanted for a while, and now that an opportunity has come along, I feel it's the right time. In fact, there's a place —" Spying something on her porch, he broke off. "Looks like someone left you flowers."

Her finely arched brows met in the middle. "What?"

A niggling feeling of unease settled deep in his gut. He scooped up the bouquet of yellow daisies tied with a ribbon and handed them to her. Lifting them to her nose, she inhaled their fragrance. Then he spotted the folded paper.

He picked it up and, handing it to her, waited for her to read it, even though it was none of his business. The color drained from her face, and her eyes darted to the woods and the yard.

He stepped closer and gripped her arm. "What is it, Kate?"

"Tyler."

Anger seizing him, he took the paper she

held out.

You are my life. I won't rest till you're home where you belong.

Crushing the note into a ball, he paced away from her. The audacity, the boldness of Matthews's actions — coming onto O'Malley property in broad daylight for the purpose of scaring Kate — spawned outrage and fury in his chest.

Had no one seen him? Obviously not. His family wouldn't have left this here for her to find.

How was he supposed to keep her safe?

He pivoted back. "From now on, I don't want you going anywhere alone."

"But —"

Going to her, he settled his hands on her shoulders. "I'm serious, Kate. If you need to go somewhere, let me or one of my brothers know. Or my father. The last thing I want is for you to encounter Matthews unprotected."

Her expression troubled, she stared up at him with trusting eyes. "All right."

"I have to make some deliveries in Sevierville next week. I'll be gone for a few days."

He'd feel a whole lot better if she knew how to protect herself. Maybe he should teach her how to handle a weapon. "I just want you to be careful."

"I know," she murmured. "The thought of being alone with him . . ." She trailed off, shuddering.

Without thinking, he pulled her close and wrapped his arms around her. She came willingly. Pressing her cheek against his chest, she looped her arms about his waist. Her hair smelled fresh and clean beneath his chin.

He didn't speak, simply held her and rubbed her back in a soothing gesture. He felt her soft sigh deep in his bones. The world around them faded. The birds' chirping and the cattle's lowing receded. Holding Kate made him forget everything else.

Like how dangerous it was to care for her.

Later that evening, she was penning letters to acquaintances back home when she heard a thump on the porch.

"Hello? Kate, are you in there?"

Recognizing Mary's voice, she set aside her fountain pen and rushed to open the door.

"Mary! Can I take that for you?" She indicated the tray in her hands.

"I brought tea." The older woman brushed past her only to hesitate at the table. "Am I interrupting your correspondence?"

Kate hurried to clear the tabletop of her

stationery. "Not at all. My hand was beginning to cramp, so a break is most welcome."

Mary poured the steaming liquid into two cups and, placing one in front of Kate, settled into the chair opposite. Her expression was one of motherly concern. "Nathan let slip what's been happening with Tyler, and I wanted to see how you're faring."

Absentmindedly she stirred the honey into her tea. "I'll admit it's unsettling. I never would've expected Charlotte's son to behave this way." Setting her spoon aside, she sipped the bracing brew. "I've heard it said that everyone has a twin. Did you know his wife?"

"In passing. Lily was a shy sort." Sighing, Mary fingered the cross at her neck. "We were all shocked to hear about the accident. And poor Tyler. He may have recovered from his injuries, but he's not been the same since."

"I wish he'd realize I'm not her."

"Don't worry." Mary patted her hand. "My boys will do everything in their power to keep you safe. More important, you're never out of the Lord's sight. He's promised not to abandon you."

"Yes, I know you're right."

God was faithful. Not like people who promised forever, then left. People like Wesley. And, yes, even Fran.

"You're not thinking of leaving anytime soon, are you? I'm enjoying having another female around. You're like the daughter I never had."

The sweet acceptance shining in Mary's eyes brought tears to her own. Not once had her mother looked at her like that. What would it have been like to grow up with a mother like Mary? To revel in the knowledge that she was special. That she was *enough.*

Swallowing the emotion clogging her throat, she shook her head. "I still have a lot of work to do here. On the other hand, I don't want to burden your family. Not only have I displaced Josh, I'm adding extra work for you —"

She held up a staying hand. "One more mouth to feed hardly matters. And Josh has admitted he'd rather be in his old room for the time being. So, please, no more talk of being a burden. It's a pleasure to have you here."

"Thank you." She lowered her gaze, emotions near the surface. "You don't know how much that means to me."

Sensitive to her mood, Mary guided the conversation to safer topics, asking questions about her life in New York and answering Kate's questions about Gatlinburg and its history. The town was originally called White Oak Flats — that surprised Kate. Mary pointed out that it was named after all the white oak trees in the area.

She was preparing to leave when Josh arrived.

Standing tall and broad-shouldered, hat in his hands, Josh was more handsome than any man had a right to be. "Evenin'."

"Hi."

"Got a minute?"

"Certainly." She moved back to give him room to enter.

His gaze swung to Mary. "Want me to take that back to the house for you, Ma?"

"No, I can manage." Her smile encompassed them both. "Did you find your supper?"

"I did. As always, it was delicious."

"Thanks again for the tea," Kate said as Mary passed by. "And the conversation."

"Anytime, dear. See you in the morning."

"Good night, Ma."

"Good night."

Tossing his hat on the cupboard, he took a step forward. Kate's pulse picked up speed. She couldn't help but remember what had happened the last time he was here. Would he kiss her again? Should she let him?

Her inner voice of reason gave a resounding "No!" Look at what happened the last time she allowed a man to take such liberties! Her heart argued that Josh was nothing like Wesley. He would never in a million years overstep the moral boundaries. Josh O'Malley loved God and lived to honor Him.

"I came to tell you that I've decided to teach you to shoot a firearm."

What? Kate tried to make sense of his words. "Excuse me?"

"Tomorrow morning, you and I are gonna take a little walk out to where I have my targets set up. I have a gun picked out for you. It's not all that difficult. Just takes practice, is all."

Laughter bubbled up. "Me? Fire a gun? You must be joking."

His brows lowered. "Why would I do that?"

"A lady does not speak of weapons, much less handle one." The mere idea was preposterous. Who did he take her for — Annie Oakley?

"Besides, where do you propose I conceal this weapon on my person?" She spread her hands wide. "In my reticule?"

Clamping his lips together, Josh said, "I'll get you a holster to wear around your waist."

Kate blushed. "That's hardly fashionable."

"This isn't about fashion, it's about safety."

"I understand your point, Josh, but it simply isn't proper."

"This isn't New York City," he bit out. "Out here, survival is more important than propriety. Matthews was bold enough to come here in the middle of the day. There's nothing stopping him from coming back. What happens if he catches you alone? What will you do then?"

She didn't have an answer.

"Look, I'd rest a whole lot easier knowing you have a way to protect yourself."

"But —"

"No 'buts.' " Snatching up his hat, he moved to the door. "I'll stop for you bright and early. Be ready."

Chapter Ten

Standing in the thick grass, dew wetting her ankle boots and fog blanketing the meadow, Kate listened as Josh explained how to use the gun, which he'd described as a nickel-plated .44 Schofield revolver. But no matter how hard she tried to focus on his words, her attention was caught by the movement of his firm lips framed by the neat, golden-brown mustache and goatee. His quiet, confident voice resonated in the hushed silence of the early morning.

They were alone in what seemed like a magical place, cut off from the rest of the world. Even the animals had yet to stir. Her entire being focused on the man before her.

Josh O'Malley was a fine, honorable man. A family man. Hardworking. Caring.

Money and material gain weren't important to him. Neither was climbing the social ladder. Serving God and others was.

Her lungs squeezed with regret as she

watched him now. She could not have him. Even if he wasn't in love with her sister, he wouldn't want her. Not if he knew her secret.

"Are you ready to try it out?" His voice broke into her thoughts.

His serious gaze was pinned to her face, questioning. Could he tell she hadn't been paying attention? He'd shown up at her door just after dawn, all business, looking as if he carried the weight of the world on his shoulders.

Clearing her throat, she nodded, despite her sudden nervousness. "I'm ready."

One brow quirked up, but he didn't comment. Moving to stand beside her, Josh transferred the gun to her hand, his warm fingers closing over hers as he demonstrated how to hold it. Her mouth went dry. Was it the fact that she was holding an instrument of death for the first time or was his nearness making her feel light-headed?

"Do you see the target there?" Letting go, he pointed to the trees not far distant.

Again, she nodded.

"Hold your arm steady, aim and pull the trigger."

He sounded so matter of fact about the process. Could it really be that simple?

Raising her arm, she pointed the gun barrel forward. It was heavier than she'd expected. Trembling, she squeezed her eyes shut and pulled the trigger. The blast startled her, and, gasping aloud, she opened one eye to see where the bullet had gone.

"Kate." He sighed, his breath stirring her hair. "You're supposed to keep your eyes on the target. How do you expect to hit it if you can't see it?"

"This may be second nature to you," she said, hiking her chin up a notch, "but the only weapons I've seen up close are the ones behind glass displays at the museum. I never imagined I'd be holding one, much less learning how to shoot someone."

"If it makes you feel any better, I taught Megan and the girls to shoot."

Her mouth fell open. "Nicole, too?"

His lips lifting in a slight grin, he gently tapped her chin closed. "Like you, Nicole had her reservations, but she turned out to be a good shot. I have every confidence you will be, as well."

"I haven't seen any of them carrying a gun."

"Gatlinburg is a relatively safe place. We all know and look out for each other. The girls do carry weapons if they leave sight of their house for any length of time. Strangers travel through this area on a regular basis, and I feel better knowing the girls have a way to protect themselves."

But Kate wasn't worried about strangers. Tyler's face flashed through her mind, and, remembering the desperation carved into his features, she shivered. He wanted her. She couldn't help wondering what he might do once he had her.

"Don't worry," Josh murmured as if reading her thoughts. "I'll make sure you feel confident using this thing."

Positioning himself behind her, his arms came around her, his hands closing over her wrists. "I'll steady your aim, and then you pull the trigger."

Encircled by his arms, close enough to feel the rise and fall of his chest, Kate couldn't think.

Slowly he lifted her arms until they were even with the target. "Okay." His mouth hovered near her ear. "I'm ready whenever you are."

With all the concentration she could muster, her eyes wide open this time, Kate squeezed the trigger. The shot veered too far to the left. After several failed attempts, she lowered the gun.

"It's harder than it looks."

"Don't give up. It takes a lot of practice." He moved back. "We can come out here every morning until I leave."

Examining the gun in the palm of her hand, she said absentmindedly, "My parents will never believe this." Her mother would be appalled. This was one aspect of her trip best kept private.

Josh took the gun from her. "Tell me about them."

She raised alarmed eyes to his. "My parents?"

"Yes."

"What do you want to know?"

"I want to know why they didn't invite you along on their trip. And why is it Francesca spoke so fondly of them and yet you appear sad, almost regretful when the subject is brought up?"

The blood in her veins turned sluggish, and dread spread through her like poison. How could she admit the truth? That she was an outcast? Unwanted? What would he think of her then?

But his eyes held a wealth of kindness, a subtle knowing, as if he'd guessed the source of her unhappiness. Perhaps she should tell him. Shatter any illusions he had about her so-called charmed life.

Unsettled, she started walking, slowly, haltingly. He fell into step beside her, his quiet, solid presence a comfort in itself.

"Francesca's relationship with our parents is vastly different than my own. She fits their idea of the perfect daughter."

Walking beside Kate, Josh noted the dejected slump of her shoulders, the resignation in her voice. Her words confused him. "And you don't?" he asked, disbelieving.

"Not at all." Her attempt at laughter falling flat.

"I don't understand."

"Fran does everything right. She's their pride and joy. I, on the other hand, am a source of consternation. Father is mostly indifferent, but my mother and sister can't understand why I'd rather read a book or tend flowers than pore through fashion magazines and dissect the latest gossip." Apprehension wrinkled her brow. "Now that Fran is settled, my mother will convince Father it's time to search for a suitable husband for me."

A hard knot formed in his gut at the idea of softhearted, lovely Kate being paraded before a string of fortune hunters. Something suspiciously like jealousy surged through him. "You're an adult. Surely they don't plan to choose your husband for you?" His jaw hardened. "After all, Francesca married her heart's desire, didn't she?"

Kate threw him a measuring glance. "Percy has all the right credentials. Besides, they've been attached since the year she turned seventeen. My parents had no reason to launch a manhunt. As I have no such attachments, I'm certain they'll take it upon themselves to *assist* me."

Francesca and that man attached? For years? Josh went numb. He'd had no clue.

"They'll be relieved to marry me off." She sighed. "In their eyes, I've always been trouble."

He stopped short. Kate? Trouble? Never! "No, Kate —"

"Yoo-hoo!" a familiar voice called from the trees. "Josh! Kate!"

Megan. He swallowed back his frustration as they both turned to greet her.

She arrived at their side, winded but smiling. "Aunt Mary said you'd gone for a walk. I'm glad I found you," she said, as she shoved unruly curls out of her eyes. "I was on my way to town and wondered if Kate would like to join me."

Josh looked at Kate. "Go if you want. I've got a pie safe to finish before the day is out. We can practice again tomorrow morning."

"Practice?" Megan's gaze volleyed between them. "You're teaching her to shoot?"

"I am."

"Why?"

"Kate needs to know how to protect herself, don't you think?" It wasn't often he kept things from Megan, but he didn't want to unduly alarm her or her sisters.

Her steady gaze left his to probe Kate's. "I suppose." She didn't look convinced, but she said no more about it.

"Where are you headed?" he said.

"Momma asked me to deliver ointment to Mrs. Irving, and she gave me a list of things we need from Clawson's." She turned to Kate. "So what do you say?"

Her pretty lips lifted. "I'd like that."

"Great. My errands will go so much faster if you're along." She tugged on his sleeve. "Have you told her about the barn dance coming up?"

He'd forgotten all about it. "No, I haven't."

"Barn dance?" She looked intrigued.

"They're great fun." Megan linked her arm through Kate's. "There's music and dancing, of course. Lots of food. A chance to visit with neighbors and friends. We always have a great time."

He could just imagine the attention she would attract. A beautiful, unattached young lady didn't stay that way for very long in these parts. If he accompanied her, there'd be no end of speculation. The fact that his wedding had recently been called off would be fresh in the townspeople's minds.

Was he ready to endure that level of scrutiny? Furthermore, did Kate even realize what she was in for?

"Kate's accustomed to celebrations on a much grander scale, Megan. I doubt she'd be interested."

Kate's eyes flashed, reminding him that beneath her gentle manners lay determination. This was a lady who knew her own mind. "As a matter of fact, I think it sounds like fun."

"So you'll come?" Megan grinned from ear to ear. "You'll escort us, won't you, Josh? Nathan already has a date, and Caleb avoids social functions as a rule."

He wanted to refuse, but with both women staring up at him expectantly, it was difficult — if not impossible — to do so. "You do realize your name will be on everyone's lips, don't you? Especially if you arrive with me."

A tiny wrinkle appeared between her brows. "If it's going to be trying for you, then of course we won't go."

Touched, his words came out as rough as sandpaper. "I can handle it. It's you I'm worried about."

Megan looked thoughtful. "Most folks around here are kind, God-fearing folks. It's not their intention to make you feel uncomfortable, but, of course, they'll be curious about you, as they would be about any newcomers. You should go, and if it's awkward for you, then I'm sure Josh or Uncle Sam would take you home. Right, Josh?"

"Of course."

Tucking a stray curl behind her ear, she grinned shyly. "What time shall I be ready?"

Josh felt the impact of that grin clear down to his toes. He was in big trouble.

Walking with Megan on the well-worn path through the woods, sharing thoughts on their favorite authors and books, Kate felt content. This is what life could be like, she thought. Spending time with friends who weren't constantly comparing themselves to you, wondering whose clothing and jewels cost more or whose suitor was a better prospect. How refreshing not to be in competition!

It wasn't just Megan who made her feel this way. Megan's mother, Alice, and her sisters, Nicole, Jessica and Jane, had all welcomed her with genuine kindness. And, of course, Josh's family, except for Caleb, had treated her as one of their own from the first day. Even Josh, who'd had every reason to resent her, had gone out of his way to make her life pleasant.

It wasn't his fault she couldn't think straight when he was near. Or that her heart melted with each unexpected smile. Or that her soul yearned to knit itself with his, to be his helpmeet the rest of her days.

A deep sigh ripped from her chest. Odd how one man could represent her dreams come true yet still cause her such upheaval. A future with him was impossible. The sooner she accepted that, the better.

"Is something bothering you?"

Swinging her basket at her side, Megan maintained an easy pace. The sun had burned off the fog and chased away the nip in the morning air, the brilliant rays now warming her skin.

Not ready to share her most private thoughts, Kate shrugged. "Nothing I can speak of at the moment."

She flashed a sympathetic smile. "Well, if you ever need someone to talk to, I'm here. I've been told I'm a good listener."

Pointing to a break in the trees, she said,

"Here's our first stop — Mrs. Irving's place. She's a widow, like Momma. Sweet lady. I'm dropping off some ointment for her."

Kate followed her onto the narrow footpath. Unlike Sam and Mary's neat lawn, the grass here was nearly as high as her knees.

"I'll have to ask Josh or Nathan to come by and tend this overgrown mess." Megan sighed. Approaching the small, squat cabin, she said over her shoulder, "Whatever you do, do *not* eat her green tomato pie. It's revolting!"

Crybabies. Tomato pie. Southerners sure had some peculiar-sounding foods. Smothering a giggle, Kate pressed her lips together in a tight line. She wouldn't dream of offending a friend of Megan's.

Having announced their arrival with a hard knock, it wasn't long before a short, plump, snow-haired lady appeared in the doorway. She surveyed them both.

"Miss Megan, did you bring your mother's special ointment? I've been waitin' since Sunday, you know." She aimed a stern glance in Kate's direction. "Who might this fancy young thing be?"

Swallowing a smile, Megan gestured with her hand. "This is my friend from New York City, Miss Kate Morgan."

Sparse brows descended over alert blue eyes. "Kate Morgan, is it?"

"It's a pleasure to meet you," she smiled.

"I can't say it's a pleasure to meet you —" she paused to stare hard at her "— 'cause I don't know you from Adam."

Kate glanced at Megan. Sweet old lady? For certain?

Mrs. Irving's stern expression eased. "But we can remedy that, can't we? Come on in, both of you." Shuffling back, she beckoned them inside. "I've a loaf of banana bread already sliced and a pie cooling on the cupboard. It's a favorite of yours, Megan! Tomato."

Megan sucked in a harsh breath, and Kate was hard put not to laugh. Surely it couldn't be that bad!

One hour later, having said their goodbyes and heading toward town, Kate gratefully accepted the peppermint stick Megan fished out of her pocket and held aloft. Perhaps it would settle her stomach.

"I simply don't understand —" Kate wrinkled her nose in disgust "— why anyone would think to combine tomatoes with sugar."

"It's a mystery," Megan groaned and clutched her stomach. "If Mrs. Irving wasn't such a kind soul, I'd tell her the truth about that pie."

Laughter bubbled up and spilled over. Kate couldn't help it. The whole situation struck her as funny. It wasn't long before Megan joined her, and they were still laughing when they reached the edge of town.

A tall, dark-haired man she'd seen at church was out on the boardwalk polishing the barbershop window. Glancing up from his work, he grinned and nodded a greeting.

"Mornin', Miss Megan." His gaze switched to Kate. "Miss."

"How are you, Tom?" Megan stopped and Kate did the same.

Still clutching the wadded-up cloth, Tom rested his hands on his hips. "Oh, fair to middlin'. You ladies out for a stroll this fine morning?"

"Just running some errands." Megan slipped her arm through Kate's. "Tom Leighton, this is Kate Morgan. She's newly arrived from New York. Kate, Tom owns the barbershop. He's a friend of Josh's."

"It's a pleasure to meet you, Miss Morgan. Welcome to Gatlinburg."

"Thank you."

"I hope I'm counted among your friends, as well," he teased Megan.

"Of course you are."

"And as a friend, you won't mind my asking if you have an escort to the barn dance?"

"Oh, well, Josh has agreed to escort both Kate and me," she hedged.

"He's a lucky man. I wonder if you all would mind if I tagged along? Make it an even foursome?"

"That would be wonderful."

Kate wondered at her friend's lack of enthusiasm. Didn't she like him? He seemed friendly enough.

"It's settled then."

They were making arrangements for Friday night when Kate happened to glance down the street. There, in a heated discussion with another man, stood Tyler. Alarm spread through her limbs, rendering her weak and breathless. Clutching the base of her throat, she pulled away from Megan.

She should run before he spotted her.

"Kate? What's wrong?"

"H-he's there. I have to go."

"Who?" She whipped her head around to scan the street.

"Tyler," Kate whispered, afraid to say it too loudly. Although surrounded by people, the last thing she wanted was to face him again. His desperation frightened her.

Tom stiffened. "Matthews is giving you trouble, Miss Morgan? Does Josh know?"

She could only nod.

Megan gasped, "What? Why didn't anyone tell me?"

"How about I take the two of you ladies home?" Tom suggested quietly.

"Would you mind?" Megan said, visibly upset.

"I'd actually feel better knowing you got home safely." Turning to the door, he flipped the sign to indicate the shop was closed. Extracting a key from his pocket, he locked it. "Let's go."

CHAPTER ELEVEN

Josh tested the cabinet doors to make sure they opened and closed smoothly. Standing back, he surveyed his work. All that was left to do was to stain and polish it.

A sense of accomplishment filled him. Not every man was fortunate enough to do what he loved. He was so close to achieving his dream. Three more orders — one cedar hope chest for Mrs. Calhoun, one dining set for the Millers, another display shelf for the mercantile — and he'd have the money to buy the store.

He was fairly confident the shop would be his. To his knowledge, no one else had come forward to buy it. Fulton would've spoken up if another prospective buyer had shown an interest.

A shadow darkened the open doorway, and Josh was surprised to see Tom Leighton standing there. Apprehension winged through him. His friend had a business to run, so the only reason for him to be here was if something was wrong.

When he moved aside to let Megan and Kate enter, Josh's pulse jumped. His gaze locked onto Kate's face, and he noticed her pallor right away. She looked shaken.

"What's happened?" Stepping around the pie safe, he strode to her side and took her slender, cold hand in his.

"I saw Tyler." She sought to reassure him. "In town. But he didn't see me, thank goodness. I was simply startled."

"Will someone explain to me what's going on?" Crossing her arms, Megan jutted out her chin. Most of the time, his cousin was easygoing and sweet as molasses. But she was an O'Malley. And every one of the O'Malleys possessed a stubborn streak. "Is Tyler the reason you're teaching Kate about guns?"

Catching Tom's pointed glance at his and Kate's joined hands, Josh dropped hers and slipped his into his pocket. "Look at her, Megan. Does she remind you of anyone?"

Frowning, her eyes full of questions, she studied Kate. "I don't —"

"Lily Matthews," Tom spoke up, incredulous.

Megan gasped and, covering her mouth, stared wide-eyed at Kate, who was begin-

ning to look embarrassed from all the attention.

"Now you understand his fascination with
her. His brain is so muddled with alcohol
and cure-alls, he can't separate fantasy from
reality."

"Cure-alls?" Tom said. "Is he sick?"

Megan lowered her hand. "I've read those
can contain addictive substances. Cocaine
is only one of them."

"I don't know if he's sick or not, but his
place is like an apothecary shop. Bottles
everywhere."

"I wonder if Charlotte is aware of all this,"
Kate murmured.

"I'm sorry you have to endure this."
Megan laid a hand on Kate's arm. "Are you
thinking of going home sooner than you'd
planned?"

Josh held his breath, suddenly feeling as if
he were standing at the edge of a deep
ravine. He shouldn't care one way or another. Stay or go. Kate meant nothing to
him. Or did she?

Squaring her shoulders, her gaze sought
his. "No, I'm not leaving."

Releasing his pent-up breath, he ignored
the way his heart danced a jig in his chest.

Tom settled his hat on his head. "We'd
best get going, Megan. I need to get back."

Tugging on the brim, he said, "Good day, Miss Morgan. Josh."

"Thanks for seeing them home safely," Josh told his friend.

"Anytime."

"I'll see you soon." With a final squeeze, Megan released Kate's arm and turned to follow Tom outside. Poking her head back inside, she smiled. "I'm glad you're staying."

"Me, too."

When she'd gone, Josh studied Kate. "Are you sure you're all right?"

"I'm fine except for a small headache. I think I'll go rest for a bit."

"I hate that he's doing this to you." He slid his knuckles down her cheek, then pivoted away to retrieve his hat from the hook by the door.

"Where are you going?" Unease crept into her features.

Putting it on, he paused in the open doorway, right hand resting on his pistol. "To end this once and for all."

"Please don't." She put a restraining hand on his arm.

Her concern touched him. "I have to."

"Not for me, you don't. I don't like the idea of you putting yourself in danger on my account. He didn't approach me today.

He didn't even see me."

"I refuse to stand by and wait for him to make his next move." He held up a hand as she started to speak. "Don't worry, Kate. I'm just gonna talk to the man."

If he could find him, that is. And if he was sober.

Josh didn't hold out much hope, but he had to try.

He left her with the admonishment to get some rest, then mounted Chestnut and headed into town. There was no sign of Matthews, and when he asked around, no one had any idea where he'd gone.

He wasted an entire afternoon searching. No sign of him anywhere. Frustrated, Josh headed home.

Riding into the yard, he noticed Kate waiting for him on her porch. Her face lit up the moment she saw him, her generous mouth curving into a smile of relief and happiness.

He felt the effect of that smile clear down to his toes. A man sure could get used to a welcome like that. He allowed himself to pretend, only for a moment, that he was important to her. Wouldn't it be nice to see this exact expression on her face each time he returned home?

It would, if this were a fantasy world. But

he lived squarely in reality.

He wasn't important to her, not in the way he was imagining. They were friends, that was all. And that was the way it had to stay.

Every morning for the following week, Josh took Kate out to practice shooting. Not an expert by any means, she managed to hit the target one out of every three attempts. He was a patient teacher, praising her progress, slow though it might be.

So the morning he left, Kate not only missed their time together. She missed him.

His smile. His laugh. The careful way he watched her when he thought she didn't notice.

It was wrong and foolhardy, she knew. But they were friends, and it was perfectly acceptable to miss a friend.

One thing she refused to do was sit around and mope about the situation.

After breakfast, she volunteered to help Mary with the week's supply of baking. Instead, Mary asked if she'd mind picking up some items at the mercantile. Eager to stay busy, Kate agreed. Too late, she remembered Josh's warning not to go anywhere alone.

She decided to seek out Nathan. Naturally, he was in the dairy barn.

"I'm sorry, Kate." He paused in forking hay into the stalls. "I can't spare the time now, but I'm free after lunch. Can you wait until then?"

"Sure."

She left him to his work, uncertain if she should put off the errand. Perhaps Mary needed those things as soon as possible. And if she took the main road, the walk to town would take all of ten minutes.

It was early. Tyler kept late hours at the saloon. He was probably still passed out in his bed.

Her mind made up, she retrieved her reticule and a shawl. A cool breeze swept through the trees, raising goose bumps on her skin despite her long sleeves and multi-layered skirt. On her way out the door, her gaze fell on the holster belt and firearm lying on the side table. Josh's doing. The man actually expected her to wear the contraption around her waist with a loaded gun strapped in. Inconceivable!

With a shake of her head, she shut the door and headed for town.

Josh slapped his hat against his thigh in frustration.

They'd been making good time. The weather was clear, the dirt roads dry in most places. Now this. A downed tree blocked the road, its trunk the span of his outstretched arms. Dense forest lined either side, so they couldn't go around it.

He and Caleb frowned at each other. What now?

His glance flicked to the furniture packed neatly in the wagon bed. The sooner he delivered it, the better. Two tarps covered the table and chairs in case of rain, but the protection wasn't foolproof.

A lot hung on this delivery. The money from the sale would make it possible for him to buy the empty store. His dream was so close to becoming reality.

Digging in his supplies in search of a saw or an ax, he imagined Kate's response the first time she entered his furniture shop. Judging from her comments, she admired his work.

"I have a feeling we're gonna be here awhile," said Caleb as he joined the search, rifling through the satchels on his side of the wagon.

"I hope not. We're wasting valuable daylight."

"This is all I got." He held up a handsaw.

Josh sighed, feeling a headache coming on. "If that's true, we'll be here a week." His fingers closed around the handle of a large ax. "Aha. I don't remember packing this, but it sure is gonna come in handy. I wonder how it got there."

"The memory is the first thing to go in old age, I've heard." Caleb shot him a mocking smirk.

"Is that so? Since you think you're so clever, I'll let you have the first shot at that monster."

Holding out the ax, he suppressed a grin at the resulting scowl on his little brother's face. If nothing else, this trip was going to give them some uninterrupted time together.

Kate strode briskly down the lane, bonnet ribbons whipping in the breeze, heels clomping on the leaf-strewn bridge leading into town. Her walk had proved uneventful. Nevertheless, she was grateful when the church spire came into view. People meant safety.

Turning the corner of the barbershop, she bumped into someone and was knocked backward. A man's hand seized her arm. She gasped.

"Watch where you're goin', missy," a wizened voice complained.

Hand pressed against her chest, she glanced at the speaker and tried to place his face. Her heartbeat thundered in her ears. For a split second, she'd thought of Tyler . . .

"I'm sorry, sir. I didn't see you —"

"Of course you didn't," he snapped, straightening his bowler hat. "How could you with your eyes on the clouds?"

"I'm afraid I haven't had the honor of your acquaintance. I'm Kate Morgan."

He ignored her outstretched hand. "Fulton. Chadwick Fulton."

Tugging down his suit jacket with a harrumph, he stomped past her. Lips parted in surprise, she lowered her hand and turned to watch him go. Interesting.

With a shrug, Kate continued toward the mercantile, taking in the length of Main Street. Her mother and sister would be scandalized at the lack of boutiques and shops in this town. She didn't mind, however. The only time she truly liked to shop was at Christmastime, when she would get a list of needy children's names from the church secretary and spend days searching for just the right gifts. Her only regret was not being there to watch them open their packages on Christmas morning.

A big For Sale sign directly across the street caught her eye. It was propped in the picture window of what looked like an unoccupied store. Waiting until a wagon passed by, she lifted her skirts and hurried to the other side. She glanced up and down the boardwalk. People milled about, but she didn't recognize anyone.

With one hand over her eyes to block the light, Kate peered inside. A wide, spacious room stood empty. Dust coated the floorboards and the bare shelves lining the back wall. Images flashed through her head — a curtained off area for taking portraits, a back room for developing prints, more shelving to hold her camera equipment.

She gasped aloud and stepped back. A portrait studio? Here? In Gatlinburg, Tennessee?

It wouldn't work. She wasn't that brave. Oh, she'd toyed with the notion for a year or more, but fear of her parents' reaction had held her back. A Morgan heiress working as a common laborer? The mere thought of the resulting uproar made her feel slightly ill.

Her parents expected her to be home by the time they returned from Europe. They had already informed her of their intentions to find her a suitable husband — someone educated and wealthy who traveled in the same social circles. Someone like Percy, Fran's husband.

In her mother's mind, their money and connections would more than compensate for Kate's lack of purity.

Georgia's cold words haunted her to this day. *Tell no one of what you've done, Katerina. No man will accept a young woman of loose morals. Wesley obviously wasn't impressed. We'll have to find someone else. Once you're married, it will be too late for the hapless fool to back out.*

Her mother expected her to hide the truth until it was too late.

Kate's conscience balked at such a prospect. An omission like that had the potential to destroy the trust between husband and wife.

No, if she couldn't have a family of her own, then she'd pursue a career.

If she stayed in East Tennessee, she'd be free to choose her own path. Make her own choices.

Of course, she couldn't live in Josh's cabin forever. She'd have to start fresh, find a permanent place to live. She had a sizable amount of money at her disposal, enough to sustain her for a year or more, and that wasn't including the inheritance she'd receive on her twenty-first birthday. Imagine, a home of her very own. And a profession she loved.

As she walked back to the cabin, the basket of goods in her hand, thoughts of the future filled her mind. The way she saw it, she had two choices — return to her old life or stay here and create a new one.

The decision was simple.

Josh and Caleb rolled into Gatlinburg mid-morning on Saturday. The downed tree had cost them half a day's travel time, delaying their return. Josh was tired, hungry and in need of a bath and a shave. But he was glad to be back.

As eager as he was to pay a visit to Chad Fulton, first he had to see Kate. Knowing her, she was worrying about his prolonged absence. And he needed to see for himself that she was safe.

When the wagon came abreast of his future furniture store, he glanced over and got the shock of his life. What was Kate doing in there?

Yanking on the reins, he guided the team to the side of the street. Caleb shot him a sharp look.

"I need to speak with Kate." He leaped down. "Would you mind waitin' a spell?"

"Never mind." He climbed down the other side. "I'll walk the rest of the way."

Josh made it to the door in four long

strides. She glanced up at the sound of the bell, her eyes widening at the sight of him. A bell? Since when had Fulton installed a bell?

"Josh!" Straightening from her spot in the midst of a mountain of trunks and crates, she approached him with a welcoming smile.

"I'm so happy you're back! When you didn't return last night, I started imagining all sorts of terrible things."

He hesitated, his befuddled brain trying to make sense of what he was seeing. "What are you doing here? Are you lost?"

She laughed. "No, I'm not lost."

"Were you looking for Mr. Fulton? Do you need to speak to him about something?"

"My business with Mr. Fulton is complete."

"What business?"

She splayed her hand wide. "I'm a new business owner."

As her words penetrated, his gaze shot to her face. She looked nervous. Expectant.

"I don't understand."

"I bought this place. You are standing in what is now my portrait studio."

Josh floundered for a response. Was he having a nightmare?

"I thought you were going back to New

York in a couple of weeks."

She crossed her arms in front of her like a shield, making her appear small and vulnerable. "I've decided to make Gatlinburg my home."

Arms at his sides, he wandered past her farther into the room. The room that was supposed to have held his furniture was instead piled with camera equipment.

His heart felt heavy, like a lead weight in his chest. Each breath was painful. So much for his grand plans.

First Francesca had crushed his dream of a family. And just when he was about to realize his dream of a business, Kate stepped in to rob him of it.

A sigh ripped from his chest. He plunged his hands in his hair, mussing it further.

No. She wasn't to blame. She'd had no clue what his intentions were regarding this place. It was his fault for not sharing them with her.

When she spoke, he had to strain to hear her quiet words. "I've already spoken with the Copelands. They will have a room to let next week. You'll soon have your cabin back."

Pivoting, he regarded her downturned face. "How am I supposed to honor my promise with you living in town?"

"Your promise?" Her head came up.

"To protect you."

"I suppose I'll have to release you of it. It isn't your job to protect me."

"I can't accept that."

Shrugging, she returned to the trunks. "What's done is done. I've already made the arrangements."

Rubbing the itchy bristle on his jaws, Josh said, "Look, I'm not in the best frame of mind right now. I'm in dire need of a decent meal and strong coffee. We'll finish this conversation later."

He needed time to sort through the implications of her decision. To figure out where to go from here.

"Fine." She didn't look up when he left, and it wasn't until he reached the barn that he realized he'd left her there alone. What if Matthews waited till she started down their lonely lane to make his move?

Spying his brother already mounted on Chance, he waved him down. "Nathan, I need a favor."

CHAPTER TWELVE

That did not go well. Hurt by Josh's cold reaction to her news, Kate stared unseeing out the plate-glass window overlooking Main Street. Weren't friends supposed to celebrate each other's good fortunes?

Perhaps he'd been merely tolerating her presence here. After all, she'd indicated that her stay was temporary. And she was Fran's sister. When Josh looked at her, he must automatically think of the grief Fran had caused him. The thought saddened her.

The bell jingled. In the doorway stood Nathan, looking more solemn than she'd ever seen him. Sweeping off his hat, he nodded in greeting.

"Mornin'."

"Nathan." She tried to muster up a smile, but couldn't. "What can I do for you?"

"Josh wanted me to check on you and ask when you planned on coming home so one of us could escort you."

"Why does he pretend to care?" she blurted out, blood rushing to her face. "I already told him not to bother."

She turned her back, blinking fast to fight back tears and the unexpected rush of emotion. Nathan's boots clomped on the weathered planks as he moved closer.

"Kate," he began hesitantly, "I, uh, think there's something you should know. Something Josh would never tell you himself."

She wiped the moisture from her eyes and turned back. "What is it?"

Nathan's kind eyes held a hint of regret. "He's been making plans for quite a while to expand his business."

"I know. He told me."

"When Mr. Fulton decided to retire and close up his law practice, Josh approached him about purchasing this place. Fulton knew he was close to having the full amount, but refused to hold it. My father offered to lend Josh the money, but he wouldn't accept it." He sighed heavily. "I don't know what is going on between you two, but I know my brother. He cares about you."

Closing her eyes, Kate pressed her palm over her heart.

Oh, no. It couldn't be.

He must despise her! First Fran's betrayal and now this . . .

205

"Wh-why didn't he tell me?" she whispered.

"He wouldn't want you to feel bad."

No wonder he'd reacted the way he did! He must've been in shock. Seeing his dreams fall to the wayside a second time. Now both Morgan sisters had dealt him a cruel blow.

"Please, I need to be alone," she managed, not daring to meet his gaze.

"He wouldn't want you to blame yourself. You couldn't have known."

She stared at the floor, unable to come up with a response.

His boots shifted. Clearing his throat, he said, "I'll be in town for a while. I'll stop back by later and see if you need anything."

The door closed behind him. The resulting silence was oppressive.

Kate sank to the floor and, burying her head in her hands, burst into tears.

Kate locked up the studio three-quarters of an hour later. She rushed down the street, head down, in an effort to avoid eye contact with passersby. No doubt her eyes were red-rimmed and bloodshot, and she wasn't in the mood to answer questions her appearance would surely spawn.

Determination fueled her long strides. She

had bought the store from Mr. Fulton. There was no reason why she couldn't turn around and sell it to Josh.

He had his heart set on opening a furniture store. She would not stand in his way.

She found him in his workshop, standing idly behind his worktable and looking as if he hadn't a clue what to do next. He'd changed out of his rumpled travel clothes and into a pair of pressed jeans and a shirt that matched his eyes. He'd shaved, his goatee neat as ever, and his hair was damp from a recent wash. The pleasing scent of soap mixed with the pungent odors of pine and varnish.

His awkward attempt at a smile brought a fresh wave of tears.

"You've been crying." A wrinkle forming between his brows, he came around the table but didn't move to touch her. "Matthews didn't —"

"I know about your plans for the furniture store," she said, hiking up her chin. "Nathan told me."

A shutter descended over his expression. "He shouldn't have done that."

"He shouldn't have had to. Why didn't *you* tell me?"

"It doesn't matter now. It obviously wasn't meant to be."

"You're wrong." She pulled the bill of sale out of her reticule and held it out. "I'm going to sell the space to you."

His eyes widened. Palms face up, he shook his head. "Sorry, not interested."

Planting one hand on her hip, Kate ignored his assertion. "You've been working toward this for a long time. I wouldn't have bought it, had I known. Surely you believe that?"

"I do. And just as you don't want to stand in the way of my dreams, neither do I want to keep you from yours." He jerked his head at the paper she dangled in front of him. "Put that away. The place is yours."

"Don't be stubborn. I refuse —"

She broke off when he snatched the document from her fingers and, carefully refolding it, tucked it back inside her reticule hanging from her wrist. Hands on his hips, his eyes challenged her. "Does your studio have a name?"

"You will not have the final say in this."

"I'm not buying the space from you, Kate."

They stood nearly toe-to-toe, gazes locked in a silent battle of wills. Her mouth thinned with displeasure, a darker emotion similar to desperation lurking beneath the surface. This conversation was not going the way she'd planned. Why was he being so stubborn?

How could she enjoy her new venture, knowing she'd denied him his dream?

"This has been an upsetting morning for both of us." Pivoting away from him, she stalked to the door, only to turn back at the last moment. "I'm not accepting this as your final answer. Take some time to think it over."

She swept out the door before he could respond. Chances were she didn't want to hear what he had to say anyway.

Not in the mood to return to her studio, Kate decided to take a stroll around the farm. Her focus was turned inward, and she didn't look up as she usually did to drink in the beauty and majesty of the mountains towering above her. When she tired of walking, she entered the orchard and sank down at the base of an apple tree to rest. She'd brought a copy of Jane Austen's *Emma* along, and, pulling it from her pocket, attempted to read.

But she couldn't concentrate.

The defeat in Josh's eyes tormented her. Somehow, someway, she had to make him agree to her suggestion.

"Kate?"

Twisting to look up the low rise, she spotted him. "I'm here."

Josh came to her, bending at the waist to peer at her beneath the low branches. "You missed lunch. I was worried."

Setting her book aside, she folded her hands in her lap. "I lost track of time. Besides, I'm not hungry."

He slipped his hat off and, crouching low, moved to sit opposite her. He skimmed his hair with an impatient hand and dropped his hat in his lap. "I know my reaction to your new studio wasn't what you'd expected. I was surprised."

"I know. And I'm sorry for that. But I meant what I said earlier. I want you to have the store. This is your birthplace. Your family and friends are here." She hitched a shoulder. "I can go anywhere to open a studio."

"Tell me something." His blue eyes quizzed her. "Why Gatlinburg?"

"I love it here. These mountains speak to my soul. I see God's fingerprint everywhere I look." She spread her hands wide. "There's a feeling I have when I'm in the forest that I haven't experienced anywhere else. When I'm surrounded by endless trees and hushed stillness, I don't ever want to leave. You probably think that's ridiculous." She laughed self-consciously.

"Not at all. In fact, I feel the same way. Still, life is different here."

"I'm aware of that."

He stared hard at her. "I think, after a time, you'd miss the creature comforts of city life."

"I'm not Francesca."

"I know that," he responded evenly. "But you and she had the same upbringing."

"Simply because we are siblings doesn't mean we share the same values. Do you and your brothers all have the same opinion about everything?"

He set his jaw. "No, we don't."

"You see?"

"I don't think you comprehend the reality of living without servants to cater to your every need. Out here, dinner doesn't just appear on the table every night. If you want something to eat, you gotta go out to the garden and pick it yourself. You have to choose one of your livestock or hunt down a wild animal and, once you've killed it, bleed it dry, skin, carve and cook it. *Then* you get to eat." His serious gaze challenged her. "Do you know how to cook?"

Lifting her chin, she retorted, "As a matter of fact, I do."

"Honestly."

Kate had made friends with the head chef, who'd agreed to teach her the basics. While her skills weren't those of a professional, those staff members who'd sampled her food said she had talent. Her mother wasn't told, of course. The daughter of Patrick Morgan doing menial work? Perish the thought!

"You think I'm lying?"

"Of course not." Shifting, he stroked his goatee. "Look, I'm sorry. It's not my intention to upset you. All I'm trying to do is make you see reality."

"This conversation is pointless. I'm not staying here because you are going to buy the store back from me."

"That's not going to happen."

Exasperated, Kate threw up her hands. "You're not making any sense! You don't want me to stay and yet you won't buy the building so that I can leave."

He stilled. "I never said I didn't want you to stay."

Her heart paused midbeat, then thudded wildly. "What do you mean?"

"I'm concerned that you won't ultimately be happy here. This is all brand-new and different from the city. For you, Gatlinburg might be a nice place to visit, but not to live in."

"Perhaps you're right."

"Really?"

"But there are no guarantees in life. Who knows? I might never get tired of country living."

Presenting her with his profile, he stared off into the distance.

"All I know is I'm no longer satisfied with my life in New York. I'm ready for a change."

"I just can't believe you'd be happy here."

"You have no idea what my life is like."

He looked at her then. "I know you're surrounded by luxury. You saw the way people stared at you the day you arrived. They only see clothes and carriages like that in magazines or when wealthy folks like you pass through these parts, which isn't often. You honestly think you'd be happy living in a two-room cabin the rest of your life?"

"You didn't doubt Francesca's ability to be happy here, so why do you doubt mine? What makes me so different?"

Kate gazed at him, a wounded look in her eyes. Her lower lip trembled, and he itched to smooth it with his thumb. If he rattled off the many wonderful qualities she possessed that Francesca lacked, she might think he harbored feelings for her. Which was ludicrous. He'd learned his lesson —

no more foolhardy decisions.

"It didn't occur to me how much I'd asked her to give up until you arrived. Watching you at the supper table that first night . . . how out of your element you were . . . We come from different worlds, you and I."

"You're speaking of material wealth. Yes, we have ladies' maids and butlers and kitchen staff. Fine art lines the hallways. Bohemian crystal bowls and vases grace Italian marble tables. My mother has fresh-cut roses delivered to her suite every day of the year. It's an extravagant lifestyle. Do I enjoy the delicious meals and having an entire library at my disposal? Of course. Does it make me happy? No." Her voice dipped. "I'm lonely there, Josh. I don't have many friends."

Her words came out in a quiet hush, yet there was no disguising their sadness.

He almost reached out and tugged her close for a hug. Somehow, he held back. "I can't imagine why not," he murmured, his voice thick.

"It's an issue of different values and interests." She sighed. "Spending time with your family and cousins has given me a glimpse of what home and family should be." Her green gaze settled on his with confidence. "I can live without the extras. I don't want to live without the things that really matter."

"Are you sure about this?" Megan regarded her with wide eyes. "You have such exquisite clothes. Why would you want to wear one of my dresses? Not that I mind, of course. I simply don't understand."

Standing in her bedroom, Kate smoothed the lightweight cotton material, then pressed her hands against the flat of her stomach. She inhaled, expanding her lungs as far as they would stretch. Her stiff, confining corset lay abandoned on the bed.

"Believe me, if you had to wear that tortuous article day after day, you'd understand." She twirled in a circle to watch her skirt flare like a bell. With a wide grin, she said, "I feel so free!" Sobering, she sought her friend's gaze. "But how do I look?"

Moving behind her, Megan gathered the excess material around Kate's waist and pulled it taut. "I'm taller than you."

"And not top-heavy." Kate grimaced.

"Don't complain about the blessings God gave you," she chided gently. "You have an attractive figure."

The simple compliment brought tears to her eyes. All she'd ever heard from her mother and sister were derogatory comments. Could it be that her figure wasn't as unbecoming as she'd been led to believe?

"The length needs to be hemmed, as well," Megan observed, unaware of Kate's reaction. "We need Aunt Mary's help. She's a much better seamstress than I am."

"I wonder if she'll have time." Today was Wednesday. Only two more days until the dance.

"She'll make time." She whirled around. "I'll see if she has a free moment now to take measurements. Be right back." She was out the door before Kate could blink an eye.

Moving to the kitchen window, she pushed the curtain aside and watched as her friend crossed the yard. When she paused to wave at someone, Kate followed the direction of her gaze and spotted Josh standing in the doorway of his workshop, long apron wrapped around his waist and one arm propped against the doorjamb.

Her breath caught. Since their conversation in the orchard, they'd spoken only in passing. He'd hardly left his workshop, even taking his meals there. There'd been no mention of resuming shooting lessons and absolutely no references to the studio.

He was avoiding her. If only he'd stop being so stubborn and agree to buy back the store.

Josh disappeared from view, and Kate let the curtain fall back in place.

No doubt he regretted his promise to escort her and Megan to the dance.

Megan's soft footfalls on the porch sounded a moment before she glided inside. "She'll be here in fifteen minutes." Perching on the edge of the sofa cushion, she looked up and frowned. "What's the matter? You look sad."

Kate sank down beside her. "Maybe I shouldn't go. After all, Josh agreed to take both of us, and now that Tom is going, it's more like a pairing off."

"What's wrong with that?"

"What if Josh doesn't like the idea of being paired with me? He did try and talk me out of it, remember?"

"Josh is a private person, that's all. He's afraid showing up with you is going to stir up a hornet's nest of speculation. I'm sure he's trying to shield you from that possibility."

"Then we shouldn't go."

"No!" Megan leaned forward and covered Kate's hands with her own. "You have to go. You'll see, it's great fun! And don't worry about anyone else. The O'Malleys stick together. There'll be enough of us there to form a buffer against curious bystanders."

"I don't know."

"What else is bothering you?"

"I don't blame him for not wanting to spend time with me. I ruined his life —" her voice wobbled "— and now he despises me."

"That's not true!" Megan curled an arm around her shoulders. "You had no idea of his plans. He may be disappointed, but I know him. He's smart. And he doesn't give up easily. He'll figure out another way to achieve his dream."

Kate sniffed. "I wish he would just agree to take it back. Why does he have to be so obstinate?"

Megan threw back her head and laughed. "He's an O'Malley."

Miserable, Kate urged her friend, "Perhaps you should talk to him. If he wants to back out, I'll honor his wishes. The last thing I want is to force my company on him."

"Don't be ridiculous," she scoffed. "As if any man wouldn't be thrilled to spend time with you! He likes you, Kate. I can tell."

"How can you say that? My sister betrayed him. Instead of welcoming his blushing bride to town, he got me — the bearer of bad tidings. And now I've single-handedly destroyed his dream of a business all his own. He must rue the day he heard the Morgan name."

Leaning against the side of the wagon, Josh tipped his head back and watched as the last remaining rays of the sun bathed the distant mountain peaks in pale pink and peach. He silently thanked God for the sight.

It had been a long, tiring day. He'd delivered the cedar hope chest right after breakfast, then got to work on his next project, not stopping until late afternoon when Nathan had poked his head in the shop and asked if he was still going to the dance tonight. And even though he hadn't eaten since early morning, he wasn't hungry. He was too wound up to think about food.

Kate dominated his thoughts.

He'd rehashed the events of the past week a thousand times. She hadn't been aware of his plans to buy the store. He knew her. She wasn't the type to deliberately hurt others.

Kate wasn't at all like her sister. She was an honest, caring woman with a heart as big as the forest.

Still, it hurt to have his dream snatched

away like that. All his planning and hard work — the late nights, missed suppers, aches and pains — had been for naught. Oh, he still had his clients and a long list of projects. But the furniture store he'd envisioned would have to wait.

He'd spent a lot of time on his knees the past few days, asking God why. He'd had such peace about his plans. Now he was confused and upset.

Hearing movement from inside her cabin, he tossed the sliver of hay to the ground and settled his black hat on his head.

Kate emerged and all thoughts of his failed plans scattered like leaves on the wind.

Josh swallowed hard. Gone was the stiff, extravagant clothing. In its place was a simply made dress that showed off her curves to perfection. Her hair only partially restrained by forest-green ribbons that matched the color of her dress, the remainder flowed down past her shoulders in thick, glossy waves. She could've been any girl in town. A country girl.

Seeing her this way was a hard blow to the gut. His breath hissed out from between his lips. In a near stupor, he approached and extended his hand to help her down the steps.

She placed her soft, bare hand in his, and he detected the slightest hint of a tremor. His fingers tightened in response. When she was standing directly in front of him, he could only stare.

Her jewel-like eyes held a thousand mysteries. "Is something the matter?"

"Uh-uh." He shook his head, feeling suddenly like a timid youth. "You're beautiful."

Her curled lashes swept down to hide her eyes, dark half-moons against her pale skin. A light breeze teased the tendrils around her face, and he resisted the urge to smooth them back.

Clearing his throat, he said, "It will get cooler as the night progresses. Do you have a shawl I can fetch for you?"

"I forgot to lay one out. I'll get it."

Slipping her hand from his, she hurried back inside and returned a few minutes later with the desired article. "Where are Tom and Megan? I thought they were going with us."

"Nathan stopped in his shop for a haircut this afternoon, and Tom was running behind. He passed along a message that he will pick up Megan. They'll meet us there."

His friend had had a crush on Megan for years, but he'd wanted to wait until his business was up and running to make his move.

No doubt he wanted to spend a few minutes alone with her.

Megan could be tough to read, though. Friendly to everybody. No telling if she viewed Tom as a romantic interest or merely a friend. Time would tell, he supposed.

He gestured to the wagon. "Shall we?"

"Wait, we don't have to do this. I won't be offended if you'd rather not."

"And deny myself the honor of escorting the most beautiful lady in town?" he challenged.

Her cheeks bloomed with color. "But after what I did —"

"Let's agree not to discuss the topic for tonight. This is your first barn dance, and I want you to have a good time."

She was quiet as they approached the wagon.

The sun dipped behind the mountains, blotting out much of the daylight. Another cool breeze rustled the leaves in the trees, and Kate shivered, her gaze darting anxiously to the shadowed woods behind the cabin.

"It's getting dark."

He wondered if there was more to her fear than she was letting on. Instead of questioning her, however, he helped her up onto the wagon seat and circled around the back to climb up on the other side. When she'd wrapped her shawl securely around her shoulders, he signaled the team to head out.

Kate sat quietly beside him, apparently content to survey their surroundings. With each passing minute, black swallowed up the sky. Here and there a star flickered on as if lit by a match. The kerosene lamps swung from their hooks, lighting their way.

Night had taken hold by the time they arrived at the Fosters' farm three miles west of town. People were still arriving, unloading baskets of food and jugs of lemonade and sweet tea from their wagons. His parents had come early to help with the setup, and since Nathan's date was Elijah Foster's daughter, he'd ridden over with them.

A lively tune drifted on the cool breeze, with snatches of conversation and laughter mixed in.

"Isn't Caleb coming?"

"Doubt it." She accepted his outstretched arm. "My little brother tends to keep to himself. Always avoids large crowds."

"Why do you think that is?"

"He's self-conscious about his scar."

"How did it happen?"

He didn't answer right away, his attention caught by the thick tangle of trees. Nothing seemed out of the ordinary. Still he couldn't shake the sensation someone was out there watching.

"Josh?"

"Sorry. What were we talking about?"

She looked at the trees. "What is it? Did you see something?"

"No, nothing. Must've imagined it."

She stiffened. "You don't think —"

"No, I don't," he said firmly. "He's not that bold. I'd say he's not that dumb, but alcohol tends to cloud reason."

"But —"

He touched a finger to her lips. "Remember my promise?"

Girlish giggles erupted to their right. A glance over his shoulder revealed three girls in pigtails watching their every move. The oldest girl's red hair shone in the moonlight.

He dropped his hand. "We should go in."

"Why the frown?"

"See the one on the far right? She reminds me of Juliana at that age. Still hard to believe she's gone. I never dreamed she'd leave Gatlinburg."

He missed their talks. Juliana had a lot of insight into relationships and wasn't afraid to share her opinion. He remembered how at her wedding reception she'd voiced her doubts about his choice of a city girl for a wife. She'd been right.

"The two of you are very close, aren't you?"

"Like brother and sister." He glanced at Kate. "You know, I have a feeling the two of you would hit it off."

"I would like to meet her someday."

"Maybe you will."

The barn doors had been thrown open to let fresh air circulate. A crush of people encircled the dance area and musicians. Lamps had been strung from post to post, suspended from inch-thick ropes high above the crowd. The Fosters and the setup crew had done their job well. There wasn't a trace of animal odor in the air, only fresh hay and a potent mix of men's cologne and women's perfume.

The women wore their finest dresses, the men their cleanest clothes, hair and beards trimmed for the occasion.

Beside him, Kate's expression was one of shy curiosity. She surely wouldn't be impressed with this backwoods gathering.

"Howdy, Josh." Ed Wilcox walked up, a pipe dangling from one corner of his mouth. His gaze switched to Kate. "Ma'am."

Josh made the introductions. "Nice to meet ya," Ed said. "Josh, the wife is mighty pleased with the new table. Impressed the in-laws, too." He grinned, setting his pipe to wobbling precariously.

Josh experienced a rush of pleasure at the compliment. Satisfied customers meant repeat business. "I'm glad to hear it."

The older man's grin grew even wider, and the pipe slipped free. He caught it before it hit the ground. "Say, when you plannin' on settin' up your store? Your pa told me all about your big plans. He's right proud of ya."

Kate stiffened beside him. Sensing her sudden anxiety and afraid she might dart off, he reached over and threaded his fingers through hers. With the other hand, he clapped the man on the shoulder. "I'd love to discuss my plans with you, but this is the young lady's very first barn dance. I don't think it'd be right to talk business. Let's talk later, okay?"

"Certainly." His eyes twinkled knowingly.

Before he could say anything else to upset Kate, Josh nodded a farewell and tugged her in the opposite direction.

"Would you like something to drink?"

"Maybe later."

She sounded dejected. Great. Why did the first person they ran into have to be Ed Wilcox? Pa shouldn't have told him. Or anyone else, for that matter. But Pa *was* proud of all three of his sons. He guessed it was natural for a father to brag about his off-spring.

He just wished Ed had chosen another time to bring up the sore subject.

"I'm sorry about that. The good thing is that not many people know about the store, so I don't think we'll have any more questions." He squeezed her hand. "Remember, we're here to enjoy ourselves."

"All right." She gave him a small smile, and he knew it was for his benefit.

Spying his parents, he led her through the crowd to their side.

His mother leaned forward with a smile. "Kate, you look beautiful. How do you feel?"

"Wonderful." She blushed. "Thanks for all your help."

"If you'd like, we can go to Clawson's next week and buy some material. It wouldn't take long to sew two or three more dresses."

Josh thought the suggestion unnecessary. Wasted money and energy, in his opinion. Kate's wardrobe was of the finest quality. Why would she want to wear homemade dresses?

"I'd like that."

He could tell by her earnest tone that she wasn't simply placating his mother. She was sincere.

Nicole appeared then, an eager bounce to her step. With a quick hello to his parents and himself, she focused her attention on Kate. "Do you have a free moment? I'd like to introduce you to some friends of mine."

"Would you mind?" She turned to him.

"Not at all."

Her wide smile conveyed her gratitude, her sparkling eyes her anticipation. Josh watched as, arm in arm, the pair wove a path through the throng to the refreshment table, where a cluster of young ladies stood chatting. They welcomed Kate with eager smiles, pressing in close to be introduced to her.

His mother excused herself to check on the refreshments. His father stared after Kate and Nicole.

"That gal looks right pretty, don't you think?"

"She does at that, Pa."

Kate was laughing, pearl-white teeth glinting in the lamplight, her face glowing with happiness. Watching her, his heart yearned to be the one to make her laugh. To bring her joy. To thrill her.

Whoa! Josh shook his head to dislodge the thought.

"Kate seems happy here," Pa continued.

"I had my doubts at first, but she fits in just fine."

"Yep." How long would her contentment last, however?

"I have to commend you, son. You're handling this whole situation better than most men would have."

He let loose a slow sigh. "I'm still trying to figure out my next move."

"Trust in the Lord's guidance," Pa said. "He has a plan for your life."

"I know. It's just that sometimes I'm impatient for Him to reveal it to me."

He felt a tap on his shoulder. "Evenin', O'Malley."

Noah Townsend stood beside him. The same age as Josh, he'd been married and widowed in the past year. A hardworking man, he didn't come to town often. Josh was surprised to see him.

"Good to see you, Townsend. How ya been?"

"Can't complain. The harvest has been plentiful this year." He glanced across the room. "I heard you have a lady visitor out at your place. That her?"

Josh's mouth tightened. He didn't like the direction this conversation was headed in. "Her name's Kate Morgan."

"Beautiful girl." Noah's tone warmed with

appreciation. "You think she'd agree to dance with me?"

"She's an adult. You'll have to ask her."

Noah pinned him with a serious gaze. "Am I overstepping my bounds, O'Malley? I know you were engaged to her sister, but if there's something between you two . . ."

Yes, he wanted to say, Kate was off-limits. But he couldn't.

He had no claim on her.

"To the best of my knowledge, Kate's not attached to anyone."

"Good. I believe I'll go on over there before someone else gets the jump on me. Evenin', gentlemen."

His stomach a hard knot, he watched Townsend approach Kate, singling her out from the rest of the group. Her expression revealed her initial surprise, quickly masked by polite acceptance. Good manners instilled from birth, he thought, wondering if she truly wanted to dance with the man or had agreed because politeness dictated it.

He watched as the pair joined the other couples on the dance floor. When Townsend took her in his arms, Josh felt ill. A sour taste coated his mouth. Heaving a sigh, he turned away from the disturbing sight.

"Want something to drink, Pa?"

"No, thanks. I believe I'll join that group

of old married men over in the corner. Catch up on the latest gossip," he said with a wink.

Josh made his way to the makeshift table in the corner near the door and helped himself to a Mason jar filled to the brim with sweet tea. He took a long chug of the full-bodied brew, his gaze once again drawn to the couples whirling to the music.

Kate moved with grace and elegance. Although she was surely unfamiliar with the rustic, enthusiastic music, she followed Townsend's lead without a single misstep. She was a natural.

Josh noticed she kept her gaze downcast, but that didn't deter Townsend. His mouth was moving a mile a minute and, on occasion, his words elicited a laugh from Kate. He wondered what the widower's motives were. Surely he wasn't already in the market for another wife!

At last the song came to an end. Straightening, he started forward only to stop when another man — Carl Howard — intercepted the couple leaving the dance floor. The music started up again, and Josh watched with dismay as Howard led Kate into a lively number. A glance around revealed a number of single men focused on his date.

The acid in his stomach churned with

frustration. He wasn't a dancer. Never had been. He hadn't planned on asking her to dance. It hadn't occurred to him that he'd be standing on the sidelines watching her whirl away the night with every young buck in town.

CHAPTER THIRTEEN

Her toes ached. Her throat was as dry as the Sahara. And if she had to dance with one more stranger, her cheeks would surely crack from the strain of her pasted-on smile.

Where was her supposed escort? Irritated and confused, Kate glanced surreptitiously about for the tall man with short, tousled hair the color of wheat. Yet there was no sign of him.

Why had he agreed to bring her, only to abandon her?

Feeling a light touch on her sleeve, she whipped her head up, expecting to see him. But it wasn't Josh. Masking her disappointment, she greeted Megan with a simple nod. She couldn't bring herself to smile.

"Kate! You sure are a popular dance partner!" Her skin was flushed, eyes bright with excitement. "Are you having fun?"

She couldn't bring herself to spoil her friend's mood. "The music is wonderful."

"I believe you've cast a spell on all the single men below the age of forty, Kate Morgan. You're the belle of the ball!"

All except one, she thought. "You're exaggerating. And what about you? I haven't seen you sitting out any of the dances."

She shrugged. "I've known most of these men my whole life. It's not exactly romantic to dance with someone who used to sneak frogs into my lunch pails."

"I noticed Tom has hardly left your side. Where is he, anyway?"

"Getting us something to drink." She glanced over her shoulder. "He's a good man. A good friend."

"A romantic friend?" Kate dared to ask.

"Not exactly." Her lips quirked. "Josh tells me I read too much. That I have fanciful notions of what a man should be."

"Do you agree with him?"

Tilting her head to the side, she considered the question. "Yes and no. I do know I don't wanna settle for less than God's best. He knows my heart. What or who will complete me. Does that make sense?"

Kate nodded, thinking it made total sense. She'd settled for less than God's best when she'd allowed Wesley to take her virtue. And now she carried around with her the shameful realization that no honorable man would want her for his wife or the mother of his children.

Megan peered closer. "Has all the dancing worn you out? There's some empty chairs against the wall. We can sit and rest awhile if you'd like."

"No, thank you." The heat was suddenly too much to bear. "If you don't mind, I'm going to step outside for some fresh air."

She turned away before Megan could protest, shouldering her way through, gaze locked on the door and the darkness beyond.

Just as she was about to leave the building, a hand caught her wrist. "Where do you think you're going?"

Kate would know that voice anywhere. She slid her gaze up to his face. Judging by his expression, he wasn't any happier than she was at the moment.

"I'm going outside for some fresh air."

Josh quirked a sardonic brow. "You do look flushed. Must be from all that dancing."

How dare he sound perturbed! She tugged on her hand, and he released it. "Isn't that what people are supposed to do at a barn *dance?*"

Folding his arms across his chest, he narrowed his gaze. "My assumption was you're supposed to spend time with the one who brought you."

"Hah!" Jamming her hands on her hips, she glared at him. "And my assumption was the one who brought me wouldn't abandon me to a procession of strange men!"

His lips parted in surprise. She didn't give him a chance to reply.

Stomping out into the night, Kate strode the length of the wooden structure and turned the corner, too angry to be intimidated by the darkness. Crisp air brushed her heated skin. Crickets chirruped. Muted music and laughter passed through the wall at her back.

Glancing up, she gazed at the fat, pearlescent moon, floating in the blue-black expanse. Not a cloud marred the view. Hundreds of stars twinkled above her.

A wide clearing bordered the Fosters' barn. Then the forest took over. The shadows were so thick there, the trees merged together.

"Kate." Josh had rounded the corner and was advancing toward her. He held a kerosene lamp aloft, the golden light sharpening the planes and angles of his face. He looked wary. And a bit sheepish, which wasn't like him. Josh was ever-confident, unwavering, a pillar of strength.

He set the lamp in the grass. "You're right. I shouldn't have left you to fend for yourself. I assumed you were enjoying the attention."

"Enjoying the —" she huffed. "If that's your attempt at an apology, you're not doing a very good job."

"What?"

"You honestly think I like being passed around like that?" Pivoting, she swung away from him.

He seized her upper arm, halting her retreat. "That's not what I meant —"

"Why didn't *you* ask me to dance?" She whirled back. "I gave you a chance to back out, remember? But no. You insisted on coming. Why?"

He grimaced. "I'm sorry. I should've explained before now that I'm not much of a dancer. I enjoy the music, but I'm horrible at keeping time. I tend to botch the steps, and I'd hate to put either of us through the embarrassment."

"Oh."

The strains seeping through the wall changed tempo, the instruments strumming a sedate, melancholy tune. The air between them stilled, stretching taut with unvoiced awareness.

In one smooth movement, Josh slid an

arm around her waist and tugged her against him. His voice a mere whisper against her hair, he said, "There aren't any spectators out here. And I really would like to dance with you, Kate. Will you do me the honor?"

Overwhelmed by the moment, she could only nod.

His large hands spanning her waist, they swayed as one to the sweet melody. Back and forth, feet barely moving, they danced beneath the stars.

Light-headed, Kate rested her cheek against his chest. His heart beat steady and sure beneath her ear. Josh held her reverently, as if she were made of fine porcelain. He was good at this. Making her feel cherished. His solicitous nature led her to believe he cared for her. *Just as you believed Wesley cared. You were wrong then, and you're wrong now.*

Easing back, his blue eyes, aflame with need, hungrily roamed her face. "I want to kiss you again," he breathed.

"Did you kiss Fran?"

He reared his head back. "No."

"But you wanted to." She didn't know why she was bringing this up now, but Fran hovered like a ghost between them. "Of course you wanted to." She grimaced, pulling away. "You asked her to marry you."

He didn't try to stop her retreat. "It's complicated."

"No, it's not. You fell in love with my sister and wanted her for your wife."

Presenting him with her back, she rubbed her palm over her heart in a vain effort to stop the stabbing pain that truth inflicted.

"That's what I thought, too," he said quietly. "Until you came."

She didn't move. Couldn't. "What are you saying?"

He circled to face her. "Our time together was brief. I got to know her facade, not her heart." Sliding a finger beneath her chin, he tipped her face up, forcing her to look at him. "Family is everything to me. Marrying her meant the start of my own, a partnership for life. All this time, what I thought was love was simple longing. Do you understand how it feels to want to belong to someone?"

His question scraped raw the wounds inside. Her eyes smarted with tears. "I do."

"I'm drawn to you, Kate."

"Y-you are?" *He wouldn't be if knew the truth about you,* an ugly voice inside her head said accusingly. *No!* Dread slithered through her. *Josh can never find out.*

"You're the sweetest woman I know. Intelligent. Honest. Above reproach."

Honest. Above reproach. The words reverberated through her brain like continued striking of a gong.

After his ordeal, of course he would place an even higher importance on these particular qualities. He couldn't know she was neither of those things.

"I'm not —"

A movement on the edge of her field of vision registered a split second before Josh was hauled backward. She heard the crack of bone striking bone as a balled-up fist connected with his face.

"Josh!" she screamed, her mind scrambling to make sense of the scene being played out in front of her.

Landing hard on the ground, he rolled away before the man's boot could find its target. He scrambled upright and rushed his attacker. They fell in a heap not far from her feet, limbs flying, grunts terrorizing the night.

The stranger's hat went flying. One look and Kate knew his identity. Tyler.

Cold fear constricted her lungs, slowing her blood flow, making her heart flounder. Help! She had to get help!

Her feet like lead, she hurried to find someone — anyone — who could stop Tyler from harming Josh. What if he had a gun? she thought frantically.

A group of men had congregated near the wagons. "Please! Come quick!" she yelled, chest heaving.

"What's the matter, Miss?"

"Josh. He's being attacked!"

They ran past her, warning her to stay put. Instead, she stumbled after them, skidding to a stop at the corner of the barn. *God in Heaven, please let him be all right.*

All she could see were Josh and Tyler scuffling in the grass near the tree line.

More men were streaming from the barn, passing her and crowding around the dueling pair, blocking her view. Nathan rushed past, shouting at her. "Go inside, Kate! Find Ma and stay with her!"

Megan appeared at her side. "Nathan's right." Putting an arm around Kate's shoulders, she urged her to leave. "It's safer inside."

"But what if he's hurt?"

"Josh can hold his own. Besides, look at all those men," she said soothingly. "They'll have it broken up in no time."

Kate reluctantly allowed herself to be led away. Sam and Mary met them outside the door. Once she explained what had happened, Sam insisted on taking the women home. Upset, but not willing to argue with her hosts, she found herself sandwiched between the two on the bench seat of their wagon.

As Sam led his team away from the Foster farm, she craned her neck in an attempt to see any sign of Josh. Mary patted her knee. "He'll be just fine, dear. Don't you worry."

"She's right," Josh's father echoed. "By now I'd wager they've got Matthews under arrest, and Josh is giving his account to the sheriff."

Adrenaline pulsed through Josh's body. He fought to free himself from the hands restraining him, preventing him from finishing what Matthews had started. His enemy lay prone on the ground, face in the dirt, hands tied behind his back. Unlike Josh, he wasn't struggling.

"Calm down," Nathan growled in Josh's ear. "Unless you wanna join him in the jail tonight."

Chest heaving, he closed his eyes and concentrated on slowing his breathing. His pulse thundered in his ears. His jaw ached from that first blow, and he suspected he might have a busted rib or two.

He twisted his head around to skewer his brother with his gaze. "Where's Kate?" he grunted.

"Safe."

Sheriff Timmons strolled over. His hand resting near his gun handle, he leveled his gaze at Josh. "You boys can let him go now."

They released him. Reaching up, he rubbed his sore jaw.

"What happened here, O'Malley?"

"Matthews ambushed me. I defended myself."

"Why would he do that?" He spit a stream of tobacco juice.

Aware of all the curious ears listening in, Josh said, "Can we speak in private, Sheriff?"

He studied Josh a long moment before waving the crowd away. "All right, go on about your business, gentlemen." To his deputy, he said, "Take Matthews and load him in the wagon."

The deputy hauled him to his feet. Matthews glared at Josh as he was led past. "Stay away from my Lily, or else," he snarled.

Josh clenched his hands in tight fists to keep from lunging at him. He reminded himself that the man was not in his right mind.

When everyone had gone, only he and Nathan were left behind.

The lawman cocked a brow.

"It's okay," Josh said. "My brother already knows what's going on."

"And what's that?"

"Matthews believes our guest, Kate Morgan, is his dead wife." He went on to explain the encounters Kate had had with him. "She and I were out here talking when he appeared out of nowhere and punched me."

He spit again. "You know I can't hold him based on your word alone. I'll keep him overnight for disturbing the peace, but he'll be free by noon."

Josh hadn't expected anything more. "I understand."

"I suggest you keep your eyes and ears open, gentlemen."

"Will do, Sheriff."

"G'night." He tipped his hat and walked toward his wagon.

Nathan turned to him. "You okay?"

"I will be as soon as I figure out what to do about Matthews."

"Tough to reason with a drunkard."

"I can't stand by and do nothing." Spotting his hat on the ground, he picked it up and slapped it against his leg to dislodge the dirt. "This man has lost all sense of reality. Kate's not safe with him walking around loose."

"So what's your plan?"

"I don't know yet. But I'll figure something out. You can count on it."

Alone in her cabin, Kate paced from one window to the next, flicking the curtains aside to peer into the darkness. Where was he? Edgy with nervousness, she was ready to jump out of her skin. Not knowing where or how he was doing was driving her mad!

Sam and Mary had volunteered to wait up and keep her company, but she'd declined their offer. Riding away from the Foster farm, she'd been sorely tempted to cast aside ingrained notions of polite behavior and demand they take her back. Somehow she'd managed to maintain an air of tranquility.

Her imagination conjured up torturous images of Josh, hurt and bleeding.

Pressing her fingers against her throbbing temples, her eyes squeezed shut, she attempted to block out the horrifying image of Tyler's fist slamming into Josh. Over and over again. Josh's grunts as he defended himself against the blows.

A light step on the porch had her running for the door. Yanking it open, she fell into his arms and sobbed. "I was so worried."

His fingers trailed lightly across her back, but he didn't return her embrace. "Please don't cry." His voice was soft.

She tightened her hold, and he sucked in a painful breath. Immediately she released him, gasping at the sight of his face.

Blood trickled from an inch-wide gash on his right cheekbone. His lower lip was busted. There were bits of grass and hay in his hair and a rip in the shoulder of his shirt. His left hand cradled his ribs.

"Oh, Josh," she whimpered, knowing this was all because of *her.* Tyler wanted her. And Josh was standing in his way.

"It's not as bad as it looks."

Taking his free hand, she led him inside and closed the door. "Have a seat at the table."

Removing his hat, he laid it aside and fluffed his hair. He pulled out a chair and eased into it, his gaze following her every move.

When she'd gathered a bowl of water and hand towels, she told him, "I have no nursing experience, but I found a stray dog once. I doctored his injured leg for him."

His mouth curled in response, reopening the cut in his lip. "Ouch." He went to touch it, but she captured his wrist before he could.

"Let me clean it." She folded the white towel into a square, submerged it in the water and squeezed out the excess.

"Wait."

Standing over him, she held the towel aloft and looked into his impossibly blue eyes. His hair was rumpled, his jawline darkened by a day's growth of stubble. The top buttons of his shirt were undone, revealing a light patch of hair beneath his collarbone.

"Before you proceed, I need to know how the dog fared."

She hid a smile. "I'm happy to say he did quite well."

"All right, then," he drawled. "Go ahead and do what you gotta do."

She studied the gash on his cheek. "I'll be as gentle as I can, okay?"

She cleaned it the best she could and applied a thin layer of ointment. Josh sat with his eyes closed the entire time.

"I think you need stitches."

"Not a big fan of needles."

"Me, either, but it might scar without them."

"Can you bandage it?"

"Sure." She did as he asked, then turned her attention to his other injury.

Bending closer, her hair swinging forward, she carefully pressed a clean cloth against his lower lip. Opening his eyes, he stared at her from beneath heavy lids, revealing a curious mix of pain and longing.

They remained that way, he sat motionless and she bent over him, her free hand braced against the back of his chair. Then he eased her hand away from his mouth. The cloth fell to the table.

Reaching up, he twined her hair around his finger. "You have beautiful hair," he rasped, "like chocolate. And so incredibly soft . . ."

Kate swallowed hard, afraid to breathe. He was going to kiss her. His words scrolled through her mind . . . *I'm drawn to you, Kate.*

He brought her mouth down to his. Fireworks exploded behind her eyes. Clinging to his shoulders, she tentatively returned the pressure of his lips, careful of his injury.

In a move that startled her, Josh shoved to his feet without releasing her. Holding her close, his hands spanning her back, he kissed her tenderly. She held tight to him, lost in a swirl of emotions.

You're playing with fire, Kate. Allowing him to kiss her, to hold her, only fanned the flames of her feelings. This man was a dream come true. He was everything she'd ever wanted in a husband. Yet he was out of reach.

Josh eased the pressure of his lips. With a shuddering sigh, he folded her in his arms and buried his face in her hair. "My sweet Kate," he whispered.

Pulling away, she touched a trembling hand to her mouth.

"Everything all right?"

Gathering her courage, she blurted out, "Don't do that again."

"What? Kiss you?" Stiffening, his eyebrows slammed together. "I didn't exactly plan it. But I got the feeling you enjoyed it as much as I did."

"It's not wise." She stared down at the smooth floorboards. "You and I aren't courting. We're friends. That's all. There's no future for us."

He was quiet so long, she at last looked up. His expression was one of acceptance tinged with regret. "You're right. I apologize. It won't happen again."

Grabbing his hat, he dropped it on his head. "It's late. I should go."

Heart heavy, she stayed rooted to the spot as he strode across the room and slipped out the door. Why did doing the right thing have to hurt so much?

CHAPTER FOURTEEN

The next morning, Josh woke to someone nudging his shoulder.

"Wake up, Josh." Nathan stood over him. "Time to get up and get your Sunday clothes on."

"It's Saturday," he grumbled, pressing his face farther into the pillow. Saturday was the only day of the week he allowed himself an extra half hour of sleep and his brother was ruining it.

"Kate's taking portraits today."

He came instantly awake at the sound of her name. Scooting up in the bed, he leveled a look at his brother. "Who decided this?"

Nathan shrugged. "I'm not in on the decision making around here. I just do what I'm told."

Josh quirked an eyebrow. They both knew that wasn't entirely true. His younger brother was easygoing, yes, but he was definitely his own man.

"What about Caleb? Did he agree to be in it?"

His youngest brother's accident had changed him from a fun-loving jokester to a quiet, embittered loner. Nothing they did or said seemed to make a difference.

Slathering the shaving soap on his face, Nathan turned down his lips. "He agreed only because Ma pleaded with him."

Caleb's behavior troubled both his parents, but Ma was taking it especially hard. It was tough not to get frustrated with his stubbornness, but all they could do at this point was pray for God to change his heart.

Swinging his legs around, Josh planted both feet on the floor. His ribs ached something terrible. Pain radiated through his chest with every breath. "Can you wrap me up?" He grimaced.

His brother regarded him through the mirror. "Yep. Give me a minute."

Josh reached up and touched the bandage on his cheek. "How am I supposed to be in a portrait with a busted-up face?" Had they forgotten what happened last night?

Nathan shrugged. "Don't ask me."

Wondering why they couldn't have simply waited, he glanced out the window at the gray, overcast day. He hoped it didn't rain and ruin Kate's plans.

Was she still upset with him? He'd acted foolishly, allowing his attraction to her to overrule his common sense, and she'd stopped him from going any further.

Thankfully it was merely infatuation driving him and not true feelings. Kate was a sweet, intelligent, lovely woman. Any man would be tempted to care for her. And he did like her . . . as a friend.

How could he not? She was sunshine in winter, a rainbow in the midst of thunderclouds. When he was with her, worries faded and all he could think about was making her smile.

But he couldn't allow himself to fall in love with her. It would only mean heartbreak for them both.

By the time Nathan had wrapped his ribs, Josh was dizzy with pain. Sweat beaded his brow. Bracing himself against the dresser, he waited for the searing pain to pass.

"You don't look so good," his brother stated flatly. "I'm going downstairs to tell Ma you're not up to this."

"Wait." He didn't want to ruin Kate's day.

"No," Nathan said, already heading for the door. "At this rate, you'll pass out before you get one leg in your pants."

Shuffling to the bed, Josh eased down

onto the feather-stuffed mattress. Between his facial injuries and his cracked ribs, he felt as if he'd gone head-to-head with an angry bull. Matthews had been furious, all right. But at least Josh had held his own.

The fight had given townsfolk even more to gossip about. Frustrated and physically weak, he drifted back to sleep. It was nearing noon when Ma entered his room with a tray bearing a bowl of vegetable soup and two dinner rolls shiny with melted butter. His stomach rumbled. He couldn't remember when he'd last eaten.

Placing it on his bedside table, she straightened and looked at him with concern. "How are you feeling?"

"Better." And he did, as long as he didn't move.

"Do you need help with this?" She touched his shoulder.

"No, thanks, Ma. I can manage."

She gazed down at him a long moment, assessing him. "All right. If you need anything just holler." She turned to leave.

"Ma?"

She turned back. "Hmm?"

"Was Kate terribly disappointed?"

The wrinkles fading from her brow, she gave him a gentle smile. "Not at all. She was very concerned about you."

"Oh?"

"Yes. I shouldn't have insisted on doing them today anyway. I didn't get a good look at your face last night. Are you hurting? I can get you something for the pain."

"It's not so bad."

"Eat something," she urged on her way out the door. "You'll feel better."

"Yes, Ma."

He managed to eat it all before lying back down and sleeping the day away. It was dusk when he finally awoke. Muscles stiff, he moved cautiously as he first sat, then stood to his feet. Not thrilled at having wasted an entire day in bed, he went downstairs in search of a cup of coffee and a bite to eat.

His parents were in the living room. "Feeling better, son?" Pa looked up from his newspaper.

"A little."

Ma looked up from her mending. "Are you sure you should be up walking around?"

He wasn't sure at all. But he wasn't one to lie around.

"I'll be fine."

"I set aside a plate for you. Want some coffee?"

"I'll get it."

Once he'd eaten his fill, he went to retrieve his fiddle from the hutch in the corner, careful not to jar his ribs. His soul was in need of soothing, and music never failed to do that.

"Are you playing outside tonight?"

"Yeah. Are you gonna sit out there for a spell?"

"I don't think so."

His mother worked from sunup to sundown. She needed to take more breaks, in his opinion. "Are you sure? The weather will be turning cold before long." He looked to his father. "What about you, Pa?"

He pushed his spectacles up his nose. "You go on ahead. I think I'll sit right here and keep your ma company."

"Want me to prop the door open then?"

"That would be nice, dear." His ma smiled over at him.

Nudging the footstool against the door, he stepped out into the dark night, lit up from one end of the sky to the other by thousands of twinkling stars. It was a pleasant night, the air sweet with the curious mix of apples and mums. His gaze went immediately to the cabin at the edge of the woods. Lamplight shined through the windows, which meant Kate was still awake. He wondered what she was doing, if she was perhaps reading or penning letters or some other pastime well-to-do young ladies indulged in.

With a sigh, he rested his weight against the railing and, tucking his instrument beneath his chin, brought the bow up and slid it along the taut strings. His eyes drifted shut. The music flowed from somewhere deep inside, and he played without conscious thought.

He played songs his father and grandfather had taught him as a child. Bit by bit, his muscles relaxed, the tension seeping from his body.

He played for nearly an hour. When he lowered his instrument and stared up at the stars, he heard soft clapping from the direction of the cabin. Squinting through the darkness, he could just make out Kate's silhouette. His heart tripped.

"You make beautiful music, Josh O'Malley," she called in her cultured, warm voice.

"I'm glad you enjoyed the impromptu concert," he answered, walking to the edge of the porch.

"I did. Very much."

He held up a finger. "Wait there. I'll be right back."

Returning his instrument to the hutch, he went back outside and crossed the yard with long strides, stopping at the base of the steps.

Standing in the shadows of the overhang, she studied him. "I'm glad to see you up and around."

With one hand on the railing, he settled a boot on the bottom step. "I'll have to take things a little slower than usual, that's all."

"I'm sorry, Josh," she said solemnly. "If it weren't for me, none of this would've happened. You wouldn't have been hurt."

"Don't say that. Your resembling Lily Matthews is an unfortunate coincidence. We'll have to find a way to deal with this."

Stepping forward into the moonlight, he could see the fear written plainly across her features. "What if he has a gun next time?"

"I'll be armed from here on out."

She worried her bottom lip with even, white teeth.

"Hey —" he climbed the steps and took hold of her hand "— remember we have a Heavenly Father who's promised never to leave us or turn His back on us. 'Where can I go from Your Spirit? Where can I flee from Your presence? If I go up to the Heavens, You are there. If I make my bed in the depths, You are there.'"

"'If I rise on the wings of the dawn,'" she continued softly, "'if I settle on the far side of the sea, even there Your hand will guide me, Your right hand will hold me fast.'"

Kate found comfort in the reminder of God's care and protection. There was nowhere she could go where He wasn't. She had to believe He would protect Josh.

She studied his dear face. His split lip didn't look too bad, but the angry gash on his cheek was edged with bruises. Seeing him battered and bruised hurt her heart.

She hadn't wanted to acknowledge the truth, but Tyler's attack had forced the issue.

What she felt for this man was not a mere passing fancy. These were not shallow feelings. No, what had started as an infatuation had taken root and blossomed into a deep, abiding love.

A love she could never express or give free rein to.

Feeling ill, she tugged her hand free and pressed it against her roiling stomach. It was a struggle to maintain an air of calm. "I'm suddenly very tired. I think I'll turn in early."

Unaware of her inner turmoil, he descended the steps. "Sweet dreams, Kate."

Clutching the post to keep from falling in a heap, she watched his tall form as he walked away, her heart aching with the knowledge he could never be hers.

■ ■ ■ ■

Kate's dreams that night and the nights following were not at all sweet. An angry Tyler chased her through the woods. Josh was there, too, just out of reach. He called to her, but no matter how hard she tried, she couldn't run fast enough.

She awoke Thursday morning with a heavy feeling in her chest. The sound of rain spattering across the roof promised a gray day to match her mood. Her plans to take photographs of the town would have to be postponed.

There was a chill in the air, the floor cold against her bare feet. She dressed quickly in an unadorned brown skirt and sunny-yellow shirtwaist in defiance of the gloomy weather. Pulling on a pair of brown leather ankle boots, she dashed through the rain to the main house.

She'd managed to avoid Josh all week and hoped to do the same today. How could she act normal around him? Pretend to be happy when her heart ached at the sight of him?

So far, no one had noticed anything amiss. Or if anyone had, no one had commented on it. Josh had kept himself busy in his workshop, so she hadn't had to endure his presence during mealtimes.

Seeing only Mary in the house, she let out a sigh of relief. But her relief was short-lived. After a simple breakfast, Mary asked if she'd mind taking a biscuit and jug of milk out to Josh's workshop. She did mind, but she couldn't refuse her hostess's simple request. Not without offending her or raising suspicions.

Praying for strength, she entered his workshop. Bent over a waist-high table with a chisel in his hand, he didn't see her at first. A half-assembled chair stood nearby.

She seized the chance to steel her resolve. *Think of him as a friend. A confidant. A buddy.*

Looking anywhere but at him, she surveyed his shop. A cozy space, well-lit with kerosene lamps, he kept it neat and orderly. Tools of all shapes and sizes hung on pegs on the wall beside him. Farther back stood saws and machines she hadn't seen before. The scents of pine and wood stain hung in the air.

"Good morning." He noticed her presence and set aside his tools.

As he straightened, his quick smile slipped into a frown.

The careful way he moved was unmistakable. "Your ribs are still hurting, aren't they?"

"They're much improved, but still a bit sore." He spied the things in her hands. "Ma sent breakfast, did she? All I had this morning was a cup of coffee."

Wiping his hands on a towel, he came around the table and took the jar and bundled napkin from her. "Thanks." Taking in the wet spots on her blouse, he said, "Doesn't look like it's gonna let up anytime soon, does it?"

"No." She grimaced. "I'd planned to take photographs of the church today."

He was standing too close. *Do not think about his tender kisses.*

The door scraped open. "Josh, I need —" Caleb stopped and stared at the two of them, his mouth firming in disapproval. Sweeping off his hat, he dipped his head. "Miss Morgan. Pardon the interruption." His gaze swung to Josh. "I need to borrow your hammer. Mine broke."

"Here you go." Josh slipped the tool off its peg and handed it to Caleb. "What are you working on?"

"Building more shelves in the barn." He turned and left without another word.

"I'm curious about something."

"What's that?"

Kate moved away from him and pretended interest in the chair he'd been assembling.

"How come you don't work in the dairy with your father and brothers?"

With a poignant smile, he carefully leaned back against the table and put his hands in his pockets. "My grandfather was a master woodworker. Every summer during our visits to his house, I'd beg to help him build something. The summer I turned ten, he decided I was old enough to help without hurting myself. He was a good teacher. Patient. Taught me everything I know.

"Soon I started collecting tools. I cleared out a space in our barn where I could work after my chores were done." He shifted his weight. "My dad was great. He gave me the freedom to choose my path. And I'm fortunate my brothers didn't mind the dairy business. Nathan's a natural animal lover, and Caleb likes the solitary nature of the job."

Glancing at the stacks of lumber in the corner, she murmured, "So you're doing what you love and making a living at it."

And I'm the reason your dream of expanding fell apart.

"I'm a fortunate man."

How could he stand to look at her after what she'd done? Flouncing into town and

262

invading his home, his family and, ultimately, his business. In that instant, she knew she couldn't stay. If he didn't want to purchase the store from her, she'd give it to him. He'd be angry, of course, his pride wounded, but she'd be long gone before he found out.

"Josh," said Nathan, as he shoved open the door, his face and hair dripping wet. "Bess is terrible sick, and Pa's getting the wagon ready for deliveries later today. Can you lend me a hand?"

"Sure." He untied his apron and hung it on the wall. When he stopped in front of Kate, his eyes held a touch of disappointment. "In case you forgot, Bess is the brand-new momma cow. I'm not sure how long I'll be. This may take a while."

Relieved at the interruption, she managed, "I'll go and see if Mary needs my help with anything."

"I'll see you later." Plucking his hat off the table and settling it on his head, he followed Nathan out into the downpour.

Kate didn't move for the longest time. As soon as she had a chance, she'd pen a letter explaining everything. Then she'd make preparations to leave Gatlinburg.

Sorrow squeezed her heart. Unable to face anyone, she decided against returning to the main house and dashed across the soggy yard to her cabin.

In an effort to push aside thoughts of leaving, she wrote her parents a letter. She also wrote to her sister, careful to keep it impersonal. If Francesca guessed Kate's feelings for Josh, who knew how she'd react.

The remainder of the day passed slowly. The rain continued through the afternoon, and eventually she grew drowsy from the unrelenting pitter-patter against the roof. Stretching out on the sofa, she pulled the quilt up to her chin and drifted to sleep.

The dream started innocently enough. Another party at the estate. Couples dancing and laughing. Soon the bright, cheerful colors dimmed. The guests disappeared. Now it was just her and Wesley. Walking down the long, dark corridors of the basement in search of the wine cellar. This was a maid's or butler's job, she mentioned. He wanted to see her father's celebrated collection for himself, he said. And glorying in his undivided attention, she happily led the way.

Inside the low, brick-walled room, Wesley stood very near. He held her hand. Told her she was beautiful. The candle flame flickered out, utter darkness descended and her childhood fears overtook her. Terror caught her in its grip. Shaking uncontrollably, she reached out frantically for Wesley.

His voice soothed her as he pulled her into his strong embrace.

"No." She shook her head. "We mustn't."

His hands gripped her shoulders. "Kate, wake up."

"No." She twisted her head away. "Wesley, stop!"

"Kate!" He gently shook her, his voice very near her ear.

But it wasn't Wesley's voice. It was Josh's.

Slowly she became aware of her surroundings. She was lying on the sofa in the cabin. And Josh was there, sitting on the edge of the cushion, leaning over her.

His eyes were dark with concern. "Kate, you were having a bad dream."

Shoving her hair out of her eyes, she scooted up into a sitting position. "I must've dozed off."

As he stood to his feet, his gaze remained fixed on her. "Who's Wesley?"

Josh watched the tumble of emotions on Kate's face. She turned her gaze away.

"He's, um, a friend of the family's."

Her reaction to a simple question had his senses on high alert.

"And you were dreaming about him?"

She stood to fold the quilt, smoothing it

into a tidy square. "People dream about friends and acquaintances all the time, don't they? Even those they don't see on a daily basis."

Her effort to remain casual told him there was something more to this than she was letting on. "It wasn't a pleasant dream. Did he hurt you?"

She hesitated a second too long. "No."

When she made to move past him, he caught her arm. Her shadowed eyes flew to his face. "Your sister deceived me. Don't do that to me, Kate."

The color drained from her face. "I would never hurt you the way she did," she insisted, anguish underscoring her words.

He believed her. Still, doubt wormed its way into his mind. She was keeping something from him.

He dropped his hand, unsettled by the entire exchange. He'd come to bring her a plate of food, since she hadn't shown up for supper. When he'd walked in and seen her asleep on the sofa, he hadn't been able to resist watching her for a moment.

She'd looked so peaceful — a sweet smile on her lips, her dark hair spread out in a curtain across the pillow. In an instant, her sleep had become troubled. And when she'd starting calling out, he'd decided to wake her.

He stoked up the fire, gritting his teeth at the pain shooting up his sides. It had been an exhausting day. Pushing and prodding a sick cow hadn't helped his injured ribs. "Your supper is on the table."

She didn't respond. He heard the scrape of chair legs on the floor and assumed she was eating. When he turned, she was sitting at the table all right. But she wasn't eating. Hands resting in her lap, she was staring out the window. Her dejected expression wrenched his heart.

Blowing out a breath, Josh went to her. Crouching down, he covered her hands with his.

When she angled her face down, her pale eyes shimmered with unshed tears.

"Please don't be upset. I wasn't comparing you to your sister. You have a sensitive, caring heart. I know you wouldn't willingly hurt anyone."

"Oh, Josh —" her lower lip trembled "— have you ever done something you later regretted?"

"Of course." He gave a sardonic laugh. Asking Francesca to marry him ranked at the top of the list.

"Me, too." Her gaze skittered away. "I

believe the Bible when it says God forgives me when I mess up. My head believes it, but at times I have a tough time convincing my heart."

"Sometimes you have to set aside your feelings and make the conscious decision to trust in His promises. 1 John 1:9 says, 'If we confess our sins, He is faithful and just and will forgive us our sins and purify us from all unrighteousness.' He forgives us, not because we deserve it, but because of His goodness and the love He has for us."

"You're right," she said softly. "I have to keep reminding myself."

"Is there something bothering you? I've been told I'm a good listener."

"I've no doubt about that." She pressed her fingertips to her temples. "Actually, I have a headache. I think I might retire for the night."

"It may be you need to eat something." Josh stood. "I'll leave you to eat your supper in peace. See you in the morning?"

"Sure." She seemed distracted.

She made to rise, but he stopped her with a hand on her shoulder. "Sit. I'll let myself out. Just remember to lock it before you go to sleep."

Walking across the damp yard, he couldn't shake the feeling of unease. Francesca had been involved with another man throughout the duration of their courtship. She'd been toying with him. Using him to make another man jealous. Any man would be distrustful after tangling with a deceitful woman.

Kate's different, he reminded himself.

Why, then, had she acted so strangely when he'd inquired about the man in her dreams?

Face facts, O'Malley. You want her for yourself, and the idea of any other man having a claim on her doesn't sit well with you.

No, that wasn't true. He'd been careful to guard his heart.

Kate Morgan wasn't the woman for him.

Keep telling yourself that, O'Malley. You just may start to believe it.

CHAPTER FIFTEEN

Something was bothering Kate.

He could see it in the slight slump of her shoulders and the sadness tingeing her smiles. Her gorgeous green eyes no longer sparkled. And she was eating even less than usual.

Despite various attempts to get her alone, he hadn't succeeded. She was deliberately avoiding him, and he couldn't figure out why.

Perhaps today he'd get answers.

Reaching into the wardrobe cabinet, he slipped his gray suit off the hook and dressed with care. She was taking photographs of their family today. The gash on his cheek had healed enough so that it wouldn't show.

"See ya downstairs," said Nathan, shaved and dressed in his dark brown suit, as he disappeared through the doorway.

Five minutes later, Josh descended the

steps in a hurry, only to jerk to a stop at the bottom. Kate was there in the living room gazing out the window, a vision in a creamy yellow confection of a dress that complemented her lustrous brown hair and green eyes. She turned at the sound of his footsteps.

Was it his imagination or had he seen a flash of longing on her face before she'd schooled her features?

"Good morning, Kate. How did you sleep?"

"I slept well, thank you."

Her polite smile wedged beneath his skin like a splinter.

"I don't believe you."

Startled, her composure slipped. "Excuse me?"

Reaching up, he lightly touched a fingertip to the bruised skin beneath her eyes. "Your face tells another story."

Sucking in a breath, she stepped back. "I — I don't know what you're talking about."

His patience snapped. Closing the distance between them, he clasped her hands. "What's wrong, Kate? I know something's bothering you. I —"

"We're ready if you are, Kate." His mother, wearing her favorite pink floral dress and the pearl necklace his father had given her on the day of their wedding, bustled in from the kitchen.

Dropping her hands, Josh paced away from her.

"I have everything set up on the front lawn."

"Lead on, then," said Mary, smiling with enthusiasm.

Out front, his father and Caleb waited beneath the branches of a hundred-year-old oak. Pa, still fit and in good health, looked dapper in his pin-striped suit. Caleb paced in his gray trousers, black brocade vest and burgundy dress shirt, his expression clearly stating he'd rather be anywhere else.

Kate approached her camera perched on its stand, removed the lens cover and peered into the viewfinder. Straightening, she moved with careful steps to survey the area, all intense concentration and focus.

The first portrait was to be of the entire family. With an easy manner and pleasant yet firm tone, she directed everyone into position, all the while avoiding eye contact with Josh.

"All right, everyone." She circled behind her camera, scalloped lace underskirts catching on the blades of grass. Framed against the dreary skies, she was a burst of sunshine. "I need for you to stand very still until the exposure is complete. It takes approximately sixty seconds."

Stooping to peer through the viewfinder, she recapped the lens only until she'd removed the cover from the dry plate. "Ready? Here goes." Then, snatching off the lens cover, she held up her hand to remind them not to move.

"Got it!" She beamed after a minute. "Now, Sam and Mary, how about one with just the two of you? Then I can take one of your sons by themselves."

Josh and his brothers stood off to the side while Kate maneuvered their parents into place. He didn't miss the love in his mother's eyes as she glanced up at his father, nor the tender way he held her close. Life on a working farm and raising three rambunctious boys couldn't have been easy. They'd faced their share of hardships, but it had only made them stronger as a couple. And they'd learned to find joy in the simple things.

He wanted that same loving partnership for himself. He studied Kate. If only things were different . . .

"Josh? Hello?" Nathan snapped his fingers in front of his face. "It's our turn."

Embarrassed to be caught woolgathering, he was quiet as he headed toward the desired spot. Passing by her, he inhaled her citrusy scent and, unable to resist, tugged on a lemon-hued ribbon entwined in her dark locks. The backs of his fingers brushed against her nape.

She sucked in a breath, turned wide, questioning eyes on him. The air between them shimmered with unspoken longing. Okay, he shouldn't have done that.

Nathan cleared his throat. Josh dropped his hand. *Get a grip, O'Malley.*

"You, ah, had a ribbon out of place," he murmured. "It's fixed now."

Cheeks blazing, she nodded and turned to direct his brothers. Her voice was not as steady as before, but she maintained her businesslike approach.

When she'd taken the photograph, Caleb groused, "Are we done? I've got work to do."

Before anyone could answer, he stomped off toward the house to change. The door slammed behind him.

"Wait —" Mary clasped her hands together "— we don't have a picture of you, Kate. Do you think you could show Samuel what to do so that you can have your picture made with the boys?"

Kate appeared uncertain. "I suppose so. Are you positive you want one?"

"Of course, dear." She patted Kate on the shoulder. "You're part of the family now."

She dipped her head, but not before Josh caught sight of the sudden tears springing to her eyes. He yearned to hold her then, to ease her loneliness. Anger rose hot and swift in his chest at the way her parents and sister had alienated her, made her feel inadequate. How could they not see how kindhearted and special she was?

When she'd finished showing Pa how to work the camera, Mary suggested, "Why don't you stand over there with Joshua and Nathan?"

Nathan settled a hand on Josh's shoulder and addressed her. "Sorry, Ma, I've got a barn full of cows waitin' to be milked. Kate, I hope you understand."

With a parting squeeze, he strode away. Josh made a mental note to take both of his brothers to task later on. While Caleb had been just plain rude, Nathan had bailed in a sly attempt to push the two of them together.

Ma linked an arm with Kate and him and guided them to the tree. "I suppose it's just the two of you, then." She sounded much too cheerful to his ears.

Flushed with embarrassment, Kate glanced over at Josh and caught his intense scrutiny. Did this make him uneasy? It certainly made her feel that way. The knowledge that she was leaving made being near him difficult.

Mary urged them closer until their shoulders touched, then went to stand beside Sam. "Look and see if that's gonna be a good shot," she urged.

"I'm curious," Josh said softly without turning his head, "how many portraits you've had taken of yourself. Since you're usually behind the camera, that is."

Still staring at the camera, she replied, "Very few. I'm sorry you've been placed in this position. Don't feel compelled to ask for a copy of the print if you don't want one."

"Why would you say that?" He did turn his head then. "Of course I want one."

Though she knew it was irrational, his vehemence pleased her deep inside.

"All right, you two," Mary called, "we're ready. Joshua, unless you want to be caught forever mooning at Kate, look over here."

Kate heard his heavy sigh and almost smiled. Hardly daring to breathe, they stood unmoving until Sam replaced the cover as she'd instructed him to do.

"I guess that's it," Mary announced with satisfaction. "Thank you so much, Kate."

"It was my pleasure," she assured her, moving to gather up her equipment. "I'll develop these as soon as possible and make sure you get a copy of each one."

Josh's hand closed over hers. "I'll help you with this."

She released the tripod stand with reluctance. "Thank you."

Mary and Sam headed for the house. Beside her, Josh was quiet as they walked across the yard. When he'd deposited her gear on the table, he slipped his hands into his pockets and regarded her with questioning eyes.

"Well?"

"Well what?"

"Are you going to tell me what's wrong?"

"Josh." She sighed.

"Is it me? Have I done something to anger you or make you upset?"

"I'm leaving."

His head jerked back. "Gatlinburg?"

Gripping the top rung of the chair rail, she nodded. "It's time."

"I don't understand," he ground out. "What about the studio? And your book?"

"I can't get over the fact that I'm standing in the way of your dream. If you don't want the store space, I'll put it up for sale. As for the book, I'm shelving that idea for the time being. Perhaps in the future . . ."

"You didn't do it intentionally."

"My intentions are irrelevant."

"What can I do to convince you that I don't blame you for any of this?"

"Simply put — I can't enjoy it. Every time I step foot in there, I think of you and your furniture and all the hard work you've done to achieve your goals. I've made up my mind, Josh. Nothing you can say will change it."

The next morning, Josh was in that drifting state between sleep and wakefulness when his mother poked her head in his room. "Joshua? Are you awake?"

"Not exactly," he mumbled into the pillow.

"Are you going to be around today?"

He struggled to open his eyes. "Yeah. I'll be in the workshop. Why?"

"Your father and I have some business to attend to. Caleb is accompanying us."

That got his attention. Pushing upward, he peered at her. "Oh? What did you use to bribe him?"

Ignoring his remark, she said, "Nathan is headed over to the Foster farm, and I'm not sure what time he plans to be back. I don't want Kate left alone. Can you keep an eye on her?"

"Sure. I'll be around all day."

"Oh, good," she said, relieved. "I'm going down to fix coffee."

When she'd left, Josh cradled his head in his hands and stared up at the ceiling.

Kate's announcement yesterday had sent him reeling. While he was touched by her concern for his happiness, he couldn't comprehend her reasoning. He'd seen her in action — it was plain as day that she loved her work. Owning a studio would not only give her an avenue to pursue her passion, it would also grant her independence from her family. She had a chance at a new life here.

She had new friends. And his family had practically adopted her. Not only that, but she loved these mountains as much as he did.

After all the sorrow in her life, she deserved this.

It also struck him as odd that he wasn't jumping at the chance to take possession of the store. Here she was, offering to hand it over, and all he could think about was her happiness.

He may not have a store to stock, but he still had customer orders to fill.

There'd be other opportunities for him to

expand, but apparently God had other plans at this time. So he'd just keep doing what he'd been doing. Taking individual orders and doing his utmost to please his customers.

Lord, I'm so confused. The thought of her leaving kills me. Help me, Father. I must keep my wits about me. Remember all the reasons we can't be together.

Downstairs in the kitchen, he asked, "Have you seen Kate this morning?"

"She stopped in earlier." Ma wrapped her shawl around her shoulders. "All she wanted was a cup of tea. Said she wasn't hungry."

"Hmm." Brows pulled together, Josh glanced out the dining room windows. Had she been eating at all the past few days? Worried, he debated going over there.

Then he noticed the sky's odd color. "Are you going far? Looks like it might rain."

"No. And I'm sure your father will keep an eye on the weather. See you later, dear."

She went to join his father and brother in the barn, and he heard the team pull out not long after. He ate his breakfast with haste, not lingering to savor his coffee as he would've if Kate had joined him at the table.

Outside, a stiff breeze raised goose bumps on his arms. Holding on to his hat, his boots ate up the distance between the main house and the cabin. Music greeted him on the front steps. One foot on the porch, his hand gripping the railing, he paused to listen.

The delicate, ethereal notes put him in mind of angels and cherubs, of lush flower gardens and flowing waterfalls. Kate's harp, he mused. Lovely music suited to a sophisticated, talented young lady.

Would she let him watch her play? he wondered.

A raindrop splattered on his hand, then another. Eyeing the rain-swollen clouds hanging low in the pale yellow sky, he realized with a pang of disappointment that he'd have to wait for another time. He was in for a soaking if he didn't get to his shop soon.

With one last glance at Kate's door, he pivoted on the step and sprinted away.

Kate discovered that weathering a thunderstorm in a solidly constructed mansion was vastly different than in a two-room, built-by-hand cabin. Huddled on the sofa beneath a mound of quilts, she winced at each flash of lightning and the resounding boom of thunder that shook the cabin's foundation right afterward. Dark clouds had rolled in about an hour earlier and the storm didn't show signs of abating.

Unceasing rain thundered against the roof. Gusts of wind rammed into the walls.

She hugged her Bible to her chest and prayed. She'd never lived through a tornado and so didn't know what to expect. What if one raged outside her door? What would she do? Where would she go?

The door flew open then, slamming back against the wall. Kate screamed.

Josh stood on the porch, water sluicing off his hat and poncho.

"The storm's getting worse," he shouted above the din. "Put your boots on. And a warm jacket. We're gonna take cover."

Spurred by the urgency in his voice, Kate did as she was told. While she didn't relish the thought of venturing outside, she'd rather ride out the storm in Josh's company than alone.

When she joined him on the porch, he reached past her to close the door.

"Ready?"

His concerned gaze searched hers, and it took all her willpower not to throw herself in his arms.

"I'm as ready as I'll ever be, I guess," she told him.

"Let's go then."

Her hand tucked safely in his, they hurried down the steps and dashed across the yard. Soaked to the skin in the space of a minute, she regretted not taking a hat to shield her face. The rain pelted her tender skin. The wind whipped her dripping hair in her eyes.

As soon as they reached the orchard, Kate realized their destination. The apple house.

She wanted to rail at him for his insensitivity! How dare he bring her *here* of all places?

Surely he hadn't forgotten her fear of dark, cramped spaces!

Shoving open the door, he put an insistent hand against her lower back, silently urging her inside.

Kate resisted, digging her heels in the wet soil. The sound of her heart roaring in her chest drowned out his words and the storm raging all around them. She would not, *could* not go in there.

Josh noticed at once the change that came over her. All color drained from her face, and she raised stricken eyes to his.

"I can't!" Terror radiated off her in waves. "I'm going back to the cabin!"

Thunderclouds roiled like boiling soup directly above their heads. Caught in the storm's fury, tree limbs thrashed wildly about. Tornados weren't a common occurrence in these parts, but he didn't want to chance being out in the open. And her cabin was surrounded by trees that could potentially be uprooted.

As much as he hated to cause her distress, he had to put her safety first.

"This is our best shelter," he said as he urged her forward. "I'll light one of the oil lamps before I close the door. You'll see — there will be plenty of light."

Her fingers dug into his arm, her expression begging him to find another alternative.

"You don't understand!" Her voice was high and shrill. "I'd rather be anywhere else! I'd rather stay right here than go in there."

"I'm sorry, sweetheart. This is our only choice." He hated to see her so upset, but what other option did he have?

An abandoned milk pail flew past their heads, missing them by mere inches. That settled it.

Snaking his arm around her waist, he propelled her inside. He had the door shut before she had time to resist.

There were no windows here. The darkness inside the low, squat building was complete. He couldn't make out her shape.

"Josh, no!" She gasped and lunged past him in a desperate bid for the door.

Stunned by her response, it took a split second for him to react. He darted forward and hauled her back against him, hugging her trembling body close.

"Hey," he murmured against her ear, "it's all right. You're safe here."

Something was terribly wrong. This was no ordinary fear of the dark. Josh determined right then and there he was going to find out the reason behind it. But first he had to calm her down.

"Let me go!"

Struggling against his hold, she attempted to pry his arms away, her fingernails scraping his skin. He held firm. She was crying in earnest now. The pitiful sound broke his heart.

"Kate, my love," he said as he pressed his face close to hers. "Remember my promise? You're safe with me. Remember? Safe."

He continued to murmur words of encouragement while praying furiously for help from the Almighty above. Gradually she ceased struggling, her sobs abating to hitched breaths.

She was silent for an eternity, the sound of their ragged breaths loud in the enclosed space.

"Kate?"

"Y-yes?"

"I'm going to light a lamp, okay?"

It seemed like a lifetime in coming, but at last she jerked a nod.

When he eased his arms from around her, he didn't move away until he was certain she wasn't going to bolt again. Or slide to the floor in a heap.

Jaw clenched tight enough to crack his teeth, he crouched low and swung his hand in a wide arc in search of the lamp he'd brought. His fingers brushed the glass and it toppled beyond his reach.

"Don't move, okay? I'm gonna open the door so I can see to light the lamp."

He could hear nothing but the wind howling outside.

"Kate?"

"O-okay."

Scuffing his boots along the dirt, he moved forward until he encountered the door. He eased it open. Caught up by the violent wind, leaves swirled in funnels about the yard. The chickens squawked in the confines of their house.

He'd lost precious time rounding up the skittish animals and securing the barn doors. But everyone else was gone, so it fell to him to do it alone.

Lord, please spare us. And the farm, too. Protect my family.

Working quickly, he located the lamp and fished the match out of his pocket. His fingers shook when he tried to light the wick. He grimaced. He must've transferred all his calm to Kate and in turn assumed her nervousness.

The wick flared to life, casting a golden glow in a wide circle. Setting it in the dirt near Kate's feet, he sucked in a deep breath. "I'm going to close the door. Is this enough light?"

She kept her face averted. "I think so."

He hurried to do the task, getting a face full of rain as the wind changed direction. He slipped off his hat and poncho, hanging them from a nail protruding from the shelf on the wall, then turned to stare at her bedraggled form.

"You're soaked. Would it help to take off your jacket?"

After a moment's thought, she undid the buttons and slipped it off. Her fingers were like ice when they brushed against his. Hanging her jacket on top of his poncho, he returned to her side. She rubbed her arms in an effort to get warm.

Uncertain as to what to do to comfort her, he sat down on the low bench. "Come sit with me. I'll warm you."

When she lifted her head, Josh nearly

gasped at the pain and vulnerability in her expression. "I shouldn't."

"Why not?"

Her gaze slipped to the floor. "Never mind."

"Kate, please." He needed to comfort her as much as he needed to be comforted. Her outburst had rattled him as nothing else ever had.

With hesitant steps, she came and sat a good six inches away, her back ramrod straight. Feeling like a youth, he curled his arm around her shoulders and scooted in close.

"You can rest your head on my shoulder if you want," he said.

About five minutes passed before he felt her relax, her head shifting against him. He recognized it as a small victory. They sat together listening to the storm rage over their heads.

When he could stand the silence no longer, he voiced the question on the tip of his tongue. His fingertips lazily stroked her arm. "What happened to make you fear the dark?"

"It was a long time ago," she said haltingly, her muscles tensing up again. "I haven't told anyone. Ever."

"Talking about it may lessen the power it

has over you."

She lifted her head but didn't move away. "Or it could make the nightmares worse."

His fingers stilled. His own body tensed. Whatever had happened, it was going to be hard to hear.

"My parents traveled quite frequently when we were young. We were left in the care of nannies and, as we got older, governesses. The spring I turned six, Mother hired Nanny Marie."

Her voice dipped so that he had to strain to hear her. "She was an angry woman. I never could figure out what I'd done to make her angry . . ."

Josh steeled himself, dreading her next words, yet knowing she needed to find release.

Her features twisted in hurt bewilderment. "Nearly every day for six months, she locked me in the supply closet. Left me there for hours in the dark. Common, everyday items took on a life of their own. From an adult's perspective, there was nothing in there that could've hurt me, but for a small child —" She broke off, shivering.

Rage burned in his gut at the vicious stranger who'd done this. Ruthlessly he pushed it down to deal with later. Kate had her hands full coping with her own emotions. She didn't need to deal with his, too.

"Did your parents prosecute this woman?"

"They never knew what happened. She resigned her position without warning, and we never heard from her again."

"You didn't tell them because she threatened you."

Releasing a shaky breath, she jerked a nod.

"All these years you've shouldered this burden alone. No more." He pulled her close, stroking her damp hair when she relaxed against him. "May I pray for you?"

"I'd like that."

"Lord Jesus, I ask You to heal Kate's wounds, the secret hurts she holds inside only You can see. Release her from the fear that binds her. In Christ's name, Amen."

Swiping at her eyes, she straightened. "Thank you, Josh."

"I didn't do anything."

"That's the first time anyone has prayed for me besides Danielle, my friend who showed me how to follow Christ. It means a lot to me."

His heart aching for what she'd endured, he covered her slender hand with his. "I hate that you were forced to suffer in that way. The nanny should've been sent to prison for what she did to you — an innocent child. If I could, I'd gladly wipe away every memory that torments you."

I'd kiss away each nightmare, the pure beauty of our love chasing away every shadow until no darkness remained.

Love? No, that was too strong a word. He cared deeply for Kate, but that wasn't the same as loving her. Or was it?

"I wish you could," she whispered mournfully.

Caressing her cheek, he murmured, "I can help you make new memories. Happy ones."

She encircled his wrist and leaned her cheek into his palm. Her black lashes fluttered down to rest against the translucent skin beneath her eyes.

Tenderness flooded him. He longed to take her into his arms and kiss her, but aware of her vulnerable state of mind, he held back.

Impatient pounding on the door broke them apart. Josh bolted to his feet.

The door flung open. "Josh? You in there?"

Striding the length of the space, his heart jerked at the lines of anxiety in Nathan's face. Behind him, the sky had lightened and the rain had abated. "I'm here. Kate, too."

"Come quick! Ma's been in an accident."

CHAPTER SIXTEEN

Fear flashed across Josh's face. He quickly masked it with grim determination. Their conversation forgotten, worry for Mary's well-being gnawed at Kate's insides. How bad was it? Would Mary be all right?

"I want to go with you," she said.

Eyes dark with worry, he held out his hand and she took it, relieved to be out of the dark, damp structure. Already the clouds were dispersing. Thunder rolled in the distance. Water dripped from the leaves and roof edges, pitter-pattering onto the soggy earth.

They sprinted to the front of the house, where Nathan had left the wagon, mud splattering the men's pants legs and the hem of Kate's dress. Josh lifted her with ease onto the seat and jumped up beside her. Nathan climbed up on the other side and, seizing the reins, ordered the horses forward.

The ride into town was a tense one. No one uttered a word. Kate waited for Josh to ask what had happened and what injuries Mary had sustained, but his jaw remained clenched in silence. Reaching over, she clasped his hand. His fingers gripped hers as if they were a lifeline.

He'd be devastated if . . . No, she stopped her mind from wandering down that path. It was too painful. Kate had grown to care a great deal for the kind, generous, loving woman. She hated to think of her in pain.

For everyone's sakes, she prayed for a positive outcome.

The lane was littered with leaves and branches snapped off by the storm. In town, the post office window was broken, and the barbershop's wooden sign was gone.

She prayed no one else had been injured.

At last they reached the doctor's home, which doubled as an office, located at the edge of town. A hand at the small of her back, Josh ushered her inside. Nathan brought up the rear.

Sam looked up from his pacing, his features softening with relief at the sight of his sons.

"How is she, Pa?"

The older man's cheek was bruised and there was a scratch on his chin, but otherwise he appeared to be fine. "Doc Owens is checking her now, but he's fairly sure she has a broken leg."

"What happened?"

"We got caught out in the storm. The horses spooked, and the wagon overturned."

Kate gaze wandered past the three men. That's when she noticed Caleb sitting in one of the parlor chairs, his head in his hands. His posture spoke of utter defeat. Despite the uneasiness he inspired in her, Kate's heart went out to him. He was obviously hurting.

Gathering her courage, she went and sat in the chair next to him. He didn't look up or acknowledge her in any way.

"Are you all right?"

"Go away."

The words were spoken without malice. In fact, she wondered at his complete lack of emotion.

"Were you with your parents when it happened?"

He was silent, utterly still for so long she assumed he'd drifted off to sleep. When he finally spoke, his words took her by surprise.

"It's my fault."

"I don't understand."

His head whipped up, his eyes spearing hers. Raw grief and bitterness burned in the dark depths. "I was leading the team when the accident happened. I couldn't control them. I'm the reason Ma is lying in there hurt."

"No, son." Sam must've overheard Caleb's remarks. He came and settled a hand on the young man's shoulder. "You're not to blame. The outcome would've been the same if one of your brothers or I had been holding the reins."

"You're wrong." Shaking off his father's touch, Caleb lunged to his feet and stalked outside, the door slamming behind him.

Sam's shoulders slumped. Nathan came up behind him, his expression sad. "Don't worry, Pa. I'll talk to him."

When he'd left, Josh crossed to the hutch where a tray was arranged with a pitcher and empty glasses. He filled one with water and handed it to his father.

"Thanks," he said absently, his gaze glued to the closed door at the end of the hall.

Josh crouched down beside Kate, balancing himself with a hand on the chair's arm. "I'm glad you're here."

"Me, too."

When the door opened and the doctor emerged, both father and son advanced on him.

"How is she?" Sam spoke first.

"As far as I can tell, her only injury, other than minor scrapes and bruises, is a broken leg. She doesn't appear to have any internal injuries, but I'd like to keep her overnight just for observation."

"I want to see her."

"Certainly." He nodded at Sam. "One visitor at a time, though. I've given her some laudanum for pain and she's drowsy."

While Sam went to see his wife, Josh asked the doctor more questions. Nathan returned without Caleb, which didn't surprise Kate. He'd been extremely upset, feeling the weight of misplaced guilt.

While she was relieved that Mary would be okay, she couldn't help worrying about the youngest O'Malley. Perhaps Josh would seek him out later. Make him see reason.

Once Josh and Nathan had peeked in on their mother and seen for themselves that she was all right, it was decided that Sam would stay the night. Back at the house, the threesome ate a simple supper of sandwiches and warmed-up soup from the day before. Lost in their own thoughts, it was a quiet meal.

The exhaustion on Josh's face mirrored how Kate felt — emotionally and physically drained.

Lying in bed not long after, Kate tossed

and turned in the dim light, her mind buzzing with all that had occurred that day.

The storm. Mary's accident. The scene in the apple house.

Josh had been incredibly tender and understanding. Recalling how he'd held her, calmed her, *prayed* for her, tears spilled over onto her pillow.

It had been difficult, divulging her childhood secret. Now there were only three people on this earth who knew — Nanny Marie, Kate herself and Josh. He'd been right. Somehow, sharing that horrifying piece of her past with him had eased the grip it had on her.

But what of your other secret? His reaction to that would be drastically different, I'd guess.

A chill gripped her heart. Curled on her side beneath the covers, her skin was warm but her insides suddenly felt encased in ice.

He couldn't find out.

Don't worry. Josh hasn't professed his love to you. And he certainly isn't going to propose to you.

He may not have come right out and said it, but he believed she belonged in New York, not Gatlinburg. There would never be a reason to tell him.

The moment Kate opened her eyes, she

knew she'd slept considerably past her usual wake-up time. Blowing out an exasperated breath, she slipped out of bed and dressed as quickly as she could in a serviceable black skirt, the plainest one in her wardrobe, and a burgundy blouse. Not bothering with jewelry, she captured her thick waves in a simple bun at the base of her head and slipped her black boots on over her stockings.

She'd planned to cook breakfast for the men this morning. Too late for that.

Crossing to the main house, she noticed downed tree limbs scattered across the yard. Yesterday's fierce winds had stripped a number of trees of their leaves. The air was clean and crisp this morning, the sky stretching a grayish-white above her — a reminder that winter hovered around the corner.

She knocked on the front door and waited, her stomach protesting the long hours since her last meal. Goose bumps racing along her skin, she anticipated a steaming cup of tea.

Josh opened the door, his gaze warming when he saw her. "Mornin', sleepyhead. Come in."

Closing the door behind her, he remarked, "You don't have to knock, ya know. Feel free to come and go as you please. You're not a visitor anymore."

"I hadn't planned on sleeping in."

He slipped his hands into his pockets. "Nathan left about an hour ago to check on Ma."

"You didn't stay behind on my account, did you?"

"I didn't want to leave you here alone."

She opened her mouth to protest, but he rushed ahead. "Besides, there's not much I can do there anyway. Aunt Alice and Megan are there, too. I'm sure Doc doesn't want his office overrun with visitors."

"But —"

He stepped close and pressed his finger to her lips. "Shh." His blue eyes darkened with emotion. He dropped his hand but didn't move away, his broad shoulders filling her vision. "How did you sleep?"

"Better than I have in a long time." For the first time in weeks, she'd slept a dreamless sleep.

"No nightmares?"

"No."

"I'm glad." Looking pleased, he nodded in the direction of the kitchen. "How do biscuits with apple butter sound? I'll even throw in a cup of your favorite tea."

Since her arrival, Kate had grown to love

Mary's fluffy "cathead" biscuits, so called because of their size. The biscuits, with their light-as-air layers of pure delight, slathered with butter and jam, were now her breakfast of choice.

In the kitchen, she stood off to the side while he stoked up the fire in the cookstove and set the kettle on to boil. She'd seen both Josh and Nathan in action in here. They seemed capable and completely at ease doing what was considered women's work.

"Do you think your mother will be able to come home today?"

"I sure hope so."

As he arranged the tea service, Kate studied his hands. Strong and tanned, his lean fingers handled the delicate china with care. She knew from experience the tenderness those hands possessed.

He frowned. "Our biggest challenge is going to be keeping her from doing too much, too soon. She's used to taking care of all of us. I'm not sure how she's going to handle being on the receiving end."

"I can help with that. I've decided to hold off on my travel arrangements."

"You're staying?" Hope lit up his features.

"Only until Mary is back on her feet." She looked away. "Starting with today's lunch, I'm taking over kitchen duty."

"Is that a fact?" One brow quirked up, mocking her, as he folded his arms across his chest.

"I do know how to cook."

"So you said. I'm just having a hard time believing it."

"Believe it. Immediately after breakfast, I'd like for you to bring me a chicken."

He dipped his head in mock seriousness. "Of course."

Kate wasn't surprised at his reaction. Josh saw her as a pampered, helpless heiress. Let him laugh. He would soon see that he was wrong about her.

Josh bit the inside of his cheek to keep from laughing as he deposited the squawking chicken on the floor. Looking domestic with her sleeves rolled up to her elbows and one of Ma's aprons tied about her waist, Kate stood at the dry sink peeling carrots.

Her fine brows shot up to meet her hairline. "What is *that?*"

"You mean you don't know?"

She edged backward as the hen strutted closer. "Of course I do! But what is it doing in here?"

"You asked for a chicken. I delivered."

She planted her fist on one hip. "I meant a slaughtered one, and you know it."

301

He smiled at the undisguised tremor of laughter in her voice. Wayward tendrils had slipped free of her loose knot to frame her face, her cheeks tinged pink from the warmth of the cookstove heating the kitchen. Her rose-petal lips beckoned him to discover their soft fullness. It seemed like a lifetime since he'd sampled their sweet promise.

She looked completely at home in Ma's kitchen. He didn't want to think how much he'd miss her once she left. They likely wouldn't cross paths again. Trips to New York didn't happen every day.

Should he try to convince her to stay? What would that mean for his business plans? More importantly, what would that mean for his personal life?

Having Kate around wouldn't be easy. Not only was he attracted to her, he cared about her. How would he find it in him to resist falling in love with her?

There were plenty of questions banging around in his mind, but few answers. Heading outside with the bird, he wondered when and if his life would ever go back to normal.

When Josh slapped the headless bird on the counter, Kate attempted to keep her expression blank. She'd never prepared an animal for cooking, but she'd seen it done many times. It couldn't be *that* difficult.

He stood near the back door, a silly grin on his face. His eyes sparkled with mischief, and she could almost read his thoughts. *Let's see how the heiress handles this one.*

She squared her shoulders, not about to let him guess at her uncertainty. He'd argued that she couldn't make it on her own. He was about to see how wrong he'd been.

"Don't you have a project to work on?"

"Nope." His grin widened, his even, white teeth flashing.

He apparently had every intention of watching her prepare lunch.

"What would you normally be doing right now?"

He shrugged. "Reading. Fishing. Playing chess."

"How about you go read something then?"

"I can help, you know. I have lots of experience. Despite Pa's objections, Ma taught us how to cook more than the basic eggs and flapjacks. Her reasoning was simple — you can't always count on a wife to cook. After a baby comes, for instance."

Kate's cheeks burned at the mention of childbirth. It wasn't acceptable to speak of such things with a man, especially if that man was single and happened to have kissed you on more than one occasion. The way his gaze caressed her face didn't help.

Being alone with Josh in his childhood home, sharing simple, everyday tasks, stirred up daydreams of him and her as husband and wife. Every fiber of her being longed for the dream to become reality.

Impossible. I'm not good enough for him.

Conflicting emotions tore at her, cutting up her peace. She loved Josh, loved his family and this town. She desperately wanted to stay forever, but being near him, knowing he was out of reach, would be bittersweet torture.

Her mother's features, twisted in cold fury, flashed in her mind. *How dare you risk our family name . . . the Morgan reputation! You'd better hope Wesley doesn't breathe a word of this to anyone. No man will want you now, Katerina! You understand you must never tell a living soul. And if you are with child, I will send you away. You will cease to exist in my mind.*

Turning away, she blinked fast to stem the threatening tears, scooping up the carrot peelings and tossing them in the waste bucket. "Thanks for the offer," she said, clearing her muddy throat, "but I'd feel more comfortable working on my own."

"All right. I'll be in the living room if you change your mind."

"Okay."

Wanting to avoid his perceptive gaze, Kate purposefully kept her back to him as he left the room. *Oh, Lord, I made a mistake coming here. I lost my heart to a man I can never have.*

But no matter how difficult it would be to say goodbye, she'd rather live without him than see the expression on his face when she told him the truth.

CHAPTER SEVENTEEN

The mouthwatering aroma of fried chicken wafted into the living room, eliciting an impatient growl from Josh's stomach. Setting aside his book, he drifted into the dining room and surveyed the bounty. Sliced bread and a crock of butter, pickled beets, a white ceramic bowl of steaming carrots and green beans topped with what appeared to be chopped almonds.

Reaching out, he nabbed a carrot and stuck it in his mouth just as Kate turned the corner, a platter full of chicken in her hands. She cocked an eyebrow in his direction. He'd been caught.

Grinning, he swallowed the morsel glazed with honey and a spice he couldn't identify. It was surprisingly tasty. Maybe he'd underestimated her abilities.

"Can I help you with anything?" he asked, rounding the table to pull out her chair.

"No, everything is ready."

When she was seated, he returned to his chair opposite her. After they bowed their heads, he gave thanks for the meal and prayed for quick healing of his mother's injuries. She was quiet as they dished out the food.

Josh bit into the chicken and closed his eyes in ecstasy. He'd been wrong. And he wasn't too proud to admit it.

"This is delicious, Kate. You're an excellent cook."

"I'm glad you like it."

"How did you learn to cook like this?" he said between bites.

He watched as she touched the corners of her mouth with her napkin and smoothed it onto her lap. Even with her tousled hair and flour-smudged blouse, she managed to retain her regal air. Her perfect manners went bone-deep.

"In the estate kitchens. The staff took time out of their busy schedules to instruct me."

"I'm guessing your parents weren't told about this?"

Her lashes drifted down. "No."

She didn't seem inclined to talk, so he concentrated on his food. When a team leading a wagon entered the lane, Josh dropped his napkin on the table and went to the door. It was his mother's good friend,

Betty Stanley, along with her youngest son, Leroy.

"Afternoon, Josh!" Betty greeted him anxiously. "Reverend Monroe announced what happened to Mary, and I wanted to check in on her."

"That's mighty nice of you, Mrs. Stanley, but Ma's not here. Doc Owens kept her overnight for observation." Spying the basket in Leroy's arms, he stepped back. "Would you like to come in for a cup of coffee? Kate and I were just finishing up lunch."

"Oh, I'm sorry I missed her. We won't stay, but we brought some loaves of bread and jars of my apple butter your ma is so fond of." Elbowing Leroy, she nodded toward Josh. Startled, the twelve-year-old handed over the basket.

"Thank you kindly, ma'am. I'm sure she'll be home later today if you'd like to stop by again."

"I'll wait until tomorrow. She'll need her rest." She elbowed the boy again. "Let's go, son."

When he placed the basket on the end of the table, Kate's brows rose in question.

"Mrs. Stanley dropped off fresh bread and apple butter."

"How thoughtful."

"I'd wager this is only the first contribution. People tend to wanna help each other out around here."

Her eyes warmed with appreciation. "I like that tradition."

He glanced out the window behind her and spotted his aunt and cousin coming down the lane. They'd just been to see his mother. Going to the door, he searched their faces as they approached, muscles loosening when he didn't detect concern or worry in their expressions.

"Josh." His aunt greeted soberly as she climbed the steps. Megan trailed behind her.

"How's Ma?"

Alice stopped to catch her breath, her kind eyes peering up at him. Five years older than her sister-in-law, her brown hair was streaked with silver and there were more pronounced worry lines on her forehead.

"A little pale for my liking, but she insists she's fine. She wants to come home this afternoon."

"Is Doc Owens going to allow it?"

"He's leaving that up to your ma and pa."

Megan piped up. "I think Uncle Sam wants her to stay another night, but she's certain she'll rest better here."

Alice shrugged. "That's probably true. And it's at most a ten-minute ride, so as long as they take it slow and keep her leg steady it shouldn't cause any harm."

Josh opened the door wide for them to enter. "Do they need me over there?"

"I don't see why. Between the three of them, they should be able to get her into the back of the wagon without any trouble. Sam can sit with her while Nathan leads the team."

While Josh was conversing with his aunt, Kate entered the living room. A tentative smile hovered about her mouth, but her manner was subdued. What was she thinking? Was she reconsidering her decision to leave? He knew how much Megan and the girls meant to her.

Megan's gaze strayed to the dining room. "It smells delicious. Josh, did you cook all this?"

"Actually, Kate prepared it." Meeting her shadowed gaze beyond Megan's shoulder, he said, "Turns out she's an excellent cook."

"Oh? You've been keeping secrets from us?"

Megan's voice was full of teasing, so Kate's reaction confused him. Her body jerked, as if startled, the color leeching from her face. "That wasn't my intention —"

"Relax." Megan patted her shoulder. "I was teasing."

Josh interrupted. "If neither of you have eaten, I'll bring extra plates. There's plenty."

"That would be wonderful," said Megan. "I'm eager to try your cooking, Kate. Who taught you?"

Her knuckles showed white where she clenched her hands together at her waist. "The estate chefs."

"That sounds like an amazing experience." She went around to sit beside Kate's empty place. "Are you hungry, Mother?"

A smile brightened the older woman's face. "Even if I wasn't, the smells alone would tempt me." Moving toward the table, she said, "I see we've interrupted your meal. Kate, come and finish. You look like a stiff wind would blow you away."

Kate's face felt like a frozen mask. How much longer she could maintain this facade of contentment she hadn't a clue, but it felt dangerously close to slipping. She'd somehow managed to get through the excruciating meal by taking frequent small bites. Her rationale? With a full mouth, she wouldn't be expected to contribute to the conversation.

Only, she hadn't been even slightly hungry to begin with. And now it felt like a rock had been wedged beneath her rib cage. Perched on the sofa beside Megan, she sat straight and tall and resisted the urge to press a hand against her upset stomach.

Megan's comment about secrets had rattled her. Megan had no way of knowing the truth, of course. Only a handful of people knew about Kate's indiscretion and not one of them was here in Tennessee.

This only confirmed her decision to leave. Her secret, if it should be revealed, would splinter Josh's good opinion of her. No longer would he look at her with kindness and admiration but with scorn and disgust. Kate wasn't certain she could survive that.

Across from her, Josh looked tense. He couldn't seem to sit still. First he'd lean forward, resting his elbows on his knees and fingering his goatee. Then he'd slump back against the cushions. When he rose to pace near the front door, his aunt commented on his apparent unease.

"What's bothering you, dear?"

"Just restless is all."

"You're going to give me indigestion," she scolded good-naturedly. "Where is your brother Caleb? I haven't seen that boy in ages."

Kate watched Josh's expression closely. The corners of his mouth turned down in a worried frown.

He stopped to stare out the window, his

fingers gripping the sill. "I haven't seen him since yesterday. He left as soon as he learned the extent of Ma's injuries."

"I hope he hasn't gone and gotten himself into trouble."

"Me, too."

His gut-deep sigh spoke volumes. This obviously wasn't the first time the youngest O'Malley had been a source of concern. Kate offered up a quick prayer for Caleb's safety and the mending of his internal wounds, both past and present.

"They're here."

Straightening, Josh breezed through the door. Kate followed, eager to see Mary for the first time since the accident. Nathan, in his extraordinary way with animals, coaxed and cajoled the team to move with extra care. It was as if the horses understood they were carrying valuable, fragile cargo.

Vaulting to the ground, Josh was in the yard and striding toward the wagon even before it eased to a stop. Kate hung back.

She was struck by Mary's vulnerable appearance. This energetic, full-of-life matriarch who toiled dawn to dusk, taking care of her family without complaint, was being tended to by grown men as if the slightest movement might break her. Seeing the older woman's pale face, the pain she tried so

313

valiantly to mask, Kate battled back tears. She loved Mary like a mother.

Her gaze sought Josh's face. His lips were pressed in a grim line, jaw rigid with emotion. How she longed to press her hand there, to smooth away his worry. He was a man of deep feeling and sensitivity to others' suffering.

But already she'd begun to withdraw, to dam the tide of love flowing from her heart. She'd stay until Mary didn't need her. Then she'd return to New York City.

"How's that, Ma?" Josh tucked the quilt around her shoulders and dropped a kiss on her forehead before standing back to study her. Color bloomed once again in her cheeks, and the lines of pain bracketing her mouth appeared less often. Thank God, she was on the mend.

In the six days since she'd been home, she had yet to leave her bedroom. Not that she hadn't protested that fact. But the O'Malley men were a stubborn lot. Overly protective, too, of their loved ones. His mother was being coddled by all of them. Kate, too.

"I'm warm now that you've stoked up the fire." She settled more firmly against the pillows. "You look tired. Why don't you go downstairs and rescue Kate from the kitchen? The two of you have been working yourselves to death ever since the accident. You deserve to relax. Play a card game. Go for a walk if it isn't too cold."

He massaged the back of his neck. "Good suggestions, but she's not one to leave work undone." *Besides, I'm fairly certain she's avoiding me.*

"She surprised us all, didn't she?"

"If you mean that she's practically stepped in and taken your place, then yeah. Don't be surprised if she approaches you to teach her how to sew. I heard her asking Nathan today if he had any mending he needed done."

He'd walked in on their conversation that morning before breakfast. Nathan had greeted him as usual. Kate, on the other hand, had barely acknowledged his presence. Apparently she preferred his brother's company to his now. He'd kept his expression blank, unwilling to let her see the depth of his hurt.

Strangely, he didn't have a clue as to what he'd done wrong.

Mary chuckled. "Sam told me she's becoming quite the laundress."

"I offered to help her, but she waved me away."

Her humor faded. "I wish she would stay.

I'm going to miss her sweet spirit and ready smile. For a time, I'd hoped . . . well, that the two of you would end up together."

Her words pierced his heart. "It wouldn't work, Ma."

"Why not? Is it because she's wealthy? Is that what's bothering you?"

"Kate is accustomed to a far different lifestyle than we have here. A month in the mountains isn't enough time for her to make a sound decision about whether or not she wants to make this her permanent home."

"I don't know. She's an intelligent woman. I trust her to know her own mind. And besides, if she loved you, it wouldn't matter where she lived as long as it was with you."

Kate? Love him? The idea settled like a warm blanket over his soul.

No. He was positive she saw him only as a friend. As Ma said, if she loved him, she wouldn't leave.

"Well, she doesn't, so it doesn't matter." He moved toward the door. "Do you need anything else? More water? A snack?"

"I can see you aren't in the mood to discuss it," she said drily. "Can you find your pa and send him up here? I'd like for him to read the Scriptures to me, if he has time."

"He always has time for you."

His hand on the doorframe, she spoke softly, "Your father and I have been blessed with an extraordinary marriage. We want the same for all three of you."

"I know."

"I'm praying for you. And Kate, too."

He turned back with a grateful smile. "Love you, Ma. Good night."

"I love you, Joshua. Good night."

He took the stairs two at a time, pausing in the living room long enough to relay his ma's message to his father before heading for the kitchen. Kate stood at the dry sink washing the supper dishes, her back to him. At the sound of footsteps, she glanced over her shoulder. Did her eyes brighten at the sight of him or was it a trick of the light?

Whatever the case, it didn't last. Her expression quickly sobered.

"How's Mary?" She turned her attention back to her work. "Does she want anything else to eat? If so, it wouldn't take me long to fix something."

He drew alongside her in order to have a clear view of her face. "No, she's still full from supper."

Eyes downcast, she shifted away from him. "She seems to improve every day. I'm relieved to see it."

The action disturbed him. Every day since the accident, he sensed her withdrawing from him a little more.

Crossing his arms, he leaned a hip against the counter. "Knowing you're here has been a huge comfort to her. We're all grateful for everything you've done to help out."

"It's nice to be able to repay your family's kindness."

Unable to stand the small talk a moment longer, he touched her sleeve. "You've been putting in long hours. You deserve a break. Take a walk with me."

The hand holding the washcloth stilled on the plate. "I've got all these dishes to finish."

"Forget the dishes. I'll do them later."

"It's dark out."

"We'll stay near the house where the light can be seen through the windows. I'll take a lamp." His voice dipped. "Trust me to keep you safe."

He waited, barely breathing, as she silently debated. Her eyes shimmered with uncertainty. "Okay."

"I'll get my jacket."

Grabbing it off the hook by the back door, he slipped it on while she dried her hands. She approached and accepted the shawl he held out to her. Head bent, she wrapped the dove-gray material snuggly around her shoulders, slender fingers fastening the row of silver clips. The lamplight glimmered off the chocolate tendrils that had escaped her chignon. He clenched his fists to keep from tucking the wayward strands behind her ear. She no longer welcomed his touch.

Outside, he held out his arm for her, and she tucked her hand in the crook of his elbow. The action brought her close to his side. He inhaled the faint scent of soap and citrus clinging to her clothes.

There was a nip in the night air, but not cold enough to be unpleasant. Kate was no doubt used to much lower temperatures than this. The stars sparkled in the velvet sky.

Walking in the direction of the barn, quiet spanned between them.

He tried to memorize everything about this night — her scent, the feel of her close to him, the whisper of her skirts brushing against his pants. Soon there'd be no more reason for her to stay. She would pack up her things and return to New York.

"What are you thinking?" he asked.

"How much I'm going to miss Tennessee and all the wonderful people I've met." Wistfulness marked her words.

"Have you told the girls?"

"No, not yet."

"Nicole will no doubt pester you for an invitation to visit."

"I would love for all of you to visit. Will you?"

He stopped and faced her. "You know I can't do that. Seeing Francesca and her husband would be awkward at best."

Shadows obscured her eyes. "I understand."

"Do you understand I don't expect you to give up your studio for me? I want to make it clear that I don't hold what happened against you. And I don't begrudge you your dream. It hasn't been easy to accept, but apparently God has other plans for me. If you want to stay, I'll support you. I'll even be your first customer."

Eyes going wide, she pressed a palm over her heart. "That means a lot to me, Josh." Her voice was wobbly. "But I can't."

"I'm going to miss you, you know," he blurted out.

Before he knew what she was doing, Kate pressed her lips to his in a tender, whisper-like touch so sweet it made his chest ache. Then she was pushing out of his arms and racing across the yard. What —

"Kate!"

Her cabin door slammed shut. He jerked

as if slapped.
It sounded like goodbye.

CHAPTER EIGHTEEN

Kate flung herself across the bed, sobs racking her body.

She'd been a fool to come here! What had she truly hoped to accomplish? To satisfy her curiosity? To see for herself the man in the photograph? Or had she come hoping for something else entirely? His eloquent letters — filled with passion for his family, his home, his mountains — had touched her lonely soul and sparked dreams of an altogether different life.

A fulfilled life. One with sincere friendships, a sense of belonging and acceptance, and that most crucial of all emotions — love.

She'd found it all right here.

From that first day, the O'Malleys had welcomed her with open arms. Sam and Mary treated her like the daughter they'd never had. Here she had brothers. Sisters. Friends.

And then there was Josh. He was a gentle, compassionate, honorable man. Aware of her feelings and sensitive to her needs. With him, she felt cherished. Safe. And, yes, loved.

Reaching up, she pressed trembling fingers to her mouth, where her lips yet tingled from the spontaneous kiss. She would savor forever the memories of his embrace. There wouldn't be another.

After what happened tonight, Kate knew she couldn't stay another day. Her emotional retreat was hurting them both.

Her mother was right. Honorable men desired virtuous wives. And while she believed God had forgiven her, she understood that a man like Josh would be hard-pressed to look past such an indiscretion.

She'd known full well that what she was doing was wrong. Believing herself to be in love with Wesley, and he with her, she'd ignored the inner warnings. Now she was paying the ultimate price — giving up the one man who could offer her the future of her dreams.

Desolate, Kate fell into a fitful sleep and awoke the next morning with a lingering headache, a dull throbbing behind her eyes. Her stomach a hard knot, she couldn't fathom facing Josh across the breakfast table. Tears threatened even now. How could she maintain her composure in his presence?

The sound of wagon wheels on the rutted ground outside startled her out of her reverie. It was early for visitors. At the sight of Alice and the twins, she uttered a soft cry of disbelief. Their arrival was like a gift.

She wouldn't have to worry about Mary or the men. Between the church people and Alice and the girls, they'd be in good hands.

Over the next hour, she carefully repacked her clothes and other belongings and tidied up the cabin. Then she dressed with care in the same outfit she'd arrived in — the seafoam-green ensemble. How long ago that day seemed . . .

Fighting a fresh wave of tears, she folded up the store's bill of sale, tucked it in an envelope and penned Josh's name across the front. She placed in the middle of the table where he'd be sure to see it. He'd be angry at first, she thought, but he'd soon come to realize it was for the best.

With only her camera and reticule, she stood in the doorway and glanced back at her temporary home. Yes, it had been built for her sister. Somehow, though, she'd come to think of it as her own.

God help me. Give me the strength to do

what I have to do.

Turning, she closed the door behind her.

He couldn't get that kiss out of his mind. She'd done it without thinking, spurred by emotion that had rocked him to the core. Was Ma right? Did Kate feel something beyond friendship for him? And, if so, what was he supposed to do with that?

Father God, my emotions are all mixed up. I don't want her to go. On the other hand, I'm afraid of what might happen if she stays. Above all, I don't want to hurt her. She's endured enough sadness in her life.

He descended the stairs, lost in thought. When he heard a gaggle of feminine voices coming from the kitchen, he paused on the bottom step. It was early for visitors.

Then he recognized his aunt's voice and those of the twins.

"Morning, ladies," he greeted, scanning the room for Kate.

She must still be in bed.

Alice paused in unpacking her basket of baked goods and jars of preserves. "We're here to keep your ma company and give Kate a break. She's been working from dawn to dusk ever since the accident, and we thought we'd take over for a day."

"Kate isn't here," auburn-haired Jessica

325

announced.

All eyes turned to where she stood in front of the woodstove. Josh was the first to question her. "What do you mean?"

"I saw her walking to town."

That didn't make any sense. "When was this?"

The young girl lifted a shoulder. "Half an hour ago, maybe?"

Jane admonished her twin. "You should've said something."

Jessica's eyes widened. "Why? What's so unusual about Kate going to town? Maybe she needed something from Clawson's."

Grabbing his hat off the hook, he opened the back door. "Never mind. I'll go check on her."

Striding across the yard, Josh tried to ignore the sinking sensation in his stomach. There could be a simple explanation for her going to town on her own. Except, she hadn't done it before as far as he knew. And she knew there was the risk of running into Matthews.

His knock was followed by silence. Were her trunks already packed?

"Kate?" He waited. "It's me, Josh. I'd like to talk to you."

Again, nothing. Opening the door, he peered inside.

"Hello?"

His gaze landed on the envelope with his name on it.

Dread settled deep in his bones. His steps measured, he took his time opening it, not wanting to see the contents. And then he saw the bill of sale.

An inventory of the bedroom confirmed his suspicions. The wardrobe stood empty, and her trunks were lined in a neat row on the far side of the bed.

She was gone.

She couldn't resist one last look around the studio.

It was just as she'd left it. Crates and trunks dominated the center of the room, a good majority of them unopened. Before coming here, she'd stopped by the mercantile and arranged for Mr. Moore to repack everything and ship it back to New York for a small wage. When he'd expressed his regrets at her leaving, she'd come near to weeping and rushed out the door.

Walking in the direction of the livery, she'd managed to stem the tide of emotion. Later, when she was alone, she'd deal with her grief.

It hadn't been easy to find someone willing to take her to Sevierville on such short notice, but, as in most situations, money made all the difference. From there she'd have no trouble finding a private carriage for hire. She was to meet the man back at the livery in exactly one hour, enough time to stop here and dream about what might've been.

Light from the plate-glass windows illuminated the front room, but the windowless back room was sheathed in shadows. She lit a lamp. In the corner sat a trunk full of portraits she'd taken of the city and the estate. Josh had expressed interest in seeing her work, so she'd had them sent along with the other supplies.

Sighing, she crouched down to rifle through the prints. Perhaps she'd leave one or two for him and his family to remember her by.

The creak of the rear door startled her. Straightening, she crossed the room and peered to her left at the entrance. A gust of wind caught the door and it swayed, creaking again. She didn't see anyone.

"Hello?"

A floorboard groaned somewhere in the front room. Her neck prickled with unease.

"Is anyone out there?" she called.

The air was still, quiet. Must've been a trick of her imagination. Still, she didn't have a lot of time to waste. Turning back, she returned to the trunk and hunkered down once more. She lifted out the first portrait.

"Hello, Lily."

Her stomach dropped. No. It couldn't be. Not him. Not here.

She was alone. Without defense.

Whirling to face him, the print slipping to the floor, she gasped at the determination carved in Tyler's features.

"Here we are, alone at last." He stepped inside and, without breaking eye contact, shut the door behind him. "You can't run from me anymore."

Her heart slammed against her rib cage, her lungs constricting with fear. "I — I don't want to run."

She had to bide her time. Appease him until she could figure out a way of escape.

Oh, God, please help me!

"Good." He advanced slowly, his eyes unnaturally bright. "Cause I'm tired. Tired of chasing you. A husband shouldn't have to chase his wife."

Her mouth cotton-dry, she tried to swallow. Her fists curled into tight balls, her fingernails dug into her palms. She forced herself to stand completely still, to mask her distaste, as he ran the pad of his thumb across her lips. Alcohol practically oozed from his pores.

Built like a prizefighter, Tyler could over-power her without breaking a sweat.

How could she defend herself?

"I've missed you, Lily."

Invading her space, he cupped her neck and yanked her against his unkempt body.

Please, no! Suddenly she couldn't stifle the instinct to fight.

Struggling, she shoved against his chest. His fingers dug into her neck. She cried out. They scuffled, and his boot connected with the lamp, sending it flying. The sound of glass breaking dimly registered in the back of her mind.

"Stop. Fighting. Me," he huffed.

Her arms began to buckle beneath his superior strength. Desperate to evade his advances, she angled her face away from his. When she felt his rough mouth scrape the sensitive skin on the column of her neck, bile rose in her throat.

The smell of smoke and flames gradually penetrated her senses. "Fire," she gasped.

"Huh?" The moment his hold slackened, she surged backward. Her foot slipped. She felt herself falling, and then her forehead struck the corner of the trunk and every-thing faded to black.

Josh was angry. How could she leave without saying goodbye? His family, especially Megan and Nicole, would be deeply hurt. He wouldn't have expected such callous behavior from Kate.

Crossing the bridge into town, he glimpsed a thin stream of kettle-black smoke spiraling into the sky. He rubbed a hand over his eyes. Was he seeing things?

He urged his horse to go faster. Apparently, no one else had noticed it, for the handful of people on the streets were going about their business as usual.

He shouted to get their attention. "Something's on fire!"

Jerking to a stop, he slid to the ground, scanning the businesses to see which ones were involved. He couldn't see a thing from this position, but smoke didn't lie.

"I'm going around back," he yelled at Mr. Moore, who'd run into the street behind him. "Pass the word."

He passed frightened women clutching children to their sides. More men came out into the streets.

"Josh!"

Tom rushed outside. "What's wrong?"

"I saw smoke," he yelled, not hesitating. If a fire were to get out of control, the whole town could go up in a matter of minutes.

"Wait!" Tom called. "I saw Kate inside her studio earlier. Do you think she's still in there?"

Josh stumbled, alarm spiraling through him. His throat closed up. "Are you sure?"

At his affirmative nod, Josh pointed to the front door. "Go in that way! I'll go around back."

Please, God, let him be wrong.

Rounding the corner, he nearly stumbled at the sight of Tyler Matthews dragging an unconscious Kate out of the burning building. When his brain finally processed what his eyes were seeing, rage claimed him. He flew at the other man.

"Get your hands off her!"

Tyler's eyes went wide. He released her and, spinning around, sprinted into the forest.

"Kate!"

He fell to his knees in the dirt beside her and hauled her half onto his lap. Her head lolled to the side, revealing a jagged gash at her temple. Blood trickled down her too-pale cheek.

"Please talk to me, my love." He pressed his face in close, his fingers stroking her soot-streaked hair. Her eyes remained closed, her breathing shallow.

Seeing her like this struck a chord of fear deep within his soul. What if . . .

It was then that the truth slammed into him.

He couldn't lose her! Life without Kate —

Shaking now, he couldn't bear to finish the thought. *I love her.*

He could deny it no longer. His love for Kate burned brightly inside him, the intensity rivaling the noonday sun, filling the empty spaces until he could see nothing but her.

He didn't hear Tom running up behind them. "The place is consumed in flames! You need to move away before the whole structure collapses." He skidded to a stop. "What happened? Is she all right?"

"I'm taking her to Doc Owens," Josh murmured grimly.

"Stay with me, sweetheart," he whispered in Kate's ear.

Cradling her in his arms, he walked as quickly as he could without jarring her. By the time he stumbled into the doctor's house, his muscles were strained from the exertion.

"Doc! I need your help!"

The middle-age man emerged from his

office, his sharp gaze quickly taking stock of the situation. "Take Miss Morgan in here." He held the door open to the same room his mother had occupied a week earlier.

Josh deposited her with care on the examination table and gently brushed the hair off her face. "There's a fire in town. She was pulled unconscious from one of the burning buildings. I don't know how she got that gash."

But he had an idea. Fear for her safety was the only thing keeping him from hunting Matthews down like the swine he was and making sure he never harmed Kate again. Not to worry. He'd deal with Matthews in due time.

"I need you to wait outside." He rinsed his hands in a basin of water.

"I can't leave her."

The doctor stared at him. "You are not her husband. I can't allow you to stay here while I examine her."

"But —"

"Josh, the longer we stand here arguing, the longer she has to wait for medical attention."

He didn't want to leave her. Taking hold of her limp hand, he tried to convey his strength to her, willing her to hear him. "I'm not leaving, Kate. I'll be right on the other side of that door," he whispered. "Doc's gonna take good care of you."

Ignoring him, the doctor lifted her right wrist to check her pulse.

He was being dismissed. Feet dragging, Josh left the room, closing the door behind him. Slumping into the nearest chair, he buried his face in his hands.

All he could think was that the woman he loved was lying unconscious in the next room, and he was powerless to do anything to help her.

Pushing to his feet, he paced the length of the parlor, his mind returning again and again to the mental image of Matthews dragging her out of the studio. Gut churning, he forced his thoughts away from what might've transpired in the moments before the fire. No use working himself up until he knew the facts. But if he found out Matthews had laid a finger on her . . .

When his father came through the front door, Josh felt a little less alone. They embraced briefly.

"How is she?"

Sam's gaze darted to the closed door, his face reflecting understanding. He knew exactly what Josh was enduring, had been in this very same position.

"I don't know. Pa, what if —"

He held up a hand. "Let's not borrow trouble."

"But I feel so helpless," he said, shoving a hand through his hair.

"There is one thing you can do for her. Pray."

Pa settled an arm on his shoulders and, bowing his head, prayed for Kate and the safety of the men working to put out the fire. Josh seconded the petition.

Dr. Owens emerged from the examination room. "Miss Morgan is awake. You may see her now."

Pulse jumping, Josh searched his features for clues. "How is she?"

"It appears her only injury is the head wound. Her lungs are clear, and she's not complaining of anything other than a head-ache."

The knot in his stomach eased as relief flooded him.

"Thank you."

With a grateful nod, he entered the room and, approaching the bed, sank into the straight-backed chair beside it. Lying flat on her back, a crisp white quilt tucked around her, her chest rose and fell with even breaths. Her cheek nestled in the pillow, lips parted and drawing in air.

Resting one arm above her head, he

leaned forward and covered her clasped hands with his own.

"Kate?" Not wanting to startle her, he spoke in a hushed voice.

Her lashes fluttered, then slowly lifted. Peridot-green eyes focused on his. "Josh?"

"Hey." His hand tightened on hers, heart swelling with compassion at the sound of her scratchy voice. "How are you feeling?"

Her lids drifted shut. "I've been better."

Her body needed rest, he knew, but the questions couldn't wait. He phrased them as best he knew how. "You were pulled from the fire. Do you remember what happened before that?"

Her lids snapped open, anger sparking in the luminous depths. "Of course I remember. Tyler cornered me in the back room. We struggled. He overturned a lamp. That's how it started."

Josh sucked in a breath. She was irate, not scared. Did that mean he hadn't succeeded in harming her?

Quashing his own fury at the man, his gaze roamed her face. "Did he hurt you?"

She shook her head, then winced. Slipping one hand free, she gingerly fingered the bandage at her temple. "No, thank God. I guess, in a way, the fire was a blessing in disguise. If it hadn't started, I don't know what he might've done."

"He pulled you out, you know."

Her brow furrowed in disbelief. "What?"

"I saw it with my own eyes."

Her expression turned thoughtful. "He wouldn't leave Lily to die."

Reminded of the terror of that moment, he ran a knuckle down her cheek. "I was terrified I was going to lose you. My lovely Kate —" his voice cracked with emotion "— I can't imagine life without you. I love you."

He held his breath, waiting for her reaction.

Joy leaped in her eyes. Her lips curled upward. Then, like a cloud eclipsing the brilliant sun, her delight vanished.

Closing her eyes tight, she turned her face away. "Please, don't."

Confused, hurt, he sank back. "Don't what? Tell you the truth?"

A single tear slipped from beneath her lashes. "You were right, after all. I — I've discovered I miss the city. I wouldn't be happy here long-term." Her pitiful, ragged breath gouged his soul. "I'm leaving as soon as I can arrange a ride to Sevierville."

"So you're saying you don't return my feelings?" He strove to maintain his composure, to hide his pain.

Oh, God, this is so much worse than I could ever have imagined. How could I have misinterpreted her behavior?

Covering her eyes with her hand, she murmured, "I care for you a great deal, but we're from different worlds, you and I. My place is in the city."

"What about your studio?"

She was quiet a long time. "It wasn't meant to be."

She was using words he himself had used to describe their situation.

"Kate —"

"Please, Josh —" her voice shook "— the pain in my head is worsening. Can you get the doctor?"

"Of course." He stood looking down at her, committing her features to memory.

So this was it. She didn't want him. Like her sister, she was captivated by the city and all its pleasures. How could he have ever thought an heiress would throw away a life of luxury to be with him? Fool. That's what he was. Worse than Megan with all her romantic notions. He wouldn't stay where he wasn't wanted. "Goodbye, Kate."

Chapter Nineteen

Against the doctor's advice, Kate got out of bed the following morning and, unable to find her clothes, dressed in the outfit she'd placed in her overnight satchel. She'd refused to take the pain medicine he'd offered, and so had passed an agonizing night in the stark examination room.

Moving around wasn't helping. Her temple throbbed beneath the bandage, her head unnaturally heavy and her neck stiff. Her eyes felt gritty, though from smoke or lack of sleep she wasn't certain.

When she straightened from pulling on her boots, the room tilted and she flung out a hand to steady herself. Thankfully, the chair was there to grab onto.

How am I going to survive a wagon ride through the mountains? she wondered.

She couldn't afford to stay. The sooner she left, the better — before her heart overruled her better judgment and she begged

Josh's forgiveness.

She'd done the unthinkable. She'd come here to right a wrong, to do the decent thing and deliver the news face-to-face. Her self-righteous anger at Fran's duplicity mocked her now.

Fran's actions seemed insignificant compared to Kate's treachery. Josh had offered her his heart, and she'd callously rejected him. Rejected by yet another Morgan sister.

The conversation replayed inside her head, the stunned sorrow in his voice echoing in her ears. How she'd longed to blurt out the truth, to say, *Yes, of course I love you! How could I not?*

Better a tiny, white lie than the truth . . . a voice reminded. But was it? Was it really?

Honestly, Katerina, how could you be so naive? Fran's disdainful expression flashed in her mind's eye. *Why would Wesley Farrington want anything to do with you? He's suave and sophisticated and you, well, you are nothing a man of his worth would desire. Imagine, my own sister willing to give herself to the first man who winks at her!*

The shame flooded her anew, firming her resolve. Josh could never know.

Standing slowly in hopes of warding off the dizziness, she slipped her reticule over her wrist and carefully reached for her satchel.

"Kate! What are you doing out of bed?" Megan appeared in the doorway, eyes widening at the sight of her travel costume and luggage. "You look awful. Where do you think you're going?"

The sight of her friend threatened the tentative hold she had on her emotions. "I thought you'd have heard by now. I'm going back to New York."

"Nathan told me. I just couldn't believe it." Her gaze was full of sadness. "Why, Kate?"

"First, tell me. How is Josh?"

"I haven't seen him since before the accident."

Kate bit her lip. She desperately needed to know whether or not he was all right.

"Do you think he went to confront Tyler?"

"It's possible. After what he did to you, Josh would want to make sure his actions didn't go unpunished."

She gripped Megan's arm. "Why would he go alone? What if something's happened?"

"If you care so much for him," she asked gently, "then why are you leaving?"

Kate broke eye contact. "I need to go

home. Let's just leave it at that."

"Are you planning on returning?"

"I don't think that would be wise." She took her hands in hers. "Please say you'll come and visit me. You, Nicole and the twins. I can't bear the thought of not seeing you again."

Her smile was tremulous. "I'd like that."

Grateful that she didn't pursue the issue, Kate hugged her friend. "You'll send Nathan or Caleb to find Josh, won't you?"

"I'll go straight there. Try not to worry. He can take care of himself."

Easier said than done. "And you'll give everyone my love? Tell them I —" her voice hitched "— I'll never forget their kindness."

She hated to leave without saying goodbye, especially to Sam and Mary, but it couldn't be helped. When she got to the city, she'd purchase appropriate gifts to send back as a token of her thanks. It wasn't ideal, but it was the best she could do given the situation.

She pulled her shawl more tightly around her shoulders. "My escort is probably outside waiting. Will you walk me out?"

Megan sniffled. "Of course."

After informing Dr. Owens of her departure and thanking him for his services, the pair walked arm in arm through the parlor and out onto the front porch. The man she'd hired was indeed there with his team and wagon. For propriety's sake, his wife was accompanying them.

"Good afternoon." He tipped his hat and took her satchel, placing it in the wagon bed.

This was it, she thought, her gaze sweeping the familiar street. Time to say goodbye to this town that had stolen its way into her heart.

When she glimpsed the burned-out shell of her studio, bittersweet sadness settled in her soul. Her dreams, and Josh's, too, had gone up in smoke.

Sensing Megan's perusal, Kate said, "I hope he rebuilds. Opens the furniture store he wanted."

"It seems to me he'd rather have you than any ole furniture business."

Gritting her teeth, she battled back the tears. She could not speak about this, her greatest heartache. Not now. Maybe not ever.

With one last, hasty hug, she murmured, "I'll write as soon as I get there. Take care, Megan."

"Kate."

There was no mistaking his voice. Why had he come? Releasing her friend, she met his intense gaze with trepidation. How could she endure this? Saying goodbye to him a second time?

"I need a word with you."

He looked as miserable as she felt. Her heart twisted with regret and longing for what might've been.

Megan slipped away without a word. Josh spoke to her driver, instructed him to give them a few minutes to speak in private.

When he neared, she saw the misery in his eyes. She alone bore the responsibility for that pain.

"I've been thinking." He measured his words carefully. "Does it have to be New York City? Knoxville isn't nearly as large, but it has a lot of the comforts you're used to. You could have your studio. I could have my furniture store. We could give it a go, don't you think?"

She gasped and pressed a hand to her heart, stunned by his offer to move to the city. "Gatlinburg is your home! Everything you love is here."

His eyes darkened. "Not everything. Not if you leave."

"I couldn't —"

"Kate Morgan —" he gently grasped her hands "— you mean the world to me. I want to share my life with you. Where we live doesn't matter as long as you're with me.

You said you care for me. Enough to marry me? To be my wife?"

Overcome with emotion, Kate couldn't speak. How she'd dreamed of this day! Josh loved *her*. He wanted to marry *her*.

But her joy was short-lived.

Tears streaming down her cheeks, she looked him full in the face. "I'm no better than my sister, Josh. I lied to you."

His brow furrowed in confusion. "About what?"

"I told you last night that the reason I'm leaving is because I miss the city. That was a lie. I also said that I don't —" she broke off on a shuddering breath "— that I don't l-love you. That, too, was a lie. I do love you, Josh, with everything in me."

His expression cleared and, smiling like a child on Christmas morning, he gripped her hands a fraction tighter. "You love me? Then why not tell me straight-out? Were you afraid?"

"Yes, I was. I am." *Lord, help me. This is the hardest thing I've ever had to do.* Heart racing, limbs trembling, she slipped her hands free of his. "I'm not the virtuous woman you believe me to be. When I was seventeen, there was a man. A very charm-ing man who came along when I desperately needed to feel loved. And he and I . . . that is, one night we —" She stumbled around for words to express what she'd done, but there was no simple way to put it. "We were intimate."

"It was the man you were dreaming about, right?" Josh's face was pale beneath his tan, his eyes cool. His fingers curled into tight fists. "Wesley?"

Kate flinched. "Yes."

"I see."

His words resonated with disappointment. He passed a hand over his face and, with a guttural sigh, turned his back on her.

The slight was like a physical blow. His rejection couldn't be clearer.

"I know this hurts you and I never meant for that to happen. I'm sorry."

Swallowing back tears, she swept up her skirts and walked with as much dignity as she could muster to the wagon. Mr. Furley appeared and, at her request, helped her into the back. The jarring movement was almost too much for her. Her head swam. She closed her eyes and waited for it to pass.

Help, Lord. Sinking down, she rested against the wagon directly behind the driver's seat, legs stretched out before her in a most unladylike position. It hardly mattered.

His back to the street, Josh didn't move to

stop her or wave goodbye.

As the wagon jerked and rolled out onto the street, her gaze didn't waver from his familiar form. Heart ripping in two, she bit her lip until it bled. She'd known it would be like this. *I'm sorry, Josh. So sorry.*

The wagon rounded the bend, and she could see him no more.

His whole body was numb. His mind. His limbs. His heart.

Kate's revelation had hit him with the full force of a cannon blast.

Walking without seeing where he was going, Josh battled anger and bitter disappointment. She'd seemed innocent. Pure. And yet, she'd given herself to a man who was not her husband.

Jealousy surged hot and fast at the thought of her with Wesley. Gritting his teeth, he rid his mind of the images. How could she do it? Didn't she know how amazing and precious she was?

First Francesca. Now Kate. He'd had enough secrets to last a lifetime.

"Josh!" Blond curls falling in her eyes, Megan rushed up. "I passed Kate's wagon. She was crying her heart out. What did you say to her? Couldn't you convince her to stay?"

"Not now, Megan," he warned, his long stride even.

"Are you the reason she's crying?"

"I'm not discussing this."

Spotting the burned-out studio, he changed direction and strode toward it. He needed to assess the structural damage and decide if any of it could be salvaged. His brothers had offered to help him rebuild. Staying busy was the key to survival.

The front entrance was impassable. He'd have to go around back.

"Aren't you going to go after her?" His cousin hurried to keep up. "She didn't seem happy about leaving. In fact, she looked miserable. You don't look much better."

What could he say? Of course he was miserable. The woman he loved wasn't who he'd thought she was.

The back door was missing. With his gloved hand, he tested the sturdiness of the frame.

Megan sighed. "This isn't the ending I'd imagined for the two of you."

Whirling around, he growled, "This is real life, Megan, not one of your novels. You can't always count on a happy ending."

Hurt flashed across her face. "Despite what you might think, I do know the difference between reality and make-believe."

"I'm sorry." He applied pressure to his temples where a headache was starting. "I shouldn't have snapped at you."

Huddling into her wrap, she shivered. "It's all right."

"Maybe you should go on home," he suggested in a gentler tone. "I've got business to tend to and it may take a while."

"I did promise Nicole I'd help her sew a dress this afternoon." Her expression had a forlorn quality. She was hurting, too.

He touched her sleeve. "See you later, then?"

"Of course." She tacked on, "I'm not giving up on you two."

"Megan," he warned.

"That's all I'm going to say. For now."

He sucked in a breath, but she flounced off before he could utter a word. Minx.

Navigating the burned-out structure wasn't easy. Kate's belongings had all succumbed to the fire. His heart was heavy with the knowledge of all she'd lost.

He glanced in the back room where the fire had started, expecting to find nothing left. His gaze lit on one of her trunks. The outside was singed, and one of the bottom corners was warped by the heat. But overall it appeared to be in one piece.

The ceiling here was intact. He advanced

carefully into the room and, hefting the heavy trunk outside, deposited it in the grass.

Prying the lid open, he sat back on his haunches. Kate's pictures.

Not from here, from her life in the city.

One by one, he sifted through the stack of images. Shot at interesting angles, she'd made clever use of shadow and light to create not pictures, but works of art. This was not the work of an amateur. Kate had talent.

Replacing the prints, he shut up the trunk and hefted it into his arms. He'd make sure she got these back.

The piercing wind battered Josh's reddened cheeks and tore at his hat as he, Nathan and Caleb hefted another hundred-pound log into place. The early November weather had turned bitter practically overnight. Sweating beneath his undershirt, he knew it was only a matter of time before one of them became sick working in these conditions. At least the end was in sight. A day or two more and they'd start on the roof.

"Hey, fellas." Megan and Nicole smiled up at them, baskets held aloft. "We brought lunch."

Josh didn't want to stop, not even to eat,

but he couldn't be selfish. His brothers needed a break. "We'll be right down," he called, watching as the girls went around to the side and entered the open doorway.

The four walls provided shelter from the wind, but their breaths puffed white in the chilly air.

"What brings you two out on a day like this?" Nathan asked around a mouthful of sandwich.

Watching as Megan extracted a long envelope from her pocket, Josh stopped midchew, anticipating her words. His pulse accelerated.

"I got a letter from New York." Her gaze speared his. "Kate sends her regards."

Swallowing hard, he tossed the sandwich back into the basket and stalked outside. He didn't want to talk about Kate, or even think about her. While he couldn't prevent her from haunting his dreams, he could at least try to harness his waking thoughts.

A month had passed since she left. One long, lonely, miserable month.

He missed her so much it was a physical pain. He walked around with a hollow, aching, cavernous sensation inside that nothing could ease.

Her presence lingered everywhere he looked. The breakfast table. The apple house. His workshop.

He avoided the cabin at all costs. Sensing his turmoil, his parents hadn't asked when he planned to move back in. Caleb hadn't been as sensitive. His offer to take the cabin had been met with stony silence from Josh and a word of admonishment from Nathan.

"Josh, wait." Megan came up behind him. "I didn't mean to upset you. I just thought you'd want to know how she's doing."

Unable to resist, he turned to face her. "So? How is she?"

She held out the letter. "Would you like to read it for yourself?"

He stuffed his hands in his coat pockets. "No. Thanks."

She pursed her lips. "Fine. I'll give you the highlights. In every other sentence she asks about you. In the rest of it, she says how much she misses us. All of us."

"Those feelings will lessen over time."

As his would, he prayed. Living like this wore a man down. He couldn't remember the last time he'd smiled. Or enjoyed a good meal. Or played his fiddle. The music, the joy, was gone from his life. All because of Kate and her secrets.

"I don't agree. It's clear to me that she loves you, Josh, and regrets leaving. I think you should go to New York."

"That's not gonna happen."

She stamped her foot. "Don't be stubborn! It's plain for all to see you're a mess without her." The wind whipped her hair around her face, and she shoved it aside. "What will it hurt to go and see her again?"

"Listen, I know your intentions are good, but there are some issues here you aren't aware of. Issues that can't be overcome."

"Tell me. Maybe I can help."

He crossed his arms over his chest. His affection for his cousin was the only reason he was standing here discussing what was a private matter. "In the books you love so much, what happens when someone turns out to be vastly different than you thought she was?"

A line formed between her brows. "How is Kate different than what we thought? Isn't she an heiress?" She clapped a hand over her open mouth. "Is she not Francesca's sister? You said they looked nothing alike."

"Of course she's an heiress and, yes, she's Francesca's sister. You didn't answer my question."

"All right, all right. If a person keeps important information hidden, it's usually for a good reason — at least in her mind."

What was Kate's reason?

Megan studied him. "Are you going to forgive her for whatever it is she lied about?"

"She didn't outright lie, exactly." *What did you expect her to do? Introduce herself and then blurt out her indiscretion?*

"The particulars are none of my business, but I want to remind you that everyone makes mistakes. Kate has a good heart. She wouldn't deliberately hurt you, not if she could help it. I know that as sure as I know my own name."

Beneath the disappointment, his heart recognized her words as the truth.

If he stepped back from his own hurt long enough to study the situation, he could see how she'd be terrified to tell him. *She didn't have to. She could've kept her secret to herself and married you anyway.*

"Put yourself in her shoes," Megan suggested, "and try to figure out the reasons driving her actions."

Kate had lived a privileged yet lonely life. Her family had made her feel as if she were less than she was, had made it clear she didn't measure up to their standards. He could only imagine how hungry she'd been for love, for acceptance. For a man without morals, Kate would've been an easy mark.

His heart spasmed painfully in his chest. *Oh, God, she chose the honorable path by telling me about her mistake. She laid bare her heart, made herself vulnerable and I turned my back on her. Another rejection in a lifetime of rejections.*

He bowed his head. "What have I done?" he groaned.

He felt Megan's hand on his arm. "It's not too late to repair things."

He had to go to her! To beg her forgiveness.

Movement registered on his left. "O'Malley?"

He'd know that voice anywhere. *Matthews.* The sound ignited a flame of fury in Josh's gut. The knowledge of all he'd done to torment Kate, the image of him dragging her unconscious from a fire his actions had started, combined to drive rational thought from his mind.

He didn't question why Matthews had approached him. He didn't care. All he could think about was Kate.

In the blink of an eye, he had the villain in a crushing throat hold and had slammed him back against the wall. Megan gasped.

Struggling for air, his eyes bulged and he clawed at Josh's fingers.

"How dare you show your face around here?" Josh growled through clenched teeth, barely registering Megan yelling for his brothers. He wanted answers.

"Hey!" Nathan seized his shoulder. "What are you lookin' to do? Kill him?"

Caleb appeared on his other side, but he didn't try to restrain him. He glared at Matthews. "He's not worth it, Josh."

Matthews glanced wildly between the three men, obviously terrified, chest heaving. Josh only tightened his grip. This sorry excuse of a man deserved to pay for hurting the woman he loved more than life itself.

"Josh, don't!" Megan cried.

Let him go, an inner voice urged. *Vengeance is Mine, says the Lord. Let Me handle him.*

Matthews's face had a chalky hue. His hands were growing limp.

With a disgusted noise, Josh released him. Blood roared in his ears. What had he almost done?

Matthews staggered a couple of steps in the opposite direction, eager to put distance between himself and the others.

"Why did you come here?" Nathan prodded.

When Josh finally looked at his enemy, he noticed the sorry condition he was in. He looked visibly weak, his eyes sunken and his skin pasty. He'd lost weight, too. But he appeared to be sober.

"I —" His dark, pained eyes settled on Josh. "I came to ask your forgiveness for what I did to your friend. Kate, I think her name is. I never meant to hurt her —"

"You expect us to believe you?" Josh couldn't stand to hear her name on his lips.

Nathan put a restraining hand on his chest, just in case Josh decided to have another go at Tyler.

Matthews hung his head. "It's true. I — My mind was so mixed up. The alcohol. The elixirs. After the fire, I threw it all out. I, ah, have been pretty sick."

Josh could see that. Still, it didn't excuse his behavior. But at least he'd come to his senses, was no longer in the clutches of whatever substances had been fueling his fantasy that Kate was his dead wife.

"I'll be moving on." He lifted his head again and looked at Josh, misery and regret in the harsh lines of his face. "Too many memories here. I can't —" He broke off, covering his eyes with one hand and rubbing his temples as if his head pounded.

Against his will, Josh experienced a shred of compassion for the man. He'd lost the light of his life, his beloved wife. How would Josh react in the same situation? How would he survive if anything ever happened to Kate? His stomach lurched.

He surprised them all by blurting out, "I gotta go."

Nathan's brows slammed together. "Go? Go where?"

"I think I know." Megan's eyes lit up with hope.

He addressed Matthews. "I accept your apology. Take my advice — stay off the booze. And I'm warning you now — stay away from my family."

Caleb piped up. "Kate isn't —"

"Not yet." Josh clapped his brother on the shoulder. "But I hope she will be. Soon."

Twenty-four hours later, he was on a train bound for New York. It couldn't go fast enough, in his mind. He'd let her leave believing he no longer cared for her, that he condemned her for her past actions. When he thought about the misery she must've endured these past weeks, his eyes grew suspiciously wet and he ducked his head so his hat's brim shielded his face.

Forgive me, Lord, for being a stubborn fool. He only hoped Kate would give him a second chance.

CHAPTER TWENTY

"Miss Katerina, you've been summoned to the lower-level drawing room."

Standing at the library window, she tore her gaze from the barren gardens below to answer the footman. "Thank you, Mr. Crandall."

With an abbreviated bow, he slipped from the room.

Her deep sigh fogged the polished glass and with a shiver, she turned and started for the door. *What now?* she wondered. Was she to be taken to task yet again for her unapproved sojourn to the wilds of Tennessee?

Her parents had arrived home a week earlier, and her mother had yet to stop berating her for her foolishness. Kate had listened without emotion. It was as if she'd cried out all the tears she possessed and was capable of no more. Now all she felt was numb.

As she swept through the wide corridors, Kate's green satin skirts rustled and the heels of her shoes tapped against the marble floor. On this gray, overcast day, weak light filtered through the floor-to-ceiling windows, barely chasing away the gloom.

The weather suited her mood.

Life without Josh was like a day without sunshine. Without joy or laughter.

Not for the first time, she wondered how he was doing. Did he miss her at all? Did he think of her? The look in his eyes in the moments before she left was burned into her consciousness.

As she descended the grand staircase and neared the drawing room, voices filtered into the hallway.

Francesca and Percy.

Her mood sank even lower. Her sister would no doubt have plenty to say about her decision to stay with the O'Malleys.

Squaring her shoulders, she held her head high as she made her entrance. There would be no avoiding this meeting. Better to get it over with so she could return to her self-imposed solitary confinement.

"Ah, here is your sister at last." Georgia's face radiated disapproval. "Katerina, come here. Francesca and Percy have arrived home from Italy."

Kate noted that Fran looked refreshed after her extended honeymoon, her golden hair and skin kissed by the sun. On the other hand, Percy appeared unchanged, his dour expression much the same as ever.

Rounding on her, Fran's blue eyes sparked fire. "Mother tells me you stayed in Gatlinburg for over a month. What, pray tell, did you find to occupy your time?"

"Good morning, Fran," she responded drily. "Nice to see you, as well. How was your honeymoon?"

"It was fine," she snapped. "I would much rather hear about your trip."

"Just fine?" Percy's face darkened.

"You know what I meant, darling." She shrugged off his protest. "I'm trying to find out what my dear little sister has been up to." Folding her arms, she swung her gaze back to Kate. "Well?"

"It was a wonderful trip. I made many friends while I was there."

Moving past the grouping of sofas and wingback chairs, she made her way to the French doors to stare out at the gardens, wishing it was instead the lush Tennessee forests and valleys she'd come to love.

From her place on the sofa, Georgia lamented, "What I can't understand is what possessed you to undertake a trip of that magnitude without our approval. And without a chaperone! Honestly, Katerina, where is your sense of decorum?"

"Personally I think she was adopted!" Fran exclaimed.

Ignoring the comment, Georgia demanded, "Answer me, young lady!"

Kate faced her mother. "I don't have an answer for you, Mother. I've apologized more times than I count. I do not know what else I can do or say to please you."

At that moment, Kate realized she was finished apologizing for the woman she'd become. She would never fit into this family or their high-class world.

"I will not tolerate such insolence from you, daughter —"

"I think I've heard about enough."

Kate gasped at the sound of the familiar voice. It couldn't be! Yet there he stood in the doorway, black hat in hand, heartbreakingly handsome in the same gray pin-striped suit he'd worn to greet her that first day.

"Josh!" Her palm covering her galloping heart, she gaped at him. "What are you doing here?"

He stepped inside the room, his gaze hungrily roaming her features. "I had to see you again. Kate, we need to talk."

Georgia rose to her feet. "Who are you?

How did you get in here?"

"Joshua," Fran said breathlessly, "it's wonderful to see you again."

Percy shot to his feet, his face a thundercloud. "Is this the backwoods hick you were engaged to?"

He ignored them all, his attention on Kate alone. An odd mix of contrition and impatience marked his features. "Is there somewhere we can talk privately?"

"Why are you looking at my sister like that?" Fran demanded suddenly, her gaze volleying back and forth between the two.

"If you must know, I'm in love with her. I've come to ask her to marry me. Again."

Wary, Josh watched Kate's expression closely. Her green eyes widened, glistening in the soft glow emitted by the ornate wall sconces. The longing he glimpsed on her face fanned the flames of hope within his chest. Would she find it in her heart to forgive him?

"Again? What —" his former fiancée sputtered. "You must be joking!"

Francesca stalked over to stand halfway between him and Kate. Hands fisted on her hips, Francesca looked about ready to explode, her beauty marred by jealousy and plain mean-spiritedness. She'd hidden it well those short weeks they'd spent together.

Looking back, there'd been hints of her true personality, but he'd been too besotted to spot them.

He could've been shackled to this woman for life. *Thank you, God, for sparing me.*

"This isn't a joke." He frowned at her.

She rounded on Kate. "You planned this all along, didn't you? Don't think I didn't notice you mooning over his picture! How could you do this to me?"

Kate lifted her chin. "You're forgetting that you're a married woman, Fran. You chose Percy over Josh. I didn't *do* anything to you."

"Joshua," Fran began, sounding like the cat who caught the mouse, "did Katerina ever mention a man by the name of Wesley Farrington?"

"Fran, no!" The color drained from her face.

"I know everything." He injected frost into his voice. "And it doesn't change the way I feel about your sister."

Francesca's husband wore a smirk. "It doesn't bother you that she's damaged goods?"

Josh took a menacing step forward, keeping a tight rein on his emotions. "I won't allow you or anyone else to say such things about Kate."

"Josh, please. You don't have to do this."

Crossing the room to stand before her, he drank in her appearance. After the misery of living without her all these weeks, the sight of her was a gift in and of itself. "Yes, I do. There are things I left unsaid back in Gatlinburg. Things I hope will change your mind."

"Mother," Francesca wailed, "aren't you going to call the footmen to remove him? This is outrageous!"

Kate motioned behind her. "Come with me."

With graceful movements, head held high like a queen, she led him through the French doors onto a maze of brick pathways, sculpted bushes standing like sentinels on either side. They walked past manicured lawns, empty fountains, and fallow flowerbeds to another wing of the mansion. The Morgans' wealth hadn't been exaggerated.

She paused outside a door to tell him shyly, "This is my studio. We'll have privacy in here."

Once inside, his boots sank into the plush Oriental rug. It took a moment for his eyes to adjust to the dim light, but once they did, his gaze was drawn to the wallpapered walls where photograph after photograph of the mountains, the town of Gatlinburg and his family were displayed.

What struck him most were the number of pictures of just him. The one of him fishing the day she'd fallen in the water. Lounging next to a picnic basket. Dressed in his suit before church services.

She avoided his questioning gaze, but the pink staining her cheeks was a telltale sign of her embarrassment.

"You have talent," he said, bypassing the photos of himself to study the ones of the town. "These are amazing. They shouldn't be locked away in here. People should see them."

"You're too kind."

"No." He turned back. "No, I'm not. I was wrong to let you go the way I did. I acted like a fool. Can you forgive me?"

"I don't blame you. After what I did —" She broke off with a helpless gesture.

"Can you tell me about it?"

"I was a foolish young girl." Her eyes darkened with shame.

Going to stand before her, he gently took her hands in his.

"There's more to the story than that," he prompted quietly, dreading her words yet needing to hear them.

"Wesley was the first boy to notice me. I was lonely. When he began to pay attention to me, I was flattered. Here was someone my parents approved of, a promising young man from an upstanding family, and he was interested in *me.*

"During one of our parties, he asked to see my father's wine collection. I didn't see any harm in it." She shrugged. "But then the candle was somehow extinguished and the room was plunged into darkness. I panicked . . ." Her voice trailed off.

"Let me guess," Josh inserted, "instead of leading you out of there, your young man took full advantage of the situation."

"I allowed it to happen."

"My darling." He reached out and gently lifted her chin, forcing her to meet his gaze. Her eyes were large in her pale face. "He lured you down there for a reason. You were young and vulnerable. A prime target for a lustful young man without morals or any sense of decency."

He couldn't fathom how anyone could be so callous as to abuse her trust in such a way and then abandon her. A fierce protectiveness rose in his chest.

"We've all made mistakes we wish we could take back. All we can do is ask for forgiveness and move on. What happened in the past doesn't define who you are today. I'm sorry it took me so long to realize that.

I've been miserable without you."

"What are you saying?" she breathed.

"You know what I admire about you?" He trailed a knuckle down her silken cheek.

Capturing her bottom lip with her teeth, she shook her head.

"After the disappointments and trials you've endured, you could've easily become bitter. Hardened your heart. Refused to trust or love others. But you didn't do any of those things. You, Kate Morgan, are a woman of integrity. A woman whose capacity to love humbles me." He slipped his hand beneath her hair to cup her neck. With his thumb, he made lazy circles on the soft skin. "I love you."

Kate let the precious words sink in. Her past hadn't destroyed his love for her.

Cradling her face with his hands, he stared deep into her eyes. "I want you for my wife. I want us to start a family of our own. We can make new memories, joyful ones to replace all that's happened in the past. We can start new traditions that we'll teach to our children and grandchildren. What do you say?"

Since childhood, she'd yearned for love and acceptance, a family who genuinely cared for one another. And here was the man she loved and admired offering her that very thing. Josh was offering himself to her. As his wife, she'd have a kind, thoughtful husband to love and share life with. To start a family with.

"Are you certain that's what you want?"

Leaning in, he brushed his lips across hers in silent declaration. "I love you. Nothing will ever change that."

Her fears laid to rest, she basked in the unconditional love shining in his eyes.

"I love you, Josh," she uttered softly, a blush stealing into her cheeks. "I would be honored to become your wife."

With a whoop that startled her, he encircled her waist and whirled her about, his husky laugh delighting her. Balancing herself with her hands on his shoulders, she couldn't help laughing right along with him. Then he lowered her feet to the floor and kissed her soundly.

"You've made me the happiest of men."

Caressing his cheek with her palm, she smiled at him. "And you, my love, have made all my dreams come true."

EPILOGUE

Two weeks later

Placing the last candle on the window ledge, Kate adjusted the bough of greenery and turned to survey the decorated church. Bouquets of orange and pink mums, yellow marigolds and goldenrod clustered around the podium, a burst of autumn colors against the white walls. Greenery entwined with cheerful orange ribbons adorned the pews.

It was a scene reminiscent of the season of bounty and harvest. Of Thanksgiving.

The perfect time for a wedding.

Her gaze settled on her fiancé. Looking handsome and relaxed, he stood in the far corner with his cousin Juliana and her husband, Evan Harrison. All three had silly grins on their faces, happy simply to be in each other's company once again.

Kate watched as Evan held his wife close, his manner loving and protective, his eyes full of love. How many times over the past week had Kate glimpsed him placing his hand tenderly over the slight swell of Juliana's abdomen where their first child nestled? Seeing them together, she found it difficult to believe the story of their meeting, of how he'd been masquerading as an outlaw and had kidnapped Juliana when she'd interrupted the robbery of Clawson's Mercantile.

Juliana had merely laughed at Kate's shocked reaction. The gorgeous redhead laughed a lot, no doubt giddy with joy to be among her family once more.

Megan appeared at her side looking radiantly happy. "I just love weddings —" she sighed dreamily as she surveyed the room "— and yours and Josh's is going to be beautiful, don't you agree? Are you happy with the way everything looks?"

"It's perfect." Grinning, she looped her arm through Megan's. "I can't wait until tomorrow."

The past two weeks had been a whirlwind of activity. They had lingered in New York only long enough for Kate to repack her traveling suitcase and arrange for her personal maid to act as chaperone on the return trip to Tennessee. Saying goodbye to her parents and sister had been more difficult than she'd anticipated, regardless of their disdainful attitudes. They were her family, and she loved them. Who knew if she'd ever return to the city of her birth?

Without Josh's support and the prospect of a new life, she might've crumbled. But God was faithful. The Healer of all wounds. He'd provided a brand-new family just for her.

Tomorrow she would walk down this aisle and join her life to his. She would be an O'Malley. An official member of the family.

As if reading her thoughts, Megan declared, "I'm so gloriously happy the two of you worked things out. Soon you and I will be family! And we'll get to see each other every day. I'll come and visit you in your new studio. I wonder who will be your first customer?"

The mention of Josh's wedding gift made her smile. Shortly after their return, he'd approached her with a blindfold and mischief in his eyes. Ignoring her questions, he'd driven her into town and, standing on the boardwalk, revealed his surprise.

Hanging above the door of the new store he'd rebuilt with his brothers was a carved sign with the words K. O'Malley Photography and J. D. O'Malley Furniture.

"Well? What do you say?" He'd tipped his

head, a smile quivering about the corners of his mouth. "Partners?"

Overwhelmed by his thoughtfulness, she'd thrown her arms around in his neck. "You're too good to me!" she'd exclaimed, words muffled against his shirt collar.

First he'd stunned her with the announcement that he and his brothers were going to build a new, larger cabin just for them. And now this!

He'd held her tight, his face pressed against hers. "Is that a yes?"

She'd eased back to stare into his dear face. "Since we are to be partners in life, it makes sense for us to be partners in business, as well. I'm not sure how I can ever thank you properly."

His lazy smile and the flare of heat in his eyes had made her insides go all quivery. "Oh, I think we can come up with something." He'd brushed a too-brief kiss across her lips. Releasing her, he'd gestured toward their combination store and studio. "For now, would you like a tour?"

"I'd like nothing better."

"Kate —" Megan nudged her "— are you listening?"

She blinked to clear her mind of the pleasant memory. "Sorry, what were you saying?"

"Never mind —" she chuckled "— as the

bride-to-be, you have an excuse to day-dream."

Kate spotted Tom off to the side with Nathan and Nicole. His gaze seemed to follow Megan around the room. "I'm curious — did you ask Tom to come and help decorate?"

The sparkle in her eyes dimmed as she shook her head. "No, Josh did that."

"He can't keep his eyes off you, you know."

Regret pulled at her generous mouth. "I was hoping . . . that is, while he's a kind, upstanding man, there's just no spark between us."

"Spark?"

"Yes, spark. Don't pretend you don't know what I mean." She gave her a look. "Whenever you and Josh are in the same room together, the air practically hums. I can see it in the way you two look at each other. It's the same with Evan and Juliana."

Kate couldn't deny it. "So you're saying there's no magic with Tom."

"Exactly."

She tugged her friend close. "One day soon you'll meet the man of your dreams."

"That's what I keep telling her," Juliana piped up, her forest-green eyes brimming with happiness and humor. "She's got her heart set on a romantic hero come to life."

Megan grinned. "That's right. No ordinary man will do for me."

Kate sought out Josh. Her heart skipped a beat when she encountered his ardent gaze. Even from this distance, the look in his eyes made her knees go weak. Yes. There was a spark all right.

"I already found my hero," she said softly, smiling at him.

With a parting word to Evan, he started toward her.

Seeing the looks exchanged between the couple, Juliana gave her a grateful smile. "You've made him more happy than I've ever seen him, Kate. And that makes *me* happy. Welcome to the family."

Her kind words meant a lot to Kate. In the few, short days she'd spent in Juliana's company, she'd become fond of the young woman and would be sorry to see her leave.

"What are you three whispering about over here?" Josh curled an arm around Kate's waist and tucked her against his side. He dropped a kiss on her cheek, something he did with pleasing regularity these days.

She had delighted in discovering his affectionate side. He was quick to hug and hold her, and he liked to steal kisses. Simply holding hands seemed to please him. Having lived in a loveless household for much of her life, she treasured his each and every touch.

"We were saying how thrilled we are to have Kate," Megan said.

"Yes, indeed." His smile was tender as he gazed down at her. "I think we'll keep her."

Evan strolled up at the same time Juliana smothered a yawn. "I think it's time we head back to the cabin." He rested a hand on her shoulder. "Little momma here needs her rest."

"I do get tired more easily these days." To Kate, she said, "I'll see you in the morning. Sleep well."

Taking their cue from the expectant couple, everyone left except for Josh and Kate.

Their arms wrapped loosely about each other's waists, he groaned good-naturedly, "I wish it was tomorrow already. I can't wait to make you my bride."

"I have a feeling the day will go by faster than you think."

And it did.

In an emotional, romantic ceremony that next afternoon, with family and friends looking on, she and Josh exchanged vows to love and cherish each other the rest of their lives. The evening passed in a blur of well-wishes, gift-opening, cake-cutting and, for the bride and groom, longing glances and stolen kisses when they thought no one was watching.

At long last alone in their cabin, Kate's stomach fluttered with nervous excitement. With one final glance in the mirror, she emerged from the bedroom wearing a lace and satin nightgown, handmade specially for her wedding night.

A soul-satisfying contentment filled her. Her past, so riddled with pain and regret, no longer haunted her. She'd let it go. What was important was the here and now, and learning to savor each moment of her new life.

This was a day of new beginnings.

At the whisper of luminous material, her husband glanced up. His eyes widened, then darkened as he took in the sight of her. He stood slowly to his feet and walked toward her.

Still dressed in his black suit pants, the top buttons of his white dress shirt undone and the sleeves rolled up to reveal muscular forearms, he was devastatingly handsome. His honey-brown hair was mussed, giving him a rakish look.

Her pulse quickened.

Reaching up, he removed the pins from

her hair one by one, watching as her tresses fell in waves about her shoulders. "You are ravishing, Mrs. O'Malley."

Kate's eyes drifted shut, and she smiled. How she treasured the sound of her new name!

"Thank you, Mr. O'Malley."

"I'm a fortunate man to have you as my bride."

She looked at him then. "I'm not the bride you initially picked out."

"True." His smile was loving and wise. "But you're the bride God wanted for me. And we all know His choices are best."

Josh enfolded her in his embrace and kissed her then, expressing his love and adoration for her with tender touches and earnest whispers.

He loved her, and she loved him. They would spend the rest of their lives celebrating the gift God had given them.

Dear Reader,

Thank you for choosing *The Bridal Swap*. When I started this story, I didn't realize how emotional Josh and Kate's journey would be. Both are hurting and lonely and in need of love — especially Kate. It was such a pleasure to give her a happy ending with an honorable, caring man like Josh. I believe she'll be quite content with him and the O'Malley clan by her side!

Like Kate, I struggle sometimes with the notion that some of my poor choices are beyond God's forgiveness. Whenever this happens, I turn to His Word for reassurance and I'm reminded that He is faithful to forgive — all we have to do is ask. Thank you, Jesus!

I'd love to hear from you! Email me at karenkirst@live.com or swing by my Facebook page. Visit my website, www.karen kirst.com, for pictures of the O'Malleys and information about my series, Smoky Mountain Matches.

Blessings,
Karen Kirst

QUESTIONS FOR DISCUSSION

1. Josh and Francesca had a whirlwind courtship. What do you suppose motivated him to propose after such a brief time?

2. How can a person distinguish between infatuation and love? (See 2 Corinthians 13)

3. We all have dreams. God's timetable, however, does not always move at the pace we'd like. Was there ever a time in your life when your impatience either side-tracked your dream or put it out of reach altogether? How did this affect your relationship with Him?

4. Despite her wealth and connections, Kate is lonely and searching for acceptance. How do the O'Malley families reach out to her and make her feel welcome? How important is it for us to be hospitable to

others? Name specific ways we can extend the hand of friendship.

5. Patrick and Georgia Morgan favored Francesca over Kate. How did this affect Kate?

6. Kate fears dark, enclosed spaces. At one point in the story, she recites verses and prays for renewed peace. Have you ever had a fear of something that affected your daily life? How did you cope?

7. Josh is understandably upset when he discovers Kate has bought the store. How would you have reacted if you were in this situation?

8. When life doesn't go the way we'd hoped, do you think we are more inclined to blame God or to trust in His plan for our lives?

9. If you had a friend who, like Kate, felt ashamed of something in his or her past, what would you tell them? Which Bible verses would you direct them to?

10. All sins separate us from God. Why then do you think we tend to categorize sin,

viewing some acts as more shameful than others?

11. What motivates people to keep secrets? How does it affect the person? Is there ever a good reason to keep a secret?

12. Kate's cooking skills take Josh by surprise. Like Josh did with Kate, we sometimes make assumptions about people based on their appearance, financial status, friendships, etc. How does this hinder our relationships? (1 Samuel 16:7b — *The Lord does not look at the things people look at. People look at the outward appearance, but the Lord looks at the heart.*)

13. Kate allows her mother's opinion of her to define how she sees herself. How can we establish our identity and self-worth in Christ Jesus? List specific passages of scripture.

14. Do you think Francesca's deception influenced Josh's initial reaction to Kate's revelation of her past with Wesley? Why or why not?

15. When others hurt us, how can we come to a place of forgiveness?

ABOUT THE AUTHOR

Karen Kirst currently lives in coastal North Carolina with her marine husband, three boys and Andy the parrot. When she's not writing or dreaming up characters, she likes to read, visit tearooms, play piano, watch romantic comedies and chat over coffee with friends. She's incredibly blessed to be able to do what she loves, and gives God the glory.